BACHELOR BROTHERS'
Bed & Breakfast
Pillow Book

Bill Richardson

A Wyatt Book *for* St. Martin's Press New York

Design and illustrations by Rose Cowles

Library of Congress Cataloging-in-Publication Data

Richardson, Bill, 1955–
    Bachelor brothers' bed & breakfast pillow book / Bill
Richardson.
        p.   cm.
    ISBN 0-312-16779-2
    1. Bed and breakfast accommodations—Canada—Fiction.
2. Eccentrics and eccentricities—Canada—Fiction.   3. Books and
reading—Canada—Fiction.   4. Bachelors—Canada—Fiction.
5. Brothers—Canada—Fiction.   6. Twins—Canada—Fiction.
I. Title.
[PR9199.3.R467B33   1997]
813'.54—dc21   97-14695
                                                                        CIP

First published in Canada by Douglas & McIntyre

First U.S. Edition: October 1997

10   9   8   7   6   5   4   3   2   1

*To everyone who sought it out
and everyone who found it.*

*And with thanks to
Sue; Margaret Frances and Robert Stanley;
Dave, Deidre and Nora; Marg and Noel;
Laurie and Dacia; Saeko and Kelly;
and especially, Wallace.*

Contents

Pleasing Things
Finding a large number of tales that one has not read before. Or
acquiring a second volume of a tale whose first volume one has
enjoyed. But often it is a disappointment . . .
—Sei Shonagon, *The Pillow Book*

What's life, we ask;
Life, Life, Life! cries the bird
As if he had heard . . .
—Virginia Woolf

BACHELOR BROTHERS'

Bed & Breakfast
Pillow Book

Every valley shall be exalted

Every valley shall be exalted. This is what the Bible tells us, and I don't wonder why. There is something about a valley that changes your mind about the world and all it contains. I imagine that during those halcyon few minutes between the inspired forging of the world and the terrible mistake of inventing a self-serving biped to run and ruin it, God took a little stroll around the blue and green garden, inhaling air that no one had ever breathed, revelling in the unsullied vivaciousness of it all, moved by sheer delight to rise now and then on tiptoe and pirouette first one way, then the other. Valleys, I submit, are the pocked reminders of this tipsy, cosmic spinning.

The earth remembers. Deep, deep, under the layers of soil and rocky strata, where magma flows and lava bubbles and all that is molten heaves and glows, are the residual traces of that hot and primal joy. Luckily for us, it's been diluted by time and interment. We could never bear its unalloyed rush. It would break our hearts. It would fry us in a second. We only sense its presence because, from time to time, the small scrap of God that lives in us still will hum like a fiddle string, vibrating sympathetically as we trudge through our days.

There is one valley where I have often felt these cosmic stirrings; a valley whose power is magnified by its placement on an island, in the Pacific Northwest, off the coast of British Columbia. There are valleys not so very far from the one I have in mind that are more spectacular to behold: valleys that are deeply carved, bisected by virile rivers, flanked by haughty peaks that are almost ridiculous in their hoary extravagance. Indeed, it must be said that in purely topographical terms, this valley, which is both narrow and shallow, is in no way distinguished. At its northern end, just before the road

1

rises up and achieves that flat normalcy called sea level (a point it proves by winding, in fairly short order, to the sea), is a driveway marked by a small and neatly painted sign: The Bachelor Brothers' Bed and Breakfast. At the end of the driveway is a big and somewhat sagging house, jauntily dressed in yellow and blue, two-and-a-half storeys, with a wraparound porch and a cupola crown. This is our journey's end and beginning both.

The Bachelor Brothers' Bed and Breakfast is the home and the inspiration of Hector and Virgil, fraternal twins born over fifty years ago under the sign of Taurus. These two men, our bachelor brothers, have lived their whole lives in this house, in this valley, on this island, without ever feeling the need to pull up stakes and move on. Their late and formidable mother was an independent and accomplished woman, a pioneer in the art of unabashed single parenting. Their father was an itinerant book salesman who passed that way but once, pausing just long enough to sow his seed so convincingly that two babies were planted where one ought properly to have flourished.

Neither Hector nor Virgil ever clapped eyes on the man whose playful, consensual dalliance made them possible. He was an unremittingly absent father. Nonetheless, he played a role in their lives that went well beyond enabling the brute fact of their two existences. He is the shadowy figure they can thank for their bibliomania. Shortly after their tandem advent, they began receiving books in the mail. Picture and story books, illustrated fairy tales, adventure books for boys, biographies, a dictionary, an atlas, a set of encyclopedia: the books followed the path of their maturation from boys into young men. The packages bore postmarks from Manitoba, from Michigan, from Alberta, from South Dakota. There was never a covering letter, never a flyleaf inscription, never a word of explanation. By the time the flow of books dried up, the boys were in their seventeenth year and the damage was done. Hector and Virgil had acquired both a thirst for reading that knew no slaking and the certainty that while their world was small, it was in no way circumscribed. On the contrary, it was rich and variegated and fairly pulsing with mystery. For how did this travelling salesman know that his hurried meshing with their mother had borne such fruit? How did he know their names, their tendencies and leanings? And why did he care? These, like most worthwhile questions, may never be answered.

Hector and Virgil opened their home to paying guests shortly after the death of their mother. Their decision to start a bed and breakfast operation was essentially a humanitarian gesture. They wanted to create a place where people who are oppressed by the notion that there are too many books and too little time to read them might carve out a retreat; where gentle souls who carry the burden of knowing that the world is too much with them can set aside a week or ten days to whittle down their list of "books to which I must one day get around." After all, the notion of a writer's retreat is well-established. Why not honour the consumer of the product with a similar prospect of quietude?

It was a notion that struck a resonant chord. From the very outset, unbidden (and in some cases, including my own, unannounced) bookish souls began arriving. By sheer force of rumour, and with never a word of paid promotion, the Bachelor Brothers' Bed and Breakfast was successfully launched. The brothers have never advertised their establishment, never publicly revealed its precise location. In an age of instant communication and fibre-optic entanglements, they prefer to let word-of-mouth be their handmaid.

Hector and Virgil, like most altruists, are not entirely innocent of self-serving motivation. They long for stories, and as they are disinclined by nature to travel out into the world to gather them, they have created a climate where tale-tellers can come to them. Much of the discussion at a B&B takes place early in the day around a communal table where the breakfasters are often strangers to one another. People thrown together haphazardly, and meeting for the first time, seek out some kind of common conversational ground. Not surprisingly, the talk almost always turns to food. Sometimes, Hector or Virgil will ask a visitor for the recipe for a savoury sounding concoction. A number of these are included in this book, along with the tales appended to them by their senders.

While the bachelor brothers are devoted to reading, neither Hector nor Virgil thinks of himself as a writer. Both profess having neither the time nor the inclination to labour long and hard at the tedious business of stringing pretty charms on a narrative bracelet. To furnish this second small account of the comings and goings and

3

doings at their establishment and in their community, they settled on the example of the pillow book: a kind of miscellany or helter-skelter journal of the kind kept, most notably, by Sei Shonagon, a noblewoman in tenth-century Japan. Her gossipy, rather waspish chronicle of court life—consisting of diary entries and odd lists—seemed just the model they required. Sei Shonagon's masterpiece was written over a period of ten years. The brothers' pillow book covers ten months and chronicles a period in their lives when they were engaged in their effort (by now well known, but nevertheless recounted in the following pages) to resurrect the reputation of Solomon Solomon, a poet of great skill and little fame.

There is something about a valley. It is a pleasant place in which to wake. Say it is spring, and you have come from away. Say you arrived in the dark, trailing the stresses and cares that are the nagging familiars of some other, harder place. All night long you have dreamed the flat dreams, the factory dreams, the fretful dreams that are the tailings of months of hard mining. Now you lie in your bed, enjoying the settling certainty that all that is behind you, if only for a short time. The house is full of the sounds of waking. Someone is already reading. Someone is cooking breakfast. Something is probably burning. It is spring. You are there.

As we were never baptized

As we were never baptized, my twin brother Hector and I know that our two linked fates weren't tampered with by an evil fairy whose knickers were in a knot because she wasn't invited to our christening. Nonetheless, I often ponder the possibility that a malevolent sprite, between official engagements, dogged our heels just for the nasty sport of it, waiting for the perfect moment to deal us a life-shaping nip. And I think I can pinpoint the very moment she chose to meddle and forged the foreordaining of our futures.

We were six years old. Our first grade teacher, who was honey-haired and sweet and went by the tantalizing name of Miss Godbehere, was making the rounds of our classroom, asking what we hoped to be when we "grew up." Our colleagues, already trained to tell their elders what they wanted to hear, responded with the usual vocational litany. Cowboy. Fireman. Nurse. Teacher.

Today, I expect modern pedagogical methods prescribe that twins be placed at a remove from each other in the classroom, or in different classes altogether, in order that their two identities not be smudged or compressed into one. But Hector and I sat side by side throughout the whole of our schooling. It pleased us to do so. No one thought to raise any objection. And because we belonged to the fraternal rather than the identical branch of twindom, we were easy enough to tell apart. None of our teachers was ever troubled or embarrassed by an inability to distinguish between us. They knew they wouldn't fall prey to the practical jokes and games of name-swapping young clones love to play. In classroom drills, whether the inquisition was conducted by following an alphabetical roster or whether it was organized by row, we were always quizzed one directly after the other. Had Miss Godbehere, on this pivotal day, first focussed her careerist attentions on Hector rather than on me, our lives might have taken on a very different cast. We might well have followed the road more travelled.

Hector, at that point in his young life—for reasons he was never willing to divulge and may not completely have understood—had fallen deeply in love with Princess Juliana (as she then was) of the Netherlands. He planned to make her his wife, conceding nothing to petty considerations of nationality, rights of succession or bigamy laws. His answer to the "What do you want to be?" query would certainly, and logically, have been "King of the Netherlands." But I was to dash his hopes and prospects with a single word when Miss Godbehere beamed down at me first.

"Little Virgil," she smiled, "what do *you* want to be when you grow up?"

The truth was that until the question was put to me directly, I didn't have the vaguest idea and didn't much care. I was too wrapped up in the world of childhood to imagine it ending in something as appalling as a profession. Were it not for what I now ascribe to supernatural interference, I would probably have aped the boy who answered before me and lisped, "A policeman." This was not to be.

"A bachelor!" I shouted, without a nanosecond's pause for consideration.

To this day, I cannot understand how or why I would have responded in such a way. Bachelor. I had never pronounced those three consecutive syllables before. Where would I have learned or even heard the word, unless some killjoy troll chose that instant to whisper it in my ear? The whys and wherefores are a knot I'll never untangle. The incontrovertible fact is that "bachelor" fell from my lips. And at the very moment I uttered "bachelor," I felt the settling of something heavy, like a leaden certainty, on my tiny shoulders. The meddlesome fey whispered "So be it" in my ear, and vanished with a chill and menacing chuckle.

Miss Godbehere was puzzled. Her mandibles twitched, and she ran her tongue over the downy shadow on her upper lip. She cleared her throat.

"Darling, you might very well grow up to be a bachelor. Many men do, and many more ought to. But I want to know what you think you might do to make a living. Being a bachelor isn't what you'd call a profession. Would you like to be a tinker or tailor? A soldier or sailor?"

I was a sweet child, devoted to compliance. I shied away from anything that remotely resembled confrontation, and I would sooner have sliced off my thumbs and made them into a sandwich than say or do anything to offend Miss Godbehere: Miss Godbehere, with her clear blue eyes and her hair rolled up in a buttery bun and her fondness for tweeds and lilac *eau de cologne* and her right leg in a brace because of some orthopaedic difficulty, about the exact nature of which we knew it would be impolite and indiscreet to make inquiries. I loved her. Indeed, she figured prominently in the baroque stories I would tell myself as I lurched toward sleep each night. Often we would be having a picnic on the savanna, and we would be set upon by a pack of jackals, and I would drive them off with a stick and a few harsh words, and she would pick me up in her arms, and I would ask her to marry me, and she would say yes yes yes, like a virginal Molly Bloom. Then she would take off her brace and cast it aside and carry me without so much as a trace of a limp across a burning plain, through tall and waving grasses where no jackal dared scamper or howl. My six-year-old love was refined and pure and hot and healing.

But not even my feelings for Miss Godbehere were febrile enough to make me back down or retract my peculiar blurting: "A bachelor." It had come from nowhere, striking me in the region of the solar plexus with the one-two punch of epiphany. I was not about to fall for the sop of tinker, tailor.

"No," I said, rather too forcefully, "I want to be a bachelor. A bachelor! A bachelor!"

"Very well," said our teacher, fearing that I might be on the brink of blue-faced tantrum. "Very well then, Virgil. We'll ask your brother. Hector, what do *you* want to be when you grow up?"

Hector and I, like most twins, have always had the kind of close psychic tie that allows us to finish each other's sentences and answer each other's unspoken questions. This was especially true in the palmy days before adolescence. As we aged, we became more and more individuated. But when we were children, we operated on a single emotional circuit. My joy was his. His distress was mine. My upset was so profound and staccato in its articulation that it osmotically infiltrated his very being. His every cell prompted him to rise to my defence. He bravely abandoned, then and there, his aspirations to the Dutch throne. In one selfless second, he signed on for a life term.

"I want to be a bachelor, too!"

He said this with such ferocity, and crossed his arms so purposefully across his chest, that Miss Godbehere saw it was senseless to offer either resistance or suggestions for employment alternatives. She retreated with a strained chuckle.

"Well, well. I suppose that we'll have to call you our bachelor brothers, then!"

Bachelor brothers. It was the first time we were tagged with that alliterative epithet. I am happy to report it didn't lodge in the brains of our classmates, nonplussed and puzzled as they must have been by my eccentric emotional outpouring. Nor, during our growing up, were we called, either through fondness or contempt, the "bachelor brothers." It is only latterly, since we took it on ourselves to open our house to paying visitors as a bed and breakfast, that the name has passed into popular currency. Still, that long-ago classroom episode had about it the pungency of prophecy. We could neither of us know that we had, at the age of six, scribbled the story of our future lives in stone.

"What's a bachelor?" Hector asked me, as we wound our way home.

"I don't know," I answered.

"Oh."

When our mother told us the meaning of the word, I was inconsolable. It was worse than I thought. Not only had I offended Miss Godbehere; now, I would never be able to marry her. And as near as I could see, her sentence was grimmer still. I, at least, would have my brother. She would live her life lame and alone, exiled from the kingdom of my love and its promises of security and wholeness. That night, my pillow soaked up my tears and muffled my sobs. Jackals tore triumphant through my dreams.

I am writing this in bed, propped up by no fewer than five pillows. I am neither alone nor unobserved. Our pretty calico cat, Waffle, has moulded herself a deck chair in the folds of the eiderdown. She sits in it and watches me write, her eyelids at half-mast, her small guttural motor idling in her chest. Every so often she lifts an interfering paw to dab at my pen. I am not sure if she does this with censure, encouragement or just plain mischief in mind. My notebook is full of misshapen words and letters marked by errant downward strokes: the result of Waffle's intermittent editing. Our parrot, Mrs. Rochester, is perched upon the bust of Edgar Allan Poe that hangs above my chamber door. Her head is tucked beneath her wing. Every so often, she peers from between the feathers and lobs a half-hearted "Nevermore" in my direction.

Mrs. Rochester was our mother's parrot. She is a yellow-fronted Amazon, powerful of beak and of mind. We have no way of knowing her precise age, but can say with a certainty that she is a tenant of long standing on the planet. The years have whittled away none of her acuity with their passing. The story of her arrival is as mysterious as her age. She came to this house of her own choosing. She was neither bidden to enter nor encouraged to stay. She simply flew in through an attic window and decided that she liked what she saw. Parrots are by nature monomaniacal in their devotions, and Mrs. Rochester directed all her love toward our mother, who was happy to receive it.

Over their long years together, they formed a tight and exclusive interspecies alliance as partners in misanthropy. In fact, I am persuaded that Mother found in her bird the perfect weapon for holding the world at bay. In the dark ages before the dawning of Mrs. Rochester, Mother was sufficiently lacquered with an acquired veneer of civility to keep the contempt she felt for the world at large to herself. Mrs. Rochester, on the other hand, was unfettered by the restraining shackles of human decency. She was a plumed poultice, willing and able to suck up or channel the antisocial humours that were the foundation of Mother's character, and give those vile vibrations voice. The two of them were a formidable team.

Mrs. Rochester's unlooked for advent coincided almost exactly with our own. She put into port shortly after Hector and I were installed in our nursery. Mother always said that the parrot and the amusement she provided were the reasons she wasn't driven mad by our incessant demands for milk and changing. "If it hadn't been for Mrs. Rochester," she told us as she tucked us in at night after reading to us from the latest issue of *Popular Mechanics* or *Scientific American*, "I'd have probably looked for a she-wolf to suckle you."

Mrs. Rochester, happily, was a diversion and a puzzle. Mother made every effort to locate her owner, but no one ever claimed her. She came with no clues, other than her lexicon, which was eclectic, to say the least. She could recite the whole of *A Shropshire Lad*, and a good bit of *Samson Agonistes*. She knew the recipe for Scripture Cake. She could sing "Alexander's Ragtime Band," "Lullaby of Broadway," "The Donkey Serenade" and "E Lucevan le Stelle." She could whistle all the airs from that infernal nonsense *Pinafore*, and she could call up from the depths of her tiny chest a siren wail that was stunning in both its amplitude and verisimilitude.

My earliest recollection is of lying beside Hector in our tandem pram, looking up at the monumental woman who was our mother and at the parrot perched on her fedora. We must have been out for a walk, and we couldn't have been much older than ten months at the time. I know that memory is a trickster, and that I might have manufactured the image from a story I heard later in childhood. But I can see it all so clearly: laughing along with Mother, who was regaled by the sight of passers-by scuttling out of the way, like leaves that before the wild hurricane fly, alarmed by the high-pitched and insistent klaxoning of her tactless bird. "Get the lead out!" Mrs. Rochester would bellow between waves of warning blare. "Drive it or park it! Step on it, lard arse!" Mother, at last, had found her true voice. And she didn't even need to open her mouth to use it.

"The fool folds his hands and eats his own flesh," Mrs. Rochester sputtered just moments ago, responding to who knows what stimulus. "Ecclesiastes 4.5," she added, with a know-it-all wink of her rimmed and beady eye. This untoward penchant for rhyming off biblical passages was the only one of her many party tricks to cause her chosen mistress any grief or pain. Mother was evangelistic about her atheism. At the same time, she was so devoted to empiricism that she could never bear to leave a source unchecked. Whenever her parrot would haul up yet another scriptural snippet from the intricate filing system of her inner noggin, Mother would be compelled to verify it, chapter and verse. Simply having a Bible in the house galled her to no end. It made her the more furious to leaf through its onion paper pages, learning against her will, by sheer force of repetition, Genesis, Exodus, Leviticus, Numbers. Over the many long years of their association, Mrs. Rochester's storehouse of biblical knowledge proved so vast—and accurate—that by the time Mother's soul was sundered from her body, she had dipped deeply into the rich well of both Testaments. I almost wish I believed in an afterlife in which rewards and punishments are disbursed according to some record of who's been naughty and who's been nice. I love the idea of Mother standing before some throne of judgment, pulling the wool over the eyes of the seraphic jury with her easy and unlikely familiarity with the Book of Job.

Not surprisingly, given our single parent's predilection for the secular and the practical, we were never taught to pray. Even so, I can't remember a time when I didn't. From a very early age, I would wrestle with the great imponderables of what preceded beginnings and what came after endings. It seemed right and natural to me to acknowledge the presence of such mysteries by whispering a few words of hope or thanks intended for the ears of whatever entity had invented the uncrackable code of being. As Mother would not have taken kindly to overt displays of piety, I said my words into my pillow: the very pillow into which I sobbed after the Miss Godbehere episode. I came to treat my little bag of feathers as a kind of celestial post office, to which I could consign my messages. The covert way I delivered them up created a bond of conspiracy between God and me that I found oddly invigorating.

I have that pillow still. It's hard as a rock, but it's where I like to lay my head. Now, as I settle back and say a fond goodnight to the quartet of angels who spin on the posts of my bed—one to watch, and one to pray, and two to bear my soul away—I think of Jacob, son of Isaac, brother of Esau, stopping in the desert at night and choosing a stone to cushion his skull. I see him pull his cloak about him against the chill of the night; see him fall into his dream of a ladder to Heaven, an angel on every rung, and God at the top, telling him his offspring will be like the dust of the earth. That, I know, I'll never hear. For I am a bachelor who sleeps alone, and always means to do so.

"Like a bird who strays from the nest is a man who strays from his home," mutters Mrs. Rochester, as she shifts from foot to foot, and settles into her own feathers for the night. "Proverbs 27.8."

She scarcely needs to tell me. It's a lesson we've both of us learned well. Look at us. We're living it. We will always be here.

Betty Bundy's Bachelor Buttons

Cream together:
  1/2 cup butter
  1 1/2 cups brown sugar

Add:
   2 *eggs*
   a dash of vanilla

Sift together and add to creamed mixture:
   2 *cups flour (1 bread, 1 pastry)*
   1 *tsp. baking powder*
   1 *tsp. baking soda*
   a pinch of salt

Add 1 tablespoon of hot water. Drop onto cookie sheet by small spoonfuls and bake at 375 degrees F. Put together with strawberry jam or date filling.

Dear Hector and Virgil,

Here, at very long last, is the recipe for Betty Bundy's Bachelor Buttons. I hope you haven't been sitting up nights pining for it! In all likelihood you've forgotten by now that you asked me to send it along. I had every good intention of doing so the minute I got home, but I was delayed in Calgary by a high school reunion that took on a life of its own and rolled on for three days longer than expected. My car broke down in Swift Current, which allowed me to sample the delights of that cosmopolitan centre for the better part of forty-eight hours. By the time I got home to Nepean (sounds like a country song, *n'est-ce pas?*) my house-sitter had decamped for a new assignment, and a group of inventive felons had taken advantage of my prolonged absence to break in and redecorate.

I mean this quite literally. Nothing was stolen. Nothing was broken. Nothing was smashed, except the basement window by which they gained access. They did nothing but move the furniture from one room to another. The first thing I saw when I came in the door was the bedroom where the living room had been. The bed, wardrobe, dresser and blanket box were artfully placed where last I had seen the sofa, chairs, lamps, and so on. The living room furniture, in its turn, had been carted up a narrow flight of stairs into the bedroom. How they managed to navigate their way from one floor to the next with a truly cumbersome couch and two overstuffed armchairs that make professional movers weep, and not so much as mark the paint, is a wonder to me even yet. The stove, mercifully, was left in the kitchen, but the refrigerator had been removed to the den. The contents were intact. Not even the newspaper clippings and dentist appointment reminders, or the fridge magnets that held them in place, had been disturbed. Whoever moved the fridge had a fastidious streak, as he or she had scrubbed away what must have been an ungodly accumulation of dust and dross from the floor and wall behind. I can't think of the last time I cleaned back there.

All my china had been taken down from the hutch. All my silver had been wrested from its drawers and *polished!* The dining room table, now also in the den, was set, very formally, for a dinner party of ten. They had even located matches—something I can never manage to do myself in my own house—and put them at the ready by the loaded candlesticks. The plates and pots and pans and dry goods had all been ferried from the kitchen cupboards and thought-fully arrayed in the bookcases, and the books themselves had been released from their orderly alphabetized ranks and placed in the kitchen cupboards. As there were more books than there was shelf space available in the kitchen, the homeless volumes were arranged in tidy piles in the bathroom. There was a narrow passageway that allowed me access to both toilet and tub.

"*Ceci n'est pas ma maison,*" I whispered, echoing Magritte, whose surrealist sympathies would surely have been aroused by this dis-play.

I finally managed to locate the phone in a salad bowl, which was on a bookshelf where the K—M authors used to live. "Not again," sighed the officer to whom I told my strange tale.

Evidently, there has been a rash of such criminal whimsy here-around of late. For want of a better term, the police have taken to calling the culprits "drive-by decorators." As it seems to be the work of young people—for who else would have the temerity, nerve and strength to undertake such an innovative break and enter—and as the jobs are quickly and thoughtfully done, they lay the blame at the feet of a consortium of mischievous university students, representing schools of engineering and interior design. I suppose you have to admire the spirit of interfaculty co-operation that makes such feats possible.

It was several days before I was able to re-establish anything like order in the house. By that time, your request that I send you the recipe for Betty Bundy's Bachelor Buttons had simply left my head. That I remembered at all is thanks to my mother, who regularly sends me obituaries from the Calgary papers: clipped summations of the lives and careers of people whose passing she thinks will interest me, but of whom I have, for the most part, little or no recall. Usually there's no word of explanation, although from time to time she will mention the deceased in her accompanying letter. "You remember Hazel, of course. She was in charge of flowers at the church the year Bonnie had that attack of sciatica." "Poor Nancy! I don't think she ever really recovered from the disappointment of losing the curling bonspiel to that team from Prince Edward Island." "Can't believe that Helga has gone. Saw her just last week and she was talking about how much she was enjoying going to Elder Fit at the Seniors' Centre." And only this morning, "You remember Betty Bundy, of course. She was always so perky on the phone! She went into hospital last month with a stomach pain. They looked inside and closed her right back up again, she was just so full of it. There was nothing they could do."

Betty Bundy never had children of her own, which was a great sadness to her. She directed her maternal urges toward the neighbourhood at large. She used to make up big batches of her Bachelor Buttons (which she also called Jam Jams), stand out on her porch and just holler into the summer air, "Come and get 'em while they're hot! Bachelor Buttons! Jam Jams are on the table!" We'd swoop down like locusts and devour them, batch after batch. I was so fond of them I begged my mother to wheedle the recipe out of Mrs. Bundy. Somehow, though, Mama's were never up to snuff. I told that to Betty once, who nodded knowingly and said it was because she used homemade jam for the filling, while my mother relied on what Mrs. Bundy scornfully called a "store boughten" product.

I have the recipe for Betty Bundy's Bachelor Buttons, carefully copied out on a file card in my mother's distinctive hand, but I've never actually made them myself. Mama sent me this, and several other recipes, shortly after I moved from Calgary. I suppose she was thinking I would want to make the familiar foods of my childhood as a charm against homesickness. For the longest time, those cards languished in their little box. Now that middle age is on me, though, I find myself in the grip of inexplicable cravings. I'll whip up a dish of Gerda Lantzinger's Foamy Lemon Pudding when a weird nostalgia settles over me. Eve Reimer's Spicy Pineapple Loaf is as potent for me as Proust's *madeleine*. But I can't imagine rolling up my sleeves and whipping up a few dozen Bachelor Buttons. I could never fold into them the qualities of love and longing that Betty Bundy invested in her Jam Jams each and every time she baked them. I'll be curious to learn how they turn out if one day you decide to give them a whirl.

The drive-by decorators had stacked my cookbooks (all fifty of them) onto one of the bedside tables, which were in the living room with the rest of the bedroom furniture. A copy of Harper Lee's *To Kill a Mockingbird* had been placed on the twin table. It was a thoughtful choice on the part of whatever prankster had selected it for my bedtime reading. I've always found it a comforting novel, above all else: comforting and affirming. I stretched out on the bed where the couch used to be. While waiting for the police to arrive, I took up the book and began to read, for the tenth time at least, about that tumultuous summer in the lives of the decent Finch family.

"Too bad you touched that," said the constable, as he surveyed the vastly reconfigured lay of the land, "it might have had prints."

As there was nothing I could tell the police to help them in their investigation, and as I couldn't offer them a cookie or a cup of coffee—having no notion where anything was—I simply remained prone and read while they made their inspection, read while they took their notes and photographs, read long after they had quit the scene of the crime. In fact, I didn't stop reading until the words ran out, and I fell asleep, puzzled, bemused and exhausted. I had pleasant dreams. When they had run their course, I was able to look around my living room, laugh, and call a moving company to send a team of friendly brutes to put things back where they belonged. All except for the blanket box, which I decided I liked in the living room and now use as a coffee table.

It's cold here today. Spring has had second thoughts, and a cossack wind is pounding down from the north. Snow is promised for later tonight. It's harsh. I wonder if it makes you feel just the tiniest bit smug, there on your island, as you look out your windows at the rhododendrons and the tulips? All the best, and again my apologies for the long delay.

Hoping to see you again soon, I remain, Elizabeth Moir, Nepean Ontario.

Last winter, to the astonishment of all

Last winter, to the astonishment of all who know me, I grew a goatee. I sought neither permission nor counsel before embarking on this course. I filed no flight plan. I just went ahead and did it. Virgil was the first to make inquiries when it became evident the fresh turf on my face had been deliberately cultivated and was not just some grievous oversight. We were sitting in the kitchen enjoying a midafternoon cup of tea and plodding through the crossword in *The Occasional Rumour*. He took his pen out of his mouth—he was sucking on it while contemplating the answer to 10 down, "traitorous eggs"—and peered at me over the top of the schoolmarmish half-glasses he has latterly taken to wearing. Middle age is full of insults, and these are among the most unsightly.

"Is that what I think it is?" he whispered, cautiously, as if we were in a cathedral looking at some shrivelled bit of holy anatomy in a reliquary.

"I beg your pardon?" I looked around the room with an exaggerated innocence, like little George Washington pretending he was hearing the word "hatchet" for the very first time.

"On your face. That fledgling growth on your face. Is that what I think it is?"

"On my face? Oh! *That* fledgling! Strange, isn't it? I woke up the other morning and there it was! I suppose it must have flown in through the window. That's what you get for leaving them open, especially at this time of year. Of course, I went right into the bathroom and started to remove it, but it cheeped at me so pathetically that I figured it must be brooding on some eggs. So I said to myself, heck! What can it hurt? I'll just leave it there until the little ones hatch and learn to fly and then it'll probably leave of its own accord."

Virgil is my brother and I love him dearly, but he takes himself too seriously at times. It's a kindness to twit him. Really, it is. He fixed me with his baleful "St. Sebastian greets the archers" look.

"Very, very funny. I can hardly contain my laughter. Please, I must ask you to remember my hernia. You know how dangerous unbridled hilarity can be to a man in my condition."

"Sorry," I said, barely concealing my smirk.

"*Why* is what I suppose I'm asking, in my passive-aggressive way."

"Oh, you know. Just another one of those mid-life, male menopause things. It was either this or a Ferrari."

"Hmmmmm. You're not planning to take up the saxophone, are you? You know how I feel about the saxophone."

Virgil has the same easy relationship with the saxophone that acid has with base. If there were a universal symbol for "No Saxophones," he would search high and low to find one on a bumper sticker and take his message with him when he goes out into the world. I reassured him on that account, and also made it clear that I had no immediate plans to start favouring black turtlenecks, garret living or Gitane cigarettes.

"However, I just might get my ear pierced," I added, half-thinking as I said it that I would look quite jaunty with a hoop through one of my lobes.

But my brother paid me no mind. The crossword had reclaimed his attention. The answer to 10 down had risen to the corrugated surface of his brain, and he was penning in "Eggs Benedict Arnold."

The goatee is not my first experiment with facial hair. Almost forty years ago, long before shaving lost its allure, when I was still a teenager and thrilled with the fuzzy testimony to manhood that was starting to insinuate itself onto my upper lip, I dared to try a moustache. It took long and careful carding before I could weave the sparse filaments into two very thin blades that looked less like handlebars than like the crazy legs of some red water strider. I used a dab or two of bacon grease as moustache wax, which I thought was a cunning if slightly malodorous way to achieve the desired look. I studied my reflection long and hard in the bathroom mirror. Over all, I was pleased. I thought I was dashing, devil-may-care and sartorial. In the right light, I was persuaded, I might be mistaken for Errol Flynn's much younger cousin. I practised a few fencing moves and lunges with the plunger, then hurried down to breakfast, eager to try out the effect on my mother and brother.

Unfortunately, Mother had agreed to baby-sit a St. Bernard for some neighbours who had been called suddenly away. Bernice— her name is forever etched in my mind—intercepted me just as I swashbuckled my way into the kitchen. She reared up on her hind legs, placed her two massive front paws on my shoulders, wrestled me to the floor and sucked the ersatz wax from my nascent moustache. Mother rushed to the scene of the accident.

"For heaven's sake, Bernice! Stop it! Stop it! You know you're supposed to be on a diet!"

Virgil, who demonstrated at an early age that he had a curious ability to match snippets of poetry to events as they unfolded, looked up from his book and cornflakes only long enough to wince in sympathy and pronounce, "Look on my works, ye mighty, and despair." Mrs. Rochester flew to the top of the door frame from where she stared down at my mussed stashes and called out, with all her accustomed helpfulness, "Cockroach, cockroach, cockroach!"

I never again invested any hope in the prospect of dressing up my lip; not, at least, until I went to visit Abel Wackaugh for my New Year's haircut. I happened to step into his barbershop, which is also our local hardware store, at the same time a salesman was trying to interest Abel in some "computer imaging" equipment. The vendor of this terribly high-tech salon gewgaw was a stranger to the valley and not at all accustomed to our ways. He must have thought it odd that hair was being styled—if so vaunted a term can be applied to Abel's slash and burn technique of barbering—at the same place where screws were being sold, keys duplicated, and paint mixed.

It could never be said of Abel that he doesn't have a malicious bone in his body. When his bonnet starts to buzz about someone or something, you can be certain the bee is the killing kind. He evidently felt he was being condescended to by this purveyor of digitized cosmetic aids, and had taken it upon himself to make the poor thing's life a misery by acting like a backwoods hick.

"Now, let me be sure I understand you, young fella," he said as I took a chair and picked up a 1967 copy of *Field and Stream*, "you're telling me that this here whaddayacallit computer imaging thingy will let my customers see how they would look if they wanted to have such and such a hair cut. Have I got that right? Well, I'd love to get such a gizmo, but I think I'll have to pay off the buddy who was through here last week and sold me that machine for dissolving kidney stones first."

Given our parentage, it is only natural that both Virgil and I have a special fondness and sympathy for travelling salespeople. We can always be counted on to buy a lint brush or vegetable peeler when someone turns up on the stoop with a sample case and a hopeful look. Sitting there in Abel's shop and watching so terrible a baiting, I couldn't help but feel sorry for this pathetic creature.

"Perhaps you'd like to give a demonstration of your machine," I suggested, volunteering myself as a guinea pig.

His look of relief and gratitude put me in mind of a puppy who is taken in from the raging storm. He set up the camera and screen and keyboard that made up his kit. A small crowd gathered round.

"Glory be and tarnation! Will wonders never cease?" Abel carried on, sounding for all the world like a rustic who had fallen beneath his plough and suffered an inadvertent lobotomy.

The salesman twiddled various dials and knobs to bring my face into focus.

"Now, how do you think you'd look with bangs?"

He waved his wand, and lo! There I was, with my forehead obscured by a lanky mop of hair.

"Wait!" called Abel, who was on a roll and really couldn't help himself, "Larry, Moe or Curly Joe?"

"And if you had a perm, you'd look like this!"

Another manipulation of the mouse, and the bangs were whipped up into a frothy storm that finally settled down into a tight coagulation of curls.

"Land o' Goshen! This thing could prove real useful the next time we have to cast the witches in *Macbeth*!"

"That's enough, Abel. I don't suppose you can show me what I'd look like with a moustache?" I asked, remembering my failed experiment of long ago. The young man obligingly punched a few buttons, and within seconds I was transformed. I could see that my adolescent instincts had not been without foundation. The moustache did add a certain *je ne sais quoi* to my overall mien.

"And this," the salesman volunteered, gleefully, "is how you'd look with a goatee!"

The moustache dissolved and regrouped on my chin. I couldn't stop myself from grinning at the picture of a me I had never before imagined. There was something so rakish, so bohemian, so very very espresso bar about it that I had the twinkling of an inkling that it was still possible I might one day become someone wholly other than who I have been. And that is a seductive notion.

"Oh, daddy-o! Now we know who to call on when we need someone who knows all the verses to 'Blowin' in the Wind!'"

The salesman sighed at Abel's final jeer and pulled the plug. It was clear he wouldn't chalk up a sale on this swing through our valley, and he could waste his time more profitably elsewhere. Abel, on the other hand, managed to convince his visitor to buy both a plastic bag sorter and a buttonhook before he made it out the door.

Unlike our father, who understood somehow that his passage through our valley had been eventful, this man will never know that his visit had its own minor consequences. My face is the proof of it. A goatee had been the last thing on my mind. I can't imagine it would ever have made it to my face had our paths not crossed that afternoon, and had I not been so taken by the possibilities for transformation I saw beaming at me from the screen. The truth is that, in this instance anyway, technology proved herself a more able craftswoman than nature. The goatee the computer designed for me was far more attractive than the one my own chin provided. Still, I have been interested to note how different people interpret the semiotics of my face, now that the thing has grown in. Some think it sinister. Mrs. Rochester, for instance, has resurrected the phrase "spawn of Satan" from her alarming memory. Some call it cool. Some think it clownish, while others say it gives me rather a professorial air. Everyone has an opinion. Altona was away at a seminar for writers of romance novels when I decided to make the change. On her return, she looked at me, gaped, and said just what I hoped she would say.

"Sexy! That is *so* sexy!"

Later on, when we were thoroughly reacquainted, and I had told her the story of the computer-imaging salesman, she turned to me and asked, "If there were a machine that could show you how you'd look wearing whole different lives instead of different hairstyles, what life would you pick?"

And how do you think I answered? Why, I said just what she hoped I would say. I meant it, too. That's the truth. I swear by the hair of my chinny chin chin.

May we recommend?
The bachelor brothers' suggestions
for cookbooks that are fine to read

Lists, which are arbitrary and idiosyncratic, should irritate and annoy as much as they inform and entertain. The reader should be provoked to raise a voice of protest, to exclaim, "Wait! You've forgotten so and so! Why have you included thus and which, when you've left out such and why?" These books have been selected as much for their literary merit as for their culinary impact. While there are many, many more titles that might have found their way into this small catalogue, and many, many more authors who are deserving of inclusion, we have chosen these with breadth of appeal in mind. While they might not be the final choices of another compiler, we are confident they would find their way onto any short list.

The Alice B. Toklas Cookbook, Alice B. Toklas

"Cook-books have always intrigued and seduced me," wrote Alice B. Toklas in this engaging memoir, in which reminiscences are interspersed with recipes, including the receipt for the famous haschich (*sic*) fudge which elevated the book to something like cult status over thirty years ago. Miss Toklas assures her readers that "almost anything St. Theresa did, you can do better." Gastronomes who might be drawn to Toklas by the famous brownies and their promise of *luxe, calme, et volupté* should not ignore the rest of the book. It is charming and poignant by turns, and is as pleasant to read as Gertrude Stein is puzzling.

American Gourmet, Jane and Michael Stern

The Sterns have carved out an enviable niche for themselves as anthropologists of the truck stop and as keen-eyed chroniclers of the shifting shape of bad taste in America. They manage to find humour and even something like beauty in such crass manifestations of American commercial culture as Elvis-mania and automobile advertisements.

The salutary effect of reading such a book, which makes us laugh, affectionately, at the pretensions and the excesses of the very recent past, is that it reminds us that there is nothing to be gained from taking ourselves too terribly seriously in the present moment. Soon enough, the day will come that present or future Sterns make merry with what we are now living through.

The Art of Eating, M. F. K. Fisher

The Art of Eating brings together in a single volume five books by a woman whose reputation as one of the finest English-language prose writers of the century continues to grow unabated. In *Serve It Forth, Consider the Oyster, How to Cook a Wolf, The Gastronomical Me* and *An Alphabet of Gourmets*, the reader discerns something of the breadth of Mrs. Fisher's learning and the depth of her humanity. Whether recounting her years in Dijon, or writing about her childhood in California, or suggesting household economies, or praising the potato, she never loses sight of her own mission and credo, set down in 1943 in the introduction to *The Gastronomical Me*: "There is food in the bowl, and more often than not, because of what honesty

I have, there is nourishment in the heart, to feed the wilder, more insistent hungers. We must eat. If, in the face of that dread fact, we can find other nourishment, and tolerance and compassion for it, we'll be no less full of human dignity."

Food and Friends, Simone Beck

We would all do well to remind ourselves that the word "companion" means, at root, "one with whom one breaks bread." Nothing complements food quite so well as a friend, and any friendship we've ever had and kept has been cemented over food. This is all to say that we are kindly disposed to this book by dint of the title alone. Simone Beck (whom her friends called Simca, which was the name of the little Renault car she drove around Paris in the '30s) was part of the triumvirate that popularized French cooking in North America in the early '60s. While her story of her friendship with Julia Child and Louisette Berthole and her recounting of the madcap years of Paris in the '20s and '30s haven't got quite the *élan* of the Alice B. Toklas memoir, they are still readable and engaging, and—for those who actually like to use a cookbook as a source of menu ideas rather than literary diversion—the recipes are very fine and varied.

Larousse Gastronomique

This classic encyclopaedia of French cuisine is one of the greatest browsing books ever devised. No one who is sufficiently steeped in the Larousse need worry about running out of conversation starters or ice-breakers at a cocktail party. You could regale the entire company with the tale of how a doctor travelled on foot with a herd of sheep from Constantinople to Paris and cured King François I of his intestinal difficulties by feeding him yogurt. You could discourse on the history of the tablecloth or the fork, settle an argument on the method for making Yorkshire pudding, discuss the best way of cooking a camel hump, and speak with some authority on the presentation of *hors d'oeuvres*. When we first began our business, Hector decided to count the egg dishes listed in the *Larousse*, but stopped when he passed 200. So far, no one has asked us for Eggs Babinski or Rothomago. In the event, however, we are prepared.

An Omelette and a Glass of Wine, Elizabeth David

There are recipes here and there in this classic volume, but it is more a collection of essays and reminiscences than a cookbook proper. What we have here is a concentrated dose of the artful writing that distinguishes Mrs. David's cookery books, such as *French Provincial Cooking*, *French Country Cooking* and *Italian Food*. She is one of those writers who expresses a whole worldview with her notes and observations about food fads and fashions, restaurants, regions and eaters she has known.

We have both tried hundreds of times to make an adequate omelette and have always been defeated. The product is too dry, too rubbery, too liquid, too crisp. It never has the feathery, airy texture that a real genius of the kitchen brings to the enterprise. We are persuaded that a talent for omelette making is precisely that: a talent, a gift, as rare and as valuable as, say, a knack for composing music or for understanding physics. This notion is buttressed by the recipe Elizabeth David includes in the title essay. It comes from an omelette black belt named Annette Poulard. Responding to a gentleman who sought the secret of her success in this regard, she wrote: "I break some good eggs in a bowl, I beat them well, I put a good piece of butter in the pan, I throw the eggs into it, and I shake it constantly." So there! This is surely the culinary equivalent of Mozart saying, "There's nothing to it. Just sit down and write the notes."

The Physiology of Taste: Or, Meditations in Transcendental Gastronomy, Jean Anthelme Brillat-Savarin

We discovered Brillat-Savarin (1755-1826) via M. F. K. Fisher (q.v.), one of his translators. Brillat-Savarin was a musician, a magistrate, a political economist, a world traveller, an essayist, an epicure, the Mayor of Bellay and a bachelor. Like Mrs. Fisher, he was a consummate literary stylist and apothegmatist. Whether he is describing the erotic effects of the truffle or the influence of the turkey on the money market, quotable quotes leap from the page:

"A *true* gourmand could not be late to dinner."

"I believe firmly that the entire gallinaceous order has been merely created to furnish our larders."

"The loveliest and most tempting of lips lose all their charms when they perform the functions of an evacuation organ."

The only hazard of reading Brillat-Savarin is the temptation to stop in your tracks, put every other project or necessity on the back burner, and sit right down and stitch his aphorisms into a sampler.

A Table in Tuscany, Leslie Forbes

A charming book by a Canadian writer who, when last sighted, was living and working in London. This is certainly one of the most beautiful cookbooks in our collection, with its delicate colour pencil drawings of things Tuscan: landscapes and tabletops and restaurants and foodstuffs and wine labels, etc. These illustrations, along with the calligraphic print and the leisurely, anecdotal presentation of recipes for dishes such as dandelion soup, eel with sage and garlic, and rabbit stuffed with olives give the impression that you are looking into someone's lovingly kept private journal. Virgil was so taken with this book that he actually spent the better part of a day making ravioli by hand for a volunteer fire department potluck: square by square by bloody square. That it dissolved into a gelatinous mess in the pot had nothing to do with laxity—or anything like it—on the part of Ms. Forbes in delivering up her instructions. It is for situations such as this that the good Lord gave us frozen pasta and grocery stores.

Early on in this Lenten season

Early on in this Lenten season—which I am observing by relinquishing my plan to take up tatting—we received a letter that caused me grave anxiety. This in itself is not so very unusual. Most letters make me nervous. Don't ask why this should be so. I have no idea. Perhaps our mother was frightened by a philatelist when she was carrying us. If so, I was the sole *in utero* victim of the psychic shock waves, for Hector and I are completely dissimilar in this regard. He waits for the arrival of each day's mail with a jigging enthusiasm. He loves to brandish the letter opener with the mother-of-pearl handle he won for his high school essay on "The Post Office in the Modern World": a concept which seems ever more foolishly optimistic, if not downright oxymoronic, by the minute. I, on the other hand, regard every piece with tremulous wariness. "Why should I open you?" is the silent question I put to each envelope and parcel, when for one reason or another Hector is not available for duty.

Some years back, as part of a cost-saving measure on the part of the post office, we valley-dwellers were stricken from the roster of those deemed worthy of receiving visits from the friendly, whistling letter carrier. Instead, as in many other rural areas in this country, our post was rerouted to a community mailbox: a shiny, silver bank of locked-up cubbies, with none of the romance of the homespun, end-of-the-driveway letter receptacles with their unique designs and tell-tale flags that served us so well for years. Now I have to deal not only with the base fact of mail; I must also put up with the inconvenience of climbing into our old pickup and driving down the road to retrieve it.

The one saving grace of this exercise is that the community mailbox is located within a flapjack lob of our local coffee bar, The Well of Loneliness. So, I am able to mitigate the insult of this imposed necessity by visiting with Rae and June. They are the co-proprietors of The Well, and we are very fond of them. While both Rae and June make a mean cappuccino, most of the coffee-making duties have fallen to Rae since their dalliance with artificial insemination proved fruitful. When they told me what they were planning to do, and that the donor was an old friend on the mainland who worked as a milkman, I thought they were pulling my leg.

"A milkman?" I roared. "Come on!"

"He's very bright," said June defensively. "I met him at my Jung reading group."

"But you're forty!"

"Exactly. And Rae's forty-seven. If one of us is going to do this, it's got to be me. And I can't wait much longer."

And lo and behold, she damned all torpedoes but one and went ahead with her procreative undertaking. It's boggling to think how radically you can alter the shape of your days and body both with tools as simple as a thermometer, a syringe, and few wiggly gifts from a willing donor. Now, June is nearing the end of her first trimester, and I find myself increasingly absorbed in the action as I watch the unaccountable and unpredictable effects of pregnancy. Nausea. Fits of energy followed by waves of fatigue. Shifting gastronomic likes and dislikes. For the last week or so, she hasn't been able to stomach the aromatic whiffs that rise from freshly ground beans. It is an occupational stumbling block, and a personal liability, too. Rae and June were moved to open The Well because they couldn't abide being in a place where a full range of caffeine products was not available.

"God," she said this morning as she tucked into one of the half-dozen yogurts she now wolfs down every day, "if anyone had told me three months ago that I'd willingly give up coffee, I'd have laughed in her face."

"Have you settled on a name yet?" I asked between sucks of the cinnamon-dotted froth that is the best part of a cappuccino. I cupped my hand protectively about the rim, trying to ensure that no wayward ambrosial wafts would pummel June's aberrantly sensitive olfactory centre.

"We're wavering between Rita Mae and Martina," said Rae.

"And you're absolutely sure there's no question of a Marcel or Oscar?"

"The tests have been wrong before," June admitted, "but we saw the ultrasound images, and there was nothing that looked like— how shall I say it—a distinguishing mark of manhood."

"Ah," I answered. I wasn't at all persuaded that such vestigial determining delicacies would be visible at this stage of development. But it was hardly my place to say so. After all, Rae and June have steeped themselves very thoroughly in prenatal lore and learning since deciding to become parents.

"Did we show you the photo of the fetching foetus? The ultrasound technician printed one for us."

I looked at the picture of a newt in aspic, a fleshy squiggle, bald and veined and vulnerable, the beginnings of a thumb tucked comfortably in what would soon be a mouth. I hardly knew what to say, I was so dumfounded by the technology that made such an image possible, and by the physical evidence that soon their lives—and inevitably, our relationship—would be vastly changed.

"What have you got there?" asked June, picking up the sheaf of mail I'd just retrieved. She leafed idly through the pile, then exclaimed, "Wow! Here's something from *Interference!*"

"What's that?"

"Virgil, Virgil. What century do you live in?"

"In what century do you live," I corrected, unable to restrain the pedant within.

"*Interference* is just about the hottest lifestyle magazine on the market."

I shuddered. I find the word "lifestyle" about as attractive as the prospect of a root canal.

"What would they want with us?"

"May I?" asked Rae.

I nodded. They are well acquainted with my aversion to opening the mail.

She ripped open the envelope, pulled a letter written on thick and creamy bond from within, read it through rapidly, and let out a low whistle.

"Holy smokes! It's from Polly Perch herself!"

"Wow!" yelped June, grabbing the letter.

"Polly Perch?"

"She's a big noise media mogul, the founder and editor, the queen bee of *Interference,*" explained Rae. She took my cup and went to make another cappuccino.

"Dear Bachelor Brothers," June read aloud. "For an upcoming issue of *Interference*, we are planning a story on innovative bed and breakfast operations, such as your own. We would like to send one of our reporters to the Bachelor Brothers' Bed and Breakfast to spend a few days as a guest, and to write about the unique aspects of your establishment. As you know, *Interference* is one of the most widely read magazines on the market today, and a feature in our pages is one of the surest ways of renewing and enriching your client base."

"Client base?" I winced.

"Of course, we ask that our journalistic representative be given a complimentary room and meals. I understand that you have avoided the bright light of publicity to this point, so you may not be aware that this is standard practice in the preparation of an industry service piece."

"Service piece?"

"Essentially," Rae explained, setting down the cappuccino, "it means they're giving you an ad for free."

"But we don't want an ad! We've never wanted an ad! What gall! What nerve! Here! Give me that letter!" And I tore it into a great many pieces and deposited it in the garbage before June had a chance to read it through to the end.

"We recycle," remonstrated June, although I think she knew that the circumstances were extenuating.

I drove home from The Well in a state of some agitation, brought on by two high-octane brews and the audacity of Polly Perch.

"Polly Perch?" asked Hector that evening, as he was going through the remainder of the mail. "Sounds like a good name for a parrot."

Mrs. Rochester let out a squawk of indignation. She hates the name Polly and rails against first-time visitors who try it out on her.

"Hello Polly! Pretty Polly! Pretty Polly! Polly wanna cracker?" they almost invariably coo.

"Halitosis! Halitosis!" she will shriek out vengefully.

The only way she can be pacified is with a fortune cookie, which is her favourite treat. She takes the prognosticatory biscuit in her scaly, primeval claw, chomps into it, and lets the pink, revelatory slip fall to the floor. At the end of the day, if she has been especially demanding and the fortunes are thick on the ground around her, I will amuse myself by assembling them into a found poem. Today, there were nearly a dozen clairvoyant clichés, and when I had culled the duplicate fortunes from the pile and mindlessly slapped them together into something that verged on the sensible, the spectre of Polly Perch came back on me, like a radish burp of the mind.

Beware of those who write from afar.
An unwanted visitor will soon appear.
Be sure you know who your real friends are.
The future for you is far from clear.
A stranger comes who is no friend.
Are wealth and fortune all they seem?
Each beginning has its end.
Pay more attention to your dreams.

So. What am I to think of all this? Just now, I'm too pooped to fret over it. Pay more attention to my dreams. There's only one place I know of where I can do that. And so, as Pepys would say, to bed, where I hope for visions of raindrops on roses, sugar plums and wagons full of bouncing, laughing babies.

Altona has a mole

Altona has a mole. It floats like an islet on the smooth and otherwise blameless expanse of her back. If her two perfect shoulder blades were waves rising up from a warm, wide ocean, this evidence of careless pigmentation would mark a point equidistant between the crests of the swells. It is small and perfectly round. A sweet speck. An innocuous eruption. To call it a mole is to overstate the case; it is little more than an enthusiastic freckle. Altona has no idea how long she has played host to this mark. It may have been with her when she was born, or it may have appeared later in life. Certainly, I have never known her without it. And I was the first to tell her it was there. It was early on in our time together. We were romping on her satin sheets, beneath the spreading canopy that hangs above her custom-made bed, which is an exact replica of the amorous playground of Catherine the Great. Altona commissioned it with part of the proceeds from her divorce settlement. I was being a Latin lover, muttering extravagant endearments in an ersatz mid-Mediterranean accent, between slurpy smooches.

"I kiss your neck! I kiss your ears! I kiss your shoulders! I even kiss your little mole!"

Altona, who was writhing and panting co-operatively, froze like a mastodon surprised in mid-mastication by an unexpected ice age.

"Mole?"

"Your little mole. I kiss your little mole, smooch smooch!"

"What mole?"

And she leapt from the bed and ran to the full-length glass on her closet door. She twisted and turned and craned her neck, and whimpered while trying to find it. I angled a hand mirror so she might see where the newly discovered dark star hung. I remember looking at the two of us reflected there, naked, twisted, middle-aged, deflated, and regretting for a brief moment the absence from our world of Hieronymous Bosch. He would surely have drawn inspiration from a vision that caused no welling of pleasure in either of us.

"Keep an eye on that mole of mine, will you?" she asked me one night as we lay in her bed, basking in the afterburn of love and the television's cathode glow. We were watching yet another doom-ridden newscast about how the depletion of the kindly ozone had turned the sun—once our cheery friend and the dispenser of some bone-strengthening vitamin—into a sworn and cancer-leeching enemy

"Aye, aye," I said, and sealed the promise with a tender, between-the-shoulders kiss. I have kept my word. And I mean to keep it as long she values and requires my watchfulness. I keep an eye on the mole when I haltingly unfasten the recalcitrant hooks of her undergarments, fumbling and hamfisted, but always with the hope that incessant practice will one day make perfect. Or conversely, I memorize its brown secrets when I zip her into some spine-revealing sheath of a dress before a cocktail party. And when we are in the thick of that crowded room, and she is standing with her back to me, a martini in one hand and a half-gnawed mushroom in the other, chewing thoughtfully while she surveys the array of dips and cold cuts, the mole is a beacon for my eyes only. I stare at it as though it were an indecipherable blot on an optometrist's chart. I fix it with my steady gaze, and watch it blur in and out of focus, pulsing while it takes on new and unlikely shapes: a sparrow, a rose, a minaret. And on those rare nights when circumstances allow us to lie together, satiated in bed, slotted like two well-worn spoons, and she has fallen asleep while I curl up against her, a pliable papoose, testing with my legs and torso all the fleshy contours of her body; and when the hated blemish is concealed by the considerate darkness, I count the vertebrae up from her sacrum, my fingers a whisper along the ridges of her spine. One's out of fashion, two gives release, three is for passion, four is for peace, five is forgiving, six says we're whole, seven is living, eight is the mole. Tickle me, tickle me, tickle me do, count down from ten again, I love you.

The attentive reader, whose sensibilities have not been heated to the point of fission by the unabashed candour of my prose, might very well want to intrude here with a perfectly logical question: If your feelings for this woman are so savage and refined, why do you stay only rare nights together? To which I would answer: Spend one night bucking in passion's lasso, and the following day attempt to be the attentive and cogent co-proprietor of a bed and breakfast, and you will ask no further.

This is a demanding job, unforgiving of those who let self-indulgence, carnal or otherwise, rob them of their rest. The exigencies of the place require that the heat be cranked up under the pressure cooker of the day by 6 A.M. By 7, full-scale percolation is underway. Before the hour is out, the lid is ready to blow right off, but none of your exertions can seem strained. No glint of panic can illumine your eye, nor bead of sweat dot your brow as your guests descend—sometimes in a trickle, sometimes in a flood—bearing with them their various matinal requirements. Only in this way can you coax confidence from those who have entrusted you with the preparation of a repast about which everyone has strong personal feelings.

The early morning is a time of fragility. Our guests come down to us with their fears and idiosyncrasies intact; fears and idiosyncrasies that have had untrammelled access to their brains all night and are still swimming close to the surface. You must be ready to listen sympathetically to their minor complaints about creaky joints, atrophying bladders and interrupted snoozes. You must be prepared to interpret their dreams, look at pictures of their grandchildren, mediate in the petty morning disputes that arise between couples, all the while accommodating the need each guest feels for inclusion in the life of the house, and not for a moment forgetting that there is sausage or bacon under the broiler, a tray of muffins in the oven, eggs softboiling, hardboiling, frying and poaching on top of the stove. In short, it doesn't do for one of the principals to be dashing in around 8:30, with his shirttail flapping and his shoes undone and telltale bruises on his neck.

It happened to me only once, in the early days of my association with Altona, when the bloom of love was full, and its sweet scent so heady that it obliterated the mitigating aromas of common sense and decency. Poor Virgil! The first thing I saw as I pelted through the kitchen door was my brother standing dazed at the sink, surrounded by the jetsam of breakfast. He looked like a soldier who was ready to throw himself onto a grenade, just to avoid more time in the trenches.

All but one of the guests—there were six of them in residence at the time—had left the table and were off about the house making their own amusement. The one happy laggard, whose name was Gladys, had just helped herself to another cup of coffee and was about to resume reading aloud from the horoscopes in *The Occasional Rumour*. She put on her glasses, looked me up and down, whistled soft and low, and said, "Well, well, well! What have we here? My goodness! Now *that's* a hickey! That's so unusual in a man of your age. Either you have a girlfriend with lips that could extract ore, or you have very tender skin. Is it your skin? You must tell me your secret. Do you use creams? Or is it just genetic? Some people have all the luck. Of course, the drawback to delicate skin is that it shows every bruise. Really and truly! I haven't seen so significant a hickey since my granddaughter started dating. How long ago would that have been? Let's see. I remember that I had just turned sixty-eight and she had just turned fourteen. Our birthdays are only a week apart, although I'm a Leo and she's a Virgo. Astrologically speaking, anyway. I'm 71 now, and she's 17, which is numerologically interesting, because it's as though we share the same age, only with the digits reversed. No wonder we're so close. Anyway, it would have been three years ago this coming May that she came to visit me one afternoon after school, and she had a hickey the size of Iceland in the vicinity of her jugular. Goodness, but I was pleased! I thought it was so *cute*, and wonderful, and a little sad, too. Here was my grandchild, turning into a woman before my very eyes. She was *dating*! She had all that happiness and excitement and discovery and disappointment ahead of her. We all have to go through it, don't we? It's part of what makes us who we are.

"I remember when I came home with my first hickey. I was almost twenty, for heaven's sake. I was engaged! But my parents didn't speak to me for a week. They treated me like dirt. *Dirt!* I don't think my father ever really got over it. Why should anyone have to go through that? I could tell she was terribly embarrassed by it, of course, and she'd tried to hide it with a really thick foundation. But a hickey is a hard thing to mask with make-up. I could have told her that, but I didn't want to upset her by noticing when she obviously didn't want me to. Still, I thought I should do something to acknowledge it, so I went out the very next morning get her a card. I drove all the way into Toronto and went to this little specialty shop in Yorkville. I asked the girl at the counter if she had any cards that said something like, 'To a wonderful granddaughter on the occasion of her first lovebite,' and she looked at me like I was completely mad. I didn't think it was so unreasonable. They have cards for everything else. Your first hickey is an important rite of passage! I meant to write to Hallmark at the time, to suggest they were missing out on a significant market, but of course I forgot. Anyway, I muttered to the shopgirl that I just hadn't been myself since the treatments began, and bought one of those blank cards with a reproduction of a Japanese woodblock print on the front, and I wrote her a little note in it. She was tickled pink! And ever since then, we've been as close as sisters. She tells me all about her boyfriends, and I tell her about mine. She has more fun with hers, I'd wager to say, but you're only young once, and I don't begrudge her any of it. Frankly, I think there's a lot to be said for—what do you call it? Oh yes! Vicarious living. Funny word, isn't it? Vicarious. Sounds like it has something to do with vicars, and it so rarely does. Anyway, dear, the point is that you shouldn't try to hide it with your shirt collar like that. We can all see what it is. We know a hickey when we see one. Did you have a nice time?"

"Yes," I said, reeling ever so slightly in the face of this inquisitive onslaught. "Yes, thank you. Quite a nice time."

"Oh, come now! Only quite?"

"Well . . . well . . . very. I had a very nice time!"

"That's the spirit! What's your sign?"

"Taurus," I answered, with a nervous sideways glance at Virgil. He was scrubbing away at a bit of congealed yolk with frothy and unnecessary vigour.

"Taurus! The bull! Well, well, that's a passionate sign, for sure. Let's see what the stars have in hold for you. Listen to this! 'Congratulations, Taurus! Now is the time to strike while the iron is hot. Love is waiting in the wings, watching for your cue. Raise your sails and catch the new wind that's blowing! The romance of your lifetime is just around the corner!' Ha! Sounds like you're in for a good time, sailor."

Even without looking at Virgil, I could sense he was biting his tongue. He knew full well that the horoscopes were among Altona's responsibilities at *The Occasional Rumour*. To his credit, he just rolled his eyes and kept his counsel. I don't doubt for a second that it was a chore for Virgil to fold Altona into the mix of our lives. Lord knows, it wasn't easy for me. She is a creature of ready emotions and considerable bombast. She leaps without looking, and her valour is in no way alloyed by discretion. But it didn't take my brother long to see through her expansive surfaces and to understand that she is also a canny and kindly woman. Whatever fears and reservations he might initially have had about the dissolution of our fraternal corporation have gone by the wayside. And while the geniality he showed Altona at the outset surely was contrived, he has come to truly love her, in his fashion; to make allowances and even appreciate her eccentricities, and to value her opinions.

"You fellows need someone to help you out," she said, not so very long ago. "Look at the way you live. Up at the crack of dawn, slaving over a hot stove, washing, scrubbing, dusting, polishing, answering the phone, doing the yard work. It's too much. You can't do everything that needs to be done. And frankly, the house is starting to show a bit of wear. The place could stand some sprucing up. A fresh coat of paint would make all the difference. Get some of those dents in the wall plastered over. Retile the bathrooms. Why not take on a hired hand to do a few things around the ranch? You can afford it. And maybe you'd even be able to take the odd afternoon off. God knows you deserve that much. Virgil, you could spend more time practising the bassoon. And as for Hector—well, who knows what Hector will get up to?"

Her meaning was plain. Over time, and out of necessity, our relationship has evolved so that our frolics take place largely during the occasionally unstructured hours between 1 and 3 P.M. I began to wonder if Altona's show of concern might not be just a tad self-serving. Still, it seemed a good idea. And I could sense that Virgil, for his own reasons, was movable on this issue.

"Why don't you take out an ad in the *Rumour*? I can get you a good rate. What with the employment situation being so bleak and all, I'm sure there are scores of people who would jump at the chance to work here."

"Scores," as it turned out, was overstating the case. We ran the ad for two full weeks. "General handyperson wanted for busy bed and breakfast. Some cleaning and outdoor maintenance. The ideal candidate will be discreet, tidy, fond of cats, birds and books. Apply to . . ." In that whole time, we had only one respondent. But he sent us twenty different letters of application.

"I'm not sure," said Virgil, as we studied the growing pile of pleas. "There's something just a little *off* about all this. His stationery seems to have been ripped from an old school scribbler . . . and what's this?"

There was a full-scale footprint on the back of one letter.

"I'd say that's a size 13 wide," said Altona, who once sold shoes at Marks and Spencer. "He must be a big fellow. Probably strong as an ox!"

"And he's certainly enthusiastic!" I chirped. We were sitting at the kitchen table. Altona was resting her hand on my thigh, and I was imagining long afternoons to come.

"He's articulate, I'll grant you that. But there's a plangency to his pleading that puts me off. And his writing has a peculiar backward slant to it," Virgil went on. "I'm not sure. We don't want to fall in with some axe murderer. And who's to say he isn't an agent of Polly Perch?"

36

Ever since we learned we were on the *Interference* hit list, Virgil has regarded every newcomer with uncharacteristic wariness.

"Oh nonsense!" said Altona, applying firm and warm pressure to a particularly erogenous province just above my left knee, "Polly Perch has bigger fish to fry. She's forgotten all about you by now. It can't hurt to meet him, can it?"

"Let's let Mrs. Rochester decide," I suggested. I gave her a fortune cookie. She snapped it deftly in half, letting the slip on which the fortune was inscribed fall to the floor beneath her perch. I bent to pick it up.

"*Voyons!*" said Altona, snatching it from my fingers. She has been brushing up on her French through correspondence. "It says, 'You will make a new and trustworthy friend.' There! That should settle it."

"All right. Okay. Fine, then," said Virgil, knowing he was beaten. "We might as well have him around for an interview. I'll set it up."

When he left the kitchen, Altona handed me the fortune.

"Oh, dear," I said. It read, "Beware of strangers."

"Fiddlesticks! Who believes this stuff, anyway?" she asked. "It's just a lot of hooey. You need someone to help around here, and this guy will work out fine. It's not as if he'll have to transplant kidneys."

I was taken aback, a little, at this brazen deception. But her fingers were sketching such promising circles that I choked back my urge to upbraid her for her duplicity. And so it has all been arranged. Tomorrow, we will meet Caedmon Harkness. Or rather, having just looked at the clock, I should say we will meet him later today. Time has done its midnight flit. I'm tuckered, and the morning will bring with it a whole new set of eggs to fry. And so to bed, and my cool sheets, and the empty space beside me. I will say "sweet dreams" to Altona's picture on my bureau. I will close my eyes and watch the last traces of light as they dwindle and fade on the backs of my lids. Then, the screens will hang blank and empty, ready for tonight's dream show. Who knows what it might be? A dream of flying. A dream of transformation. Perhaps I will dream I am a neural impulse, coursing up and down the spine of a wide smooth back, ferrying all kinds of naughty thoughts, furtive messages and electric sensations to the willing brain at the highway's terminus. Oh, I can't wait for darkness to come. I welcome it, like a mole. Tickle me. Tickle me. I love you.

Application: To whom it may concern

To whom it may concern:
I am writing once again in reply to your advertisement in *The Occasional Rumour*. I am wondering if I did not make my purpose plain in my first 17 letters. This time, I will be blunt. You are looking for a handyman. I am looking for a job. Please—may we meet?

My main reason for applying for this position is that I have fallen on hard times, and I can't recall ever asking for them. I'm no whiner. I would never disavow responsibility for anything I've done, or for what I've become. I believe we get what we're after in this world, even if we don't know it at the time. It may very well be that I've led a hand-to-mouth existence because near penury is precisely what I craved. Even though my conscious mind was set on success, maybe there was some deep, deep part of my soul that harboured the impulse to involve myself in business ventures that had as much chance of succeeding as a sieve has of holding water. Why else would I have tried to make my living as a thatcher in a place where there are no thatched roofs? Why else would I try to sell bread dough saint's medals, when the age in which we live is relentlessly secular?

These are the facts of my life. I set them before you without apology and without regrets. I am of a clinically sunny disposition and can manage to find the good in most circumstances. It has never been my ambition to become rich or famous. I have never wanted more than to simply get by. But now, even that modest requirement exceeds my grasp. I guess this is what happens when your deeper motivations insist on pulling the rug out from under your more superficial ambitions.

Let me reassure you that I have searched long and hard in the present instance, and believe with every ounce of every fibre of my being that my application for the advertised job of handyman at your bed and breakfast represents a union of my conscious and subconscious mind. I have undertaken several courses of spiritual clearing, as recommended by Buddhist, Trappist and Wicca masters. I feel awash with an ecumenical purity of intention. No subliminal subterfuge will subvert my overt purpose this time round. The head and the heart are one. I enclose a résumé. Its peculiarities are best explained in person. I look forward to hearing from you at your earliest convenience and to meeting you for an interview.

Yours very truly, Caedmon Harkness.

Uncle Henry Miller's Sex in a Pan

A day ahead, prepare crust:
  ½ cup chopped pecans
  ½ cup butter or margarine
  1 cup flour

Mix well and press into 9" by 13" pan. Bake at 325 degrees F for 20 minutes.

  8 oz. cream cheese, softened
  1 cup icing sugar
  16 oz. Cool Whip

Cream the cheese and icing sugar. Add half the Cool Whip, saving the rest for topping, and beat. Spread over the crumb crust.

1 small box instant chocolate pudding
1 small box instant vanilla pudding
3 cups milk
1 tsp. vanilla
1 chocolate bar, grated

Beat both pudding powders with milk and vanilla. Spread over the second layer. Spread the rest of the Cool Whip on the third layer, then garnish with a grated chocolate bar. Refrigerate.

Well boys, here it is. Like I said to you last week, make it at your own peril. I can't stand the stuff myself, but Uncle Henry couldn't get enough, and he lived to be damn near ninety. Of course, he lost his teeth before he was sixty. But heck! As they say, this is not a dress rehearsal. You might as well enjoy yourself while you're here. And besides, they're doing wonderful things with dental prosthetics.

Uncle Henry was not a big reader. He subscribed to the Reader's Digest Condensed Books series, but I don't know that he ever opened one, other than to paste his bookplate on the inside cover. I packed up his stuff when he moved into the rest home, and all his books had stiff spines, which suggested they'd never been cracked. His reasons for buying them were largely aesthetic, or at least ornamental. I think he felt a house was not a home unless it had a library and a piano. He liked the way the Condensed Books looked when they were arranged on the shelves, all uniform in size and colour. They took up a portion of the wall that would otherwise have to be hung with pictures, which were troublesome in their own way. Similarly, he appreciated the silent heft of the upright piano that stood mute in one corner of his living room, its teeth white, complete and discreetly concealed behind their wooden mouthguard. No one ever heard him play it, and he was known to be completely tone deaf.

I tell you this to underscore the fact that Uncle Henry had never heard of the other Henry Miller, had never read *The Tropic of Capri-*

corn or *Cancer*. He had never paid any attention to the controversies that surrounded the publication and importation of those books, never taken any interest in the bannings and condemnations that sprang up around them. Why should he? He had a busy life. He had his garden to tend. He belonged to a bowling league. And he was very active in his professional association, the International Brotherhood of Crematorium Engineers. He was well regarded among his peers for the work he did on temperature enhancement and emissions control.

One year, when the big conference was in Cleveland, he attended a session called "From Burning Bodies to Building Bridges: Improving the Image of Crematoriums in Your Community." One of the conferees advanced the idea that the association produce a cookbook to which members would contribute recipes. The book, with illustrations and discreet advertisements, could be published privately and given as a presentation gift to bereaved family members. I can only suppose the other crematorium engineers were, like Uncle Henry, fairly impervious to the evident ironies of this plan. They all seemed to think it would help ease the burden of loss, put a human face on death, and raise the profile of the association, too.

Uncle Henry had only two dishes in his repertoire. He could make a tasty egg and chip casserole. And he could make Sex in a Pan. Directly he returned home, he copied out the recipes and sent them off to the volunteer co-ordinator of the project, as he had promised he would.

Time passed. Uncle Henry forgot about the cookbook. He did some valuable experiments with heat-resistant alloys. His bowling league made it to the city finals. He was astonished one day to find a watermelon growing in his garden, the bastard offspring of a rogue tendril that had snuck in from the neighbour's garden. He phoned me to ask what I thought he should do about it. Uncle Henry hated watermelon, but he had the kind of reverence for life you'd hope to find in a crematorium engineer. The watermelon that had foisted itself upon him was looking a little droopy. He was concerned his neighbours might not be watering the mother plant sufficiently. Should he speak to them about it?

That was the last I heard from or of him until I picked up the paper one day and saw his picture splashed all over the front page.

At first, I thought he'd been involved in one of the dreadful tragedies that sometimes darken the days of a crematorium engineer. An explosion. A leak. A cry for help that went unanswered. But no. It was the cookbook. *Lovin' Ovens: All-Time Favorite Cremation Creations* had been published. The volunteer co-ordinator had sent Uncle Henry Miller a complimentary copy, along with an order form advising him to act expeditiously. A customs officer, relying on the heightened instincts all such officials must possess, seized on the innocuous package as one that bore investigating. He opened it up, flipped to the table of contents, and surveyed the long list of contributors. Now, *he* had heard of Henry Miller. And when he saw that name appended to a recipe for Sex in a Pan, he sounded the alarm.

I've never been sure how word of this seizure reached the media. Doubtless some mole within the customs branch alerted a civil libertarian organization, which took it from there. You can imagine the brouhaha that erupted. The papers had a field day. Here was a lighter side of the news that everyone could enjoy. Uncle Henry, who remained rather perplexed about the kerfuffle, received calls from reporters as far away as Delhi. Sales of *Lovin' Ovens* were brisker than anyone could have anticipated. He even had a brief note from the other Henry Miller, who said it was a relief to him to see someone else taking the heat.

After Uncle Henry died, I donated his Condensed Books to the rummage sale at the church. I keep up his subscriptions to his professional journals, for no other reason than that the personal ads are so entertaining. And a curious thing happened to me just last week. I was shopping in one of those Scandinavian furniture stores, where they keep old books around as accent pieces. One entertainment unit had half a dozen of the Reader's Digest series buttressed up against a television. I picked one up, idly flipped it open, and what to my wondering eyes should appear but a bookplate on which were written the words "Ex Libris Henry Miller."

I tucked it under my coat and took it home. Since then, I've wondered how many other people have found a volume from his dispersed library and thought they'd stumbled on a valuable artifact. It wouldn't surprise me if one day soon, one of your guests tells you about how he found one of Henry Miller's books in a Sally

Ann in Nanaimo. If I were you, I'd let him go on believing. What's the harm?

All the best, Aelwyn Pritchard, Vancouver.

P.S. I was at a party a few nights back, the kind of media schmooze fest you have to attend when you're a lowly book review editor such as I. I was standing about, chitting and chatting, the way one does, and happened to mention, just in passing, that I'd recently visited the BBB&B. That attracted the attention of a woman called Polly Perch, who happened to be in town on business. She said she had written you several times and hadn't received "the courtesy of a reply." I must say she seemed a little hot under the collar about it all. I didn't much like the way she jabbed the air with her satay skewer. Yikes! Do you know her? Which one of her parents was the barracuda?

This morning, as I was standing on my head

This morning, as I was standing on my head in the garden, I saw a balloon, yellow and blue, silent and looming, pass through the valley from over the hills and far away. It flew with considerable speed through the untried light of the dawning day. I was doing the yoga practice I've taken up latterly on the advice of one of our guests. She is an enthusiastic contortionist and winced to hear my knees crack like Christmas nuts every time I crouched in the kitchen to retrieve a bread pan or skillet. With regular yoga sessions, she assured me, my body would reclaim the flexibility it long ago forsook, and I would prance into my declining years—which are not so very far off—with the elastic grace of a young gazelle. I was sceptical, of course. But if we can look for proof where the proverb claims it lies, then this woman is one persuasive pudding. She is nearly seventy and likes nothing better than to throw herself face downward on the ground, haul her leg up over her head and swallow her heel while rocking about on the hull of her sternum like Rimbaud's drunken boat. It's impressive to watch, if a little daunting. She was so insistent that I could benefit by following the yogic path that I purchased the requisite texts and started in, trying to adapt my recalcitrant limbs to the poses and my tongue to their Sanskrit syllables. Parsvottanasana, Virabhadrasana, Upavistha Konasana. What have I got to lose? Any one of these exotic names could one day prove useful as a crossword solution. And if nothing else, I eventually might acquire a sufficient repertoire of tricks that I will be more in demand at parties.

The balloon was such an unexpected and arresting sight that for a moment or two I wondered if I might be having an episode, brought on by the clamour of excessive blood in the brain. The world seen upside-down is a very different place. There have been times, while pressing my crown to the ground and bisecting the air with my reversed torso, that I have mistaken common sparrows for garden fairies, or thought I heard the ravenous slugs sing "Hallelujah!" I righted myself rather too quickly and watched a dizzy dance of rosy coloured spots as gravity did its work and tugged my fluids to my feet. I shook my head, inhaled deeply, and looked again. Yes. There it was—a big balloon, with vibrant vertical stripes, the aerialist's basket dangling beneath, carving a colourful swath through the thick of the mist.

I stood there, all alone, in the middle of the lawn, wearing the loose and lumpy duds that yoga requires, watching the high, silent and formal passage of a stranger in a strange craft. He must certainly have been looking down at our little valley, at its patterns and random scatterings. I felt a sharp pang of something like jealousy. I have never seen this familiar terrain from such a perspective, and I would love to! It would be so novel to view the well-known contours of the place that has sustained me my whole life long with eyes made fresh by distance, to feel hardened attitudes crumble in the face of altitude.

I imagined that the pilot was on some unlikely and quixotic mission: crossing an ocean, breaking a record, honouring a promise made to himself in childhood. Although he surely had a great deal on his mind, I still allowed myself the vain belief that he, from his great height, was peering down at me and wondering if I was a man, a statue, a fence post, a scarecrow. And in that moment, I wanted him to know that he had an early morning confederate, that there was at least one other person awake and watching, bearing witness to his anomalous passage across our private sky. So, I waved. I waved a little sheepishly and hesitantly at first, waved with just one hand, decorous and contained, waved rather like the queen on parade.

Action can excite memory. I was visited by the thrilling recall of how, as little boys, my twin brother Hector and I would rush down to the tracks to greet the passing trains. We would practically throw our arms out of joint trying to interest first the engineer, then the caboose man, in the small fact of our living. We were hungry for acknowledgement, and we were thrilled to the point of shrieking giddiness when we were rewarded with a solemn salute or, more rarely, a blast from the steam whistle.

I waved harder. The agitated blood stirred in my fingertips. I felt an electric tingling and waved more extravagantly still, moving first one arm, then the other, then both together, like a windmill chopping, as if making a misguided attempt to fly myself. A fevered happiness took me over and commandeered my whole body. I began to jump, and then to run. I raced to the end of the driveway and hurtled down the road, following the balloon along its wind-driven trajectory, waving and leaping, my every motion calling out: Me! Me! Me! Look at me! I'm here, I'm here, I'm here!

I ran and cavorted until breathlessness and the thumping of my heart finally took me up short. I stood in the middle of the road, panting, watching the balloon do its "now you see me, now you don't" routine among the clouds, watching as it disappeared from view.

I kept staring stupidly into the sky, until I was satisfied it was wholly gone. My skin was clammy with sweat from the unaccustomed exertion. My pulse drummed in my ears: ha-ha, ha-ha, ha-ha! "I'm here!" I said, rather pathetically, as if such a declaration could make a difference.

There was nothing more to be done but to turn and head in a leisurely way back to the house. There was no need to hurry. All was in readiness for our half-dozen guests, none of whom seemed much inclined to appear for breakfast before 8. I knew that Hector would be up, and undertaking his own morning exercise programme: twisting the tops off marmalade and jam jars, dipping his spoon in them, testing the contents to see they were fit for presentation.

One by one, the sounds of the stirring day overtook the mocking thud of my own heart. I heard the whack whack whack of axe on wood as Rae and June down at The Well of Loneliness reduced a log to kindling. I heard a coughing report of what might have been our cat, Waffle, expunging a hair ball. In fact, Abel Wackaugh had stepped out onto his porch and was coaxing his bagpipes into action. Every morning he plays a wheezy hymn. Today, it was "Red River Valley." From the golf course on the hill, I caught the cry of "Fore!" as J. MacDonald Bellweather II teed off. My flip-flop sandals clucked as I walked. I'm here, I'm here, I'm here.

"I'm here!" I said to Waffle, when I came through the front door. The little bell she wears to give birds a sporting chance dingled as she twisted around my ankles, mewing for her breakfast.

"I'm here!" I said to Mrs. Rochester, passing by the stairway. She was perched on the newel post, like some basilisk roosting on the cosmic egg.

"Your teeth are like a flock of shorn ewes," she answered, sweetly quoting the Song of Solomon. She fluttered onto my shoulder.

"I'm here!" I informed the still and recumbent air as I walked into the library. The sun was doing its ribbon dance through the windows, and dusty motes dallied in its broad beams.

"And very welcome you are, too!" came a voice from the obscure depths of the room.

I started, then stared, peering down toward the fireplace. Caedmon Harkness emerged from the gloom, a feather duster in hand. Mrs. Rochester eyed it suspiciously.

"Getting an early start," he said, by way of explanation. "It must be years since anyone dusted the tops of these picture frames."

Caedmon has scarcely been with us a week, and I don't know him well enough yet to divine whether he meant this as an innocent comment or as a critical response to our shoddy housekeeping. Either way, there was no quibbling with his observation.

46

"Would that be your mother, then?" asked Caedmon. He pointed to a portrait that hangs above the fireplace. It's a rendering of a young and saucy woman in what appears to be a hunting costume. She poses in a verdant garden, improbably overgrown and lush. On her gloved right hand perches a parrot, who is not so very unlike Mrs. Rochester. By her side—all sad-eyed, thin and neurasthenic—sits a greyhound. We understand, from his forlorn look and defeated posture, that the bird is the cause of his misery: he wishes his mistress would get a proper falcon.

Everyone believes this to be a whimsical tribute to Mother. It's a logical assumption, given the conspicuous presence in our house of a bird that is very much like the one on the canvas. Indeed, both Hector and I thought it to be her until we were almost in our teens. Mother herself told the us the facts behind the painting's origins. The truth, as is so very often the case, proved far more banal than our own fanciful fabrications.

Mother's father, who built the house in the first place, was an avid card player. He reached a novel debt-deferring arrangement with one of his cronies, an antique dealer whom he had bested time and again at whist. The unlucky antiquarian agreed to relinquish to Grandpapa a container that was part of a shipment he had just imported from Belgium. It was a true gambler's settlement, since the contents of the crate were a mystery. Gold jewelry, ancient seals, chipped moustache cups: no one could say what might be found when the thing was cracked open. A Pandora's bargain. The container proved to hold a great many rather bad paintings, portraits for the most part, which had once graced the halls of some stately Belgian manor. No one could identify the minor gentry immortalized by equally minor painters. They were works of no historical worth and even less artistic merit. Still, Grandpapa thought they would lend the house a certain baronial grandeur, and he hung them liberally throughout the place. Now, we have consigned most of these to church rummage sales or to the attic. But during the whole of our childhood, fleshy Flemish faces gazed down upon our games from where they hung, far from home, exiled to our halls and stairways, our library and various bedrooms.

Those displaced, ruddy burghers and lost, gentle dames, with their beaver hats and stiff white collars and self-satisfied looks, were a comfort to us. Children are curious about their ancestors. They need bloodline stories to fix a place for themselves in the world. We were cut off from those connections. We knew nothing of our father, and Mother was not inclined to speak of her parents.

In the old and faded portraits, we found the possibility of both invention and reconciliation. It didn't matter to us in the slightest that the presence of the paintings in our home was purely accidental. Our hungering after history obviated that small detail. They were our instant ancestors, acquired in bulk: good old worthies about whom we could spin fictions detailing their talents, their wiles, their grand and sordid histories. In this way, we were able to provide ourselves with a sense of rootedness from which we would have been otherwise completely abstracted.

"Whoever she is, she certainly has an impish grin," said Caedmon when I had told him the dull truth of the portrait. "She looks like a woman who has something to hide!"

It was a perspicacious remark, for it's no accident that *The Lady with the Parrot* (as that portrait has come to be called) hangs where she hangs. Grandpapa placed her there in order to conceal another of his *nouveau riche* amenities: a wall safe. I lifted down the portrait and showed the vault to Caedmon.

"What's in it?"

"Nothing," I answered. "At least, that's what we were always told. As little boys, we were fascinated by it. We couldn't believe it was empty. We'd spend hours balancing on the mantel, twiddling the dial, listening for the tumblers to click, hoping we'd find a way to get into it, sure as all get-out we'd find a pirate treasure. Of course, we never managed it."

"You've never once looked inside?"

"Once, yes. A long time ago. It was after Hector took a fall and managed to concuss himself. Mother decided to put an end to the nonsense once and for all and lifted the veil."

"And it was empty?"

"Absolutely. A void," I answered.

"Were you disappointed?"

"Crushed. But Mother's purpose was served. We lost interest, and there were no more falls. We never did learn the combination, and Mother took it with her when she left the stage, so to speak."

"27—52—5," said Caedmon.

"I beg your pardon?"

"27—52—5. It was the combination for my lock at high school. Sometimes I worry my last words will be 27—52—5. Everyone will stand around my deathbed or the scene of the accident, scratching their heads. They'll wonder what on earth I meant, and no one will ever know. 27—52—5."

I had my doubts about taking on some hired help at first, I must confess. And Caedmon's eccentricities, which are many, gave me even further pause. However, anyone who can obsess about so arcane a likelihood as dying with his high school locker combination on his lips must have something to recommend him. And giving credit where it's due, he·does seem self-motivated. Not satisfied with simply dusting the frames of the few portraits we've left hanging, he wants to tackle the canvases themselves.

"All you need is a little window cleaner and an old toothbrush," he told us. "I once took a night school class in art restoration."

Mrs. Rochester willingly left my shoulder and hopped onto Caedmon's head. She is rarely so demonstrative with relative strangers, and this speaks well for his qualities. Over the years, I have learned to trust her judgment better than I trust my own.

Upstairs, I could hear the sound of guests bestirring themselves. Breakfast beckoned, and the question of garnishes remained to be settled. I left the bird and hired hand to their own devices, and stepped outside to pick a few early strawberries. I looked up, half hoping my balloonist might be making another pass. No such luck. There were only a couple of crows sitting in the chestnut tree. They studied me closely, hopping from branch to branch, cawing and preening, splendid in their pallbearer's black.

One crow brings sorrow, two crows bring joy. Isn't that how the nursery rhyme begins? I think so. I hope so. The promise of joy isn't one to turn your back on, even if crows are the bearers. Joy comes along rarely enough. When it does, with all its lovely surprises in tow, you have to be alert and ready and attentive. If you don't look up at just the right minute, your chance will pass you by. Tell me. What's sadder? The chance you see and miss? Or the chance you never knew was there? Tell me. I'm listening. I want to know.

May we recommend?
Hector's books for bathroom browsing

There is absolutely no reason why we shouldn't seek to enliven the time we spend attending to the baser dictates of biology. Nor is there any reason why we shouldn't feed, or at least tickle, the mind while we disabuse ourselves of the slag for which the body has no further use. A good bathroom book (as opposed to a good bathtub book, which is something else altogether) should be provocative, enduring, entertaining, educational, and sufficiently pithy that it can be absorbed in brief spurts. It should be easy to put down and inviting to come back to, but not so enthralling that it keeps the reader enthroned for hours at a stretch, mindless of the queue that might be forming outside the door. Here are a few of my current favourites for those times when I've skipped to the loo, my darling.

Another World Than This . . . , **Vita Sackville-West and Harold Nicolson**
Published in 1945, this is a commonplace book assembled jointly by a spousal team as famous for their extramarital sexual escapades and gardening prowess as for their literary accomplishments. It's a month by month collection of poems and prose extracts, sometimes drawn from rather obscure sources; or, at least, I find them so. Mostly, it's interesting to have a glimpse into the mind of another reader, to see what he or she underlined in some book, then took the time to copy out for further reflection.

Butterfly Cooing Like a Dove, **Miriam Rothschild**
A British zoologist, and a member of the banking family, Miss Roth-

schild has compiled a beautifully illustrated and entertainingly rambling anthology of paintings, poems and prose pieces about the spirit (the dove) and the soul (the butterfly). Jung, Neruda, Proust, Nabokov, Chagall, Picasso and Greco all come together at a wonderful crossroads that is neither purely art nor wholly science but a healthy intersection of the two. This is one of the most beautiful books I've ever seen, and one of which no one could grow tired.

A Dictionary of Angels, Including the Fallen Angels, Gustav Davidson

This is just the sort of book you want to have on hand if you find yourself with a cat who's in need of naming. Iax, Marchosias, Nuriel, Chabril, Jinn, Sizouze: every letter of the alphabet is rich with possibility. Each angel's qualities and areas of governance are described, and there is a plenitude of angelic lore. Care to know the number of angels abroad throughout creation, according to fourteenth-century cabalists? You'll find it here: 301, 655, 722.

A Dictionary of Fairies, Katherine Briggs

A mumpoker is a bogie from the Isle of Wight. A hob is a mischievous but generally kindly sprite. Among the many other names for fairies are: scrags, breaknecks, dobbies, fetches, Jemmy-burties, Dick-a-Tuesdays, hudskins, nickers, trows, caddies and gallytrots. William Blake once alarmed a woman sitting next to him with a tale of a fairy funeral he had witnessed the night before. You could protect yourself against unwanted fairy ministrations with churchyard mould, or by carrying a piece of dry bread in your pocket. Fairy pigs can bring you luck. There is much to be culled from this book, and the bathroom is as good a place as any to do so.

A Dictionary of Superstitions, Iona Opie and Moira Tatem

A miner who finds his boots toppled over in the morning won't work, for fear of disaster. Only a witch will say thank you if you lend her soap, and actors think it's bad luck to leave soap behind them in a theatre. Crying on Sunday morning brings bad luck, and sneezing on a Sunday is a surefire guarantee that the devil will rule over the week ahead. Sneezing while making a bed brings bad luck, and the bed has to lie in the same direction as the floorboards, or you'll never sleep well. The overall import of this collection of folklore from the British Isles is that regardless of what you do, or what you see, or where you go, something nasty is about to happen. After a while, this is a comforting, even a liberating, thought.

The Faber Book of Aphorisms, edited by W. H. Auden and Louis Kronenberger

Organized by such broad topics as "Religion and God," "Self-Knowledge," and "Opinions and Beliefs," this invigorating assemblage represents the siphoning of two formidable minds. The trenchant, witty thoughts of Bacon, Goethe, Nietzsche and Santayana butt up against the selected musings of Xenophone of Colophon, Simone Weil and Max Beerbohm. It is easy to memorize one of these gems while ensconced in the bathroom, and then impress the dickens out of whomever you might meet on the other side of the door. "Ah! Prisons are built with stones of law, brothels with bricks of religion! Blake," you can say, casually, while ambling down the hall.

The Oxford Dictionary of Saints, David Hugh Farmer

This is a remarkable gallery of men and women, all of whom were either native to Great Britain or Ireland, or are venerated there. Their stories, briefly told, are fascinating, outlandish and inspiring by turn, from the big gun saints like Thomas of Canterbury or the Venerable Bede to the lesser known objects of minor cults, such as Wendreda or Dingad or Erkengotta, whose grave smelled of balm for three days after her burial and whose encapsulated life makes especially fine bathroom reading.

Shrinklits: Seventy of the World's Towering Classics Cut Down to Size, Maurice Sagoff

If you've never read *The Count of Monte Cristo* or *Critique of Pure Reason*, and are in need of a very quick plot synopsis before going to a dinner party where they are likely to be discussed, this is the book for you. Mr. Sagoff has distilled the essence of seventy great, or at least famous, works of literature, both ancient and modern, and set down everything you'd ever need to know in verse. My personal favourite is his rendering of *Beowulf*, which begins:

> Monster Grendel's tastes are plainish.
> Breakfast? Just a couple Danish.

Symptoms, Isadore Rosenfeld, M.D

With its eye-catching chapter titles—"When you vomit blood," "When your legs swell," "Why are you so tired?"—this is certainly the most dangerous book on this list. No one can read it without falling prey to the dangers of self-diagnosis, and I regularly emerge from the loo convinced that I am suffering from blocked bile ducts, or an enlarged prostate, or pressure on the carotid sinus. You would be well advised not to leave it lying atop the tank or at the side of the tub for guests or friends to find, unless you are prepared to have them walking about the house with their fingers on their pulse points, speculating aloud that they might be suffering from an infection of the pericardium.

What Jane Austen Ate and Charles Dickens Knew: From Fox-Hunting to Whist—the Facts of Daily Life in Nineteenth-Century England, Daniel Pool

According to Mr. Pool, and I don't doubt him for a second, the bathrooms of nineteenth-century England were far from savoury places. Pipes were small and prone to leaks or breakage, water pressure was inconstant or nonexistent, and in the middle of the 1800s, there were fifty-three overflowing cesspools in Windsor Park. One day, a carriage simply disappeared into one and was never seen again. There is more palatable information to be had herein, however, about the quotidian life of the century before our own: calling cards, employment, domestic arrangements, the life of the orphan, courting and marriage, and much more are outlined in bite-size bits. Certainly, you'll bring a whole new frame of reference to reading the Victorian novel if you're steeped in some of this intelligence.

Thursday afternoons I like to lie

Thursday afternoons I like to lie in bed, whenever I can manage it, and listen to the radio. There is always a special broadcast of organ music on Thursday afternoon; and while the feelings I harbour for organ music are only slightly more charitable than those I keep in reserve for organ meat, I am completely mad for the man who presents the programme. In fact, I am so deeply moved by the un-natural passion he evinces for those shiny ranks of perforated pipes, and for the hooty songs they squeeze from their constricted throats, that I find myself dragged against my will into something like a fleeting fondness for the music itself. When he gets a real fever on, I am so transported beyond the trivial bounds of personal likes and dislikes that I can almost imagine a day when I'll willingly embrace the concept of, say, liver and onions. Or sweetbreads.

"From the mighty console of the eighteenth-century Florsheim organ in Bruges, which is ever so much more resonant and fluty, I find, especially in its upper registers, than its sister organ at the Cathedral of St. Catherine of Siena in Antwerp, that was Q. Powell Prescott with his own adaptation, for pedals alone, of both the Pachelbel *Canon* and the Albinoni *Adagio*.

"That's from an old Angel recording, sadly no longer in the cata-logue, and I really do hope that some record company executive might one day have the brains to dig around in the vault and find the master tape so that it can be digitized and brought out on CD, hopefully with more complete liner notes than are present on the album. Something along those lines might be organized to mark the tenth anniversary of the passing away of Q. Powell Prescott, of whom so many young people know nothing at all, apart from the rather spectacular manner of his death, which resulted in the introduction of the so-called 'Prescott Bill,' which saw more stringent safety controls being introduced to home espresso machines."

Listening to this announcer is rather like watching a geyser, or a salmon run, or some other force of nature. You can't credit that there was a time when it wasn't there, or that it might one day disappear. His crankiness, his originality, his intelligence, his evident and unassailable belief that it somehow makes a difference, his straightforward nerve in presenting two hours of *organ* music in the middle of the afternoon: all these things make me want to sing "Oh come, let us adore him." This is not a universal response. Not everyone is in love with Organ Thursday, as it is fondly known in this part of the world.

"By God, I *hate* Organ Thursday," I overheard one of our guests exclaim just last week. He was a very nice geological engineer who was reading *Tristram Shandy* and seemed in every other way reasonable. "Oh, I know just what you mean," said the woman at whom he was directing his bile. "I know, I know. You can never tell when he might play some Bruckner. I can't abide Bruckner. He just never knew when to quit. Rather like Tolstoy," she added, picking up *Anna Karenina* with the resigned sigh of someone who is determined to finish her dinner, even if it will make her ill to do so.

People are as evenly divided on the merits of Organ Thursday as they are on methods for cooking rice. Just as the world can be divvied equally into those who peek to see if it's done and those who wait it out patiently, so does Organ Thursday split civilization into two distinct camps. Trying to love someone who holds an opposing view would be tantamount to a Montagu courting a Capulet. Luckily, I can report that Altona and I see eye to eye in this regard.

Only today, when the house was quiet, and our guests had retired to their rooms for their meditations and siestas, Altona and I lay snuggled beneath the covers, listening to Karlheinz Krumbtray plumb the depths of Bach. Wave after textured sonic wave rolled from my tinny, tiny clock radio. I lay patiently on my side, not budging, while Altona used my back as a writing desk to prop up her notebook. Inspiration, summoned to the fore by that unbeatable team of love and music, had seized her by the very throat. She was a woman possessed, filled with the unstoppable urge to commit to the page a new chapter in her ongoing romance novel, *Passion's Sweet Tempest*.

When Altona writes, a firm and joyful purpose settles over her features. Her eyes are lasers, her nostrils flare, her breath comes in short, explosive snorts. She scribbles with a stunning rapidity, as though the force that guides her hand comes from some high-voltage source in the great beyond. In her altered state of this afternoon, the rhythms of her writing galloped apace with the unfolding of the music. Through the pages and the cover of her notebook, I could feel the pressure of her pen, insistent and rapid, like the needle of an earthquake-measuring device registering a full 10 on the Richter scale. Sometimes, she would dot an "i" or place a period with such ferocity that I feared for the future of my kidneys. On and on she drove, uttering moans of ecstasy, her respiration ever more hot and shallow until I heard the telltale whinny that indicates she has reached the very peak of achievement. I felt her shudder, and with a final convulsion, she moaned and collapsed onto her back. It was done.

I watched with something akin to relief as her face and features slid back to normalcy. I studied her throat's pulse point, watched its frantic hammering as it strained against her skin, traced the progress of its slowing: presto, allegro, moderato, andante. When she had regained her composure and was once again a part of this world, she read me what she had written:

"Oh, Umberto," whimpered Annalise, her breath as sweet as anise, her hair a dense and honey hedgerow full of unimagined possibilities, "I do love a fugue in the middle of the afternoon! Especially when the Bach shows no sign of strain."

They lay on the Umbrian hillside overlooking the colourful clutter of Assisi, safe from the censuring gaze of the devout village folk: everyday Assisians who trudged about the narrow, antique streets of the town, the very streets where St. Francis had walked while praying his prayers and befriending the birds. In the gnarled branches of the overhanging trees, wrens and robins—generations removed from the tiny, feathered meistersingers who first heard the friar—warmly warbled. From a distant church came the rich, variegated groan of a pipe organ, dark and brooding, like an elephant trumpeting for her lost calf.

Annalise rose and stretched like a lioness, rising to her feet after a lunch of zebra. She raised her arms into the air and tilted back her head, feeling the warmth of the May sun on her face. "Brother Sun and Sister Moon," she whispered into the fragrant breeze that strummed the green trees like a gypsy guitar. Her breasts were as white and as tempting as the meringue she and Umberto had devoured as a prelude to their wanton sport. She turned to him, naked and unashamed, and observed how the pale crumbs from their sweet feast had come to rest in the wiry mat of his chest hair, like happy insects. She wished she were one of the birds that sang from the leafy canopy. She would swoop down and daringly peck the crumbs from that tempting picnic blanket. But Annalise was not a bird. And that was something she could never hope to change.

She pretended for a moment that her lover's body was a book and started to read him, taking his toes as chapter one. She smiled at the lesson of his shins, shivered at the lovely poetry of his knees, moved her full and ruby lips while reading the sermon of his thighs: thighs that were the colour and texture and hardness of the bricks he made to support himself, his wife and their six musically gifted children, each of whom now required orthodontic work as well as lessons at the conservatory, and one of whom was even then stroking the keys and pumping the pedals of the organ in the distant church.

Annalise listened. Annalise looked. Annalise knew the truth. This man who was splayed before her now, splendidly spread-eagled on the grass, would never leave his family for her. But in that moment it did not matter. Now, he was here. Now, he was hers. And he was all man.

Oh, the book of his body was a joy! She never wanted it to end! Toes, shins, knees, thighs. But nothing was as lovely as chapter five. As if he read her thoughts—as indeed, she believed he could—Umberto tossed her a glance whose meaning there was no mistaking. Come, come, come, it said. Come here for a closer look. And forsaking despair, and mindless of whatever the future might bring, and watched only by the nonjudgmental birds and one passing goat, she did just that.

A long silence settled on the room when Altona came to the end of her recitation. I searched my heart and mind for some adequate response, but brute words failed me. I simply encircled her with my arm and drew her as near as I could, and thus entwined we slipped into the more comfortable realm of sleep. God knows how long we might have lingered there had Caedmon Harkness not roused us, round about 3, by holding a raucous tutoring session with his rooster just outside the window.

It was scarcely a month ago that Virgil, Altona and I met with him, as a committee, to assess his suitability to serve as first mate on a ship that has never had anything other than two captains. The interview took place in the afternoon. When it was done, we three sat on the porch and conducted a post-mortem over a glass of sherry.

"I hadn't imagined he'd be our age," Virgil began. "I'd pictured him as younger, somehow."

"He seems in good shape, though," said Altona, "and doesn't he have a magnificent beak?"

"It's prominent, that's for certain. We'll always have plenty of advance warning before he comes round corners."

I thought Virgil's remark a little unkind, even if there is some truth to it. Both my brother and I tend toward the aquiline; but next to Caedmon's alpine proboscis, we look quite button-nosed.

"And his feet!" Altona continued. "Mind you, he needs a big base to support his frame. How tall do you think he is—6 foot 9, maybe? Goodness! Of course, it's hard to tell where his skull leaves off and his hair begins with that Harpo Marx do. It's an intriguing shade, isn't it? Straw-coloured, I guess you could say. Although, some of that might be because of the actual straw."

There was indeed straw in Caedmon's hair: and not just a stick or two, either. Every so often, he would run his fingers through his locks and dislodge the better part of a bale. We watched in wide-eyed wonderment when one yellow filament spun from the region of his left temple and landed squarely in his teacup. Without so much as blinking, he fished it out, licked it off, and tucked it behind his ear. I was reminded of a childhood teddy bear whose skull slowly gave way under the weight of the love I lavished on him. Stuffing oozed from between his seams, until finally he was nothing but a pale and flaccid image of his former self.

Caedmon looked for all the world as though he'd come to audition for the role of Rumpelstiltskin in the community pageant, and hoped to show his insight into the character by emphasizing "rumple." Like the nasty elf who tormented the miller's daughter in the fairy tale, Caedmon worked at spinning straw into gold: metaphorically at least. For years he had tried to earn his bread as a thatcher: a trade which is admirable, but for which there is not much call herearound. Violetta, as he named the tubercular sounding bus in which he lives, is the only thatched dwelling in the valley, and probably the only thatched mobile home in all of creation. I suspect the accumulation of straw in Caedmon's topknot is due to the incompatibility of his great height with Violetta's low ceiling. If his upper extremities are forever rubbing against her, it's little wonder their two thatchings have so much materially in common.

"He's very sweet, even if he is a bit of a flake," said Altona.

"Flake" is a harsh sounding summation, but it has a poetic accuracy to it. I can't think of a more applicable sobriquet to attach to the unanchored, flighty, whimsical, drifting, exotic specimens who fall from the sky and into our valley with no visible means of support and no two of whom are the same.

"I brought you a St. Christopher's medal," he said, directly he had folded his lanky frame into an armchair. He had the look of a praying mantis who woke one Kafkaesque morning to find he had been transformed into a man, and who wasn't yet confident of his spindly and disproportionate extenders.

"I beg your pardon?" asked Virgil, who was determined to be hardheaded and businesslike about the hiring process. He had prepared a list of questions and was poised with a notebook, open at the ready, to record our prospective employee's responses. I think he wanted to give the impression that the position of general dogsbody at the Bachelor Brothers' Bed and Breakfast was hotly contested.

"St. Christopher," Caedmon explained, "is discredited now, of course, but still a beloved figure. He was the patron saint of travellers, as well as of bachelors. What better guardian for an establishment such as your own? He'll watch over you, and your guests, too."

He handed over the medal, which is made of bread dough that's been fired and varnished, and has the look of an elementary school art project. It's the size of a saucer and shows the familiar figure of the towering Christopher helping the child Jesus across the river.

"Christopher," Caedmon continued, "is also responsible for bus drivers, police officers, truckers, ferryboat captains and skiers. He's invoked against the dangers of storms, plagues, perilous water journeys, nightmares and sudden death. In the Middle Ages, his cult's adherents believed they would never die if they gazed upon his image every day."

"Ah," said Virgil. "I'll try to get into the habit of giving it a good gander, then. Maybe after flossing. Now, Mr. Harkness—"

"Please call me Caedmon."

"Fine. Caedmon. Perhaps you can tell us why you feel you're suited to—"

He stopped mid-question and stared at our interviewee's left chest. "Tell me," said Virgil, clearing his throat delicately, "what exactly is that in your shirt pocket? It seems to be moving."

"Oh," Caedmon answered, brightly. "That's my lizard, Francesca." He reached into his pocket and extracted a thin reptile of an almost translucent greenness. She had a lost and slightly tragic look about her, with her bright black eyes, elegant tail and squat determined stance.

"*Ciao, bella,*" cooed Caedmon into what I suppose must be her ear. "*Come stai?* I speak to her in Italian. She seems to like it. She's a very good lizard, and a wonderful friend to Paolo."

"Paolo?"

"My rooster. He's resting in Violetta just now. He's mute, poor thing, although I'm fairly sure it's a psychosomatic condition rather than organic. I'm trying to restore his voice with a massage technique I've read about."

Virgil closed the notebook.

"Massage?"

"Oh, yes. It's a very powerful tool for interspecies communication. I stroke him under his wings and around the wattles to try to rechannel his energies to his throat. He seems to love it, and every so often he makes a little wheezing sound that makes me sure I'm on the right track."

"I would have thought a lizard might look very much like breakfast to a rooster," ventured Virgil.

"Oh, no! Paolo adores Francesca. He often carries her around in his beak, and he's always very gentle with her."

Virgil looked from our would-be hired hand to me, and sighed. He picked up the bread dough medal and studied it closely. The light coming through the library window made Caedmon's explosion of hair look uncommonly like a halo. Francesca stuck out her head from his pocket and blinked her pretty eyes.

"Actually, you look like you could use a good massage, too," he went on. "I can feel you're carrying a lot of tension in your neck and in your jaw. Often that's a sign of repressed sexual longing."

Before Virgil could muster a mutter of protest, Caedmon had jumped to his feet and was standing behind him, kneading away at his shoulders.

"Careful," said Altona, "God only knows how much sexual longing is built up in there. If it all lets go at once, we could be done for."

A measure of the effect of Caedmon's ministrations is that Virgil, whose prudery has a decidedly nineteenth-century cast to it and who hasn't been seen in public in a bathing suit since he was a child, didn't even bother to answer this salvo. He was beginning to purr.

"Do you do windows?" asked Altona, taking up the inquisitorial slack.

"I haven't so far," Caedmon answered with the thoughtful hesitancy of one who feels he is being tested. "But I'm sure I could learn."

"Did I hear you ask him if he did widows?" asked Virgil, when the newly employed Caedmon had taken his pets and ailing vehicle into the fading afternoon, and we were sitting with our sherry on the porch.

"Har-dee-har-har," answered Altona. "You'll be glad I talked you into this."

"I don't doubt for a second that he's bright enough," he continued, "and I grant you that a massage now and then is all to the good. But will he be able to plunge a toilet? Fix a faucet? Unclog a sink? Snake a bathtub?"

"I've often heard that men in their fifties obsess about their plumbing, and now I see it's true," said Altona. "Don't be such a fretter. Anyone who can keep a bus like that on the road is sure to have some kind of mechanical aptitude. You boys need someone around here, especially with summer coming on. As near as I can tell, he's your man."

She had a point, as we knew very well. The place has been sagging since Mother went to her reward. She was extremely proprietary about the business of home maintenance and repair. Nothing gave her more pleasure than the solitary pursuits of putting up screens, or cleaning the eaves, or attaching crown mouldings. As both my brother and I ducked when the gene that governs the transference of such skills went whizzing by, and as Mother had no patience for trying to instruct her maladroit sons in the use of her many tools, we simply left it all to her. It was an arrangement that suited us all. It seemed impossible to believe that Caedmon could be any less accomplished than we when it came to the world of hammers, nails and table saws.

And so we welcomed him on board. Now, the process of habituation is well underway. It is no longer a shock when I look from my window onto the garden below, to see the colourful hulk of Violetta, her thatched roof punctuated by the chimney protruding from the oven Caedmon uses to bake his medals. She is certainly a striking landmark, painted to a Peter Max fare-thee-well with tropical flowers, birds and butterflies. And I have come to quite enjoy the whistled renditions of arias from *Turandot* and *Tosca* that are Caedmon's dependable soundtrack as he wipes down a bathtub or wrests morsels of hardened egg from between the tines of a fork. I am no longer surprised when I find him standing in the hallway, a feather duster in one hand, a lizard in his pocket, and a few bits of straw protruding from his crazy crown, staring into the middle distance. And we have come to an agreement about the hours during which he will conduct his therapy sessions with Paolo.

It is quite a spectacle, really, to watch Caedmon set his voiceless pet on the ground and caress him about the wattles and wings; then Caedmon places his hands in his own armpits, flaps his arms about as though they were wings, faces the east, throws back his head, and crows in two languages: COCKADOODLEDOO! CHI-

CHIRICHI! Over and over Caedmon bellows this hymn while his student, Paolo, scratches the ground for grubs and pays him absolutely no mind.

Our guests have been fascinated to witness so odd and localized a ritual, especially since we ensured it would be enacted between 3 and 5 P.M., rather than during the A.M. spectrum of the day, which was what happened on Caedmon's first morning with us. Imagine our surprise!

No one could fault him his thoroughness in cleaning long-overlooked surfaces and crevices. His zeal knows no bounds. It is, in some respects, even uncanny. I wandered into the library only yesterday to see *The Lady with the Parrot* propped up against the wall, and Caedmon whistling "Nessun Dorma" while staring into the small and open mouth of the safe that the painting conceals. I gasped aloud to see this. He turned, grinned widely, and said, *"Ecco!"* Then he stepped aside, motioning for me to look into the musty cavity. He left off his whistling as I marked my measured steps toward it. I stood on tiptoe and peered in at the bundles of papers jammed inside. What were they? How long had they languished there? Why were there no thick and gothic chords of music announcing that one mystery had been revealed and another was about to begin?

Clipping from *The Occasional Rumour*
November 1, 1959

Lightning Takes Life of Solomon Solomon!

Solomon Solomon, believed to be 54, died yesterday when the giant cigarette foil ball on which he was working was struck by lightning.

Solomon was a poet well known to readers of this newspaper. His works were published in these pages for almost 35 years. He was a quiet and in some ways secretive man, and never spoke of his life before he came to this valley, except to say that he wouldn't go back to Moosejaw if burning coals were held to the soles of his feet.

Solomon's chief passion in life, other than his compulsive crafting of verse, was the ongoing construction of his cigarette foil ball. An indefatigable smoker, Solomon began fashioning his shiny orb by layering strip on silver strip shortly after his arrival in our community. Over time, the ball came to measure 12 feet in diameter. Many people will remember the day he removed a wall from his cottage in order to roll the glistening globe out into his yard, so that he would not be constrained by the limits imposed on him by the dimensions of his dwelling. It was an impressive sight, out there on the lawn, and Solomon was justifiably proud of his work. Indeed, he had applied for official landmark status for it only last week.

The bolt that killed the poet also obliterated the ball. The body of his writing must therefore stand as his enduring monument. There is no need for cremation, and respecting his oft-expressed wishes, there will be no memorial service.

> When I'm dead and when I'm done,
> Then I'll be done and dead.
> Let there be no pious words
> Or tender sermons said.
> Let the maggots feast in peace
> Upon me in the sod.
> Let me go off quietly
> To yank the beard of God.

For a complete obituary and appreciation, please turn to page C6.

VIRGIL

In the wee hours of the morning

In the wee hours of the morning I was wakened by the sound of my own laughter. In the right hands and under the right circumstances, so rare and mirthful a rousing might become fodder for poetry. Unfortunately, this episode would be more suited to a frank and unsettling chapter in a laryngological textbook.

No gay and tinkling silvery peal stirred the waters of my sleep. Rather, a rattle and wheeze sucked me to the surface. A snorting exhalation. A phlegm-filtered chuckle that might have been the report of an engine left dormant all winter turning over in the spring. I opened my eyes, half-believing some hopelessly optimistic and shortsighted felon was in the yard trying to jump-start our doddering old pickup, and stared straight into the jaundiced beacons of Waffle.

She was sitting on my chest, her lantern eyes ablaze, skewering me with the accusing look I know so well. She calls it up from her extensive repertoire of "how dare you" glances when I wrest a living vole from her jaws, or prise her from my bassoon case where she likes to curl up while I practice, or prevent her from licking the butter. Waffle, like most cats, is very much the intolerant pilot of her own barque. She has no patience with events or individuals that compel her, however minutely, to change her course. Evidently, her predawn umbrage was born of having been ripped, untimely, from slumber's dark and cosy womb by the same hacking racket that brought me back to life. And she was not amused.

"Puss, puss," I croaked, and stroked her calico noggin. She dug her claws vengefully into my upper chest, stretched, rumbled and released a not so very ladylike belch which completely subverted her punishing purpose. This unexpected gaseous expulsion, the accompanying waft of tuna and the way her expression of profound annoyance gave way to a kind of purse-lipped chagrin, made me laugh out loud. A grim burbling, like the expert expectorations of possibly four-and-twenty cowboys deftly landing their well-chewed plugs in a distant brass spittoon.

The bridges linking my synapses were still thick with fog. It took fully twenty seconds for a rudimentary understanding to shuffle across the brain: here was the very same chortling alarm I had heard mere moments ago!

Laughing in my sleep? And just when I had finally resolved myself to being an old dog, hopelessly estranged from new tricks! I lay back in bed and closed my eyes again. I tried to sort through the half-shuffled deck of dreaming, examining each card to discover the image that had excited so ribald a rippling. Waffle stretched herself across my throat, a menacing muffler with an eight-cylinder purr. It was reassuring to feel her insistent heart thud against my Adam's apple, and the lulling vibratory rumble of this plush, plump puss— whom I love, for her coat is so warm—coaxed the dream-bearing alpha waves out of their caves.

"Ha!" I called, and sat bolt upright. I had a momentary insight into the origins of the word "catapult" as Waffle described a flailing arc and landed at the foot of the bed. This was too much for her to bear. She turned her back. She lifted her posterior. She wiggled it derisively and leapt into an armchair. There, she got an early start at her chosen work of upholstery shredding.

In my dream, I had been reading my own palm: staring into my hands, first the left, then the right, trying to make sense of the hieroglyphic scribblings traced there. But something was amiss. These were not the same palms I have owned for more than fifty years. They had been completely rearranged. The familiar lines of fate, life, head, heart and all the ancillary fissures had been scrambled, tossed around like twigs scattered on the lawn by a blustery storm. Though I looked and looked, I could discern nothing from the faint chalk marks on these slates of hands. There was no clue to who I was or what I might become.

Puzzlement turned to frank delight when the lines began to shift and change, kaleidoscopically. They seemed to lift up and out of the cup of the palm, taking on the added heft of dimension, shape and form. I blinked my dreamtime eyes, looked again, and saw that I was holding a coconut in my left hand and a perfect Edenic apple in my right. I studied them, contemplating their disparate weights and textures, rolling their names about in my mouth. And then, in a twinkling, I got it. I twigged on the joke that one part of my mind was playing on the other. For covert reasons of its own—maybe to release some pent-up punning energy—the subconscious had cooked up this odd image to tickle the analytical part of the brain: a confusion of palmar lines, transmogrified and changed into—what? A coconut. An apple. The fruit of the palm, and a beautiful *pomme!* Of course! I have never been one to laugh out loud at my own puns. But in that unguarded moment of first waking, it struck me as uproarious.

I am one of those people to whom sleep, once it has been routed, is unlikely to return. I lay back in bed and stared at the ceiling, mentally flipping through the album of my souvenirs while the digital clock counted its sheep. It taunted me with its irresponsibly cheerful glow and with the relentless certainty of its opinions: 3:37. 3:38. There was nothing to be gained by arguing with that.

I flicked on my bedside light and picked up my reading, an anthology of twentieth-century French poetry. As though the cosmos had decided to continue its teasing even into my waking hours, I flipped the book open randomly (if not accidentally) to "Palme," that celebrated poem by Paul Valéry. Obviously, there was no escape from the *leitmotif* established by my dreaming. The cat shot me a warning glance when I snickered again at the strangeness of it all. For want of any other occupation, I tried to work out a suitable English rendering of the famous refrain, "*Calme, calme, reste calme, connait le poids d'une palme portant sa profusion!*" Like most French poetry, it just seemed so much tripe and nonsense when forced into the straitjacket of translation: "Calm, calm, stay calm, stay calm, be like the spreading palm, serene in its own heaviness." It had none of the catchiness of the original and sounded too much like a slogan that might be used by a support group for people who are rotund and are determined to be happy about it.

I rose up out of bed and stood naked for a few appraising moments before the mirror. Everything was as I had left it. My half-dozen chest hairs were still white. The slight hernia I developed some years back still puckered out from my abdominal wall. One day, I suppose, I will have to have it tended to. I whispered a line from Mallarmé: "The flesh is sad, alas, and all the books are read." The breath that bore this muttered snippet shape-shifted into a light mist when it collided with the mirror.

Reflecting on how Mallarmé bore a syllabic resemblance to marmalade and how my fondness for sugary condiments was in some measure responsible for the ever more Buddha-like topography of my belly, I donned my robe (maroon terry cloth, ironically appliquéd across the back with the slogan "Stud Muffin," a Christmas gift from Altona), and picked up the cat from the chair where she lay, resting her chest on folded paws. She squeaked a soft and unconvincing mew of protest, then went limp in my hands and allowed me to drape her over my shoulders like a stole. Imagining myself a Renaissance pope with an ermine collar, I walked to the window and peered out at the late May morning. There was already a faint and narrow wash of rosy mother-of-pearl in the eastern sky, proof that the reliable planet had stuck to its schedule and was once more cosying up to the sun. False dawn. What was the phrase for false dawn in the Fitzgerald translation of Khayyam? I put the question to Waffle, but her answering rumble was scarcely articulate. I went to my bookcase and took down my well-worn Omar (which, for reasons of phonetic felicity, I keep next to Homer) and found the relevant quatrain. I cleared my throat and read it aloud, both for the cat's elucidation and because—I confess it—I flatter myself to think that my voice is well suited to the oral presentation of verse.

> Dreaming when dawn's left hand was in the sky,
> I heard a voice within the tavern cry,
> Awake, my little ones, and fill the cup
> Before life's liquor in its cup be dry.

"Dawn's left hand." Surely this was the phrase Solomon Solomon had in mind when he wrote:

> How sinister, the coming of the dawn!
> How spiteful too, the birds out on the lawn!

I'd join their choir and sing unto the sun:
"Begone, wan pawn who shone on fond Don Juan!"

In the several days that have passed since his manuscripts surfaced in our wall safe, Solomon Solomon has been much in the news. Few poets, living or dead, have been accorded such extravagant attention by the popular press. In part, of course, this is due to Altona's journalistic affiliation with our local organ of record, *The Occasional Rumour*. Her breathless and ongoing reportage of the story and the editorial musings of J. MacDonald Bellweather II have caused a tidal wave of excitement and interest to cascade up and down the length of the valley. From my file of clippings, I have selected a few of the more salient stories to reproduce here.

* * *

Long-shut Safe Finally Opened
by Altona Winkler

A wall safe, whose combination was long ago forgotten and which has remained shut tight for almost 50 years, harbouring, it was believed, nothing but darkness and stale air, and which was furthermore concealed from view behind a portrait in the library of the Bachelor Brothers' Bed and Breakfast, one of the valley's premier hostelries, is reported to have been opened.

When questioned by this reporter, Hector, who declined to give his age but is one of the two twin brothers who are the proprietors of the bed and breakfast, confirmed, "Yes, it has been opened. You could have knocked me over with a feather," he added, with a cockeyed grin and a charming chuckle.

Rumours that the long-shut safe had been opened by Caedmon Harkness, who is on the shady side of 50, a thatcher and hagiographer currently employed as a manservant at the Bachelor Brothers' Bed and Breakfast, could not be confirmed as Mr. Harkness was attending to the needs of his rooster, Paolo, 3, a mute, at press time. However, Henrietta Spatsworth, 46, a resident of Detroit, and a paying guest at the B&B, and who is very happy with everything she has found so far at this excellent inn, when asked about the alleged involvement of Mr. Harkness, confirmed it was he who opened the safe.

"I was there," said Ms. Spatsworth, with prim assurance, "and I saw it all. I saw everything."

*   *   *

Dear Sir:

Further to the story of the opening of the safe at the Bachelor Brothers' Bed and Breakfast as reported in your paper, I am writing to say it was my father, the locksmith Willy Wackaugh, who installed the safe in the library of the house when it was built, in 1919. He was newly returned from having served his country ably and well in France and in Belgium, and deserved the thanks and high regard of all who knew him. I regret to say he did not receive it. He was never adequately paid for the job he undertook in the house that presently harbours the Bachelor Brothers' Bed and Breakfast. The work was demanding and rigorous, especially for one such as he who had endured the mud and the shelling and the gas and the terrible Huns, in order that we might live as free men and women today, and the inadequate remuneration he received was a thorn in his flesh to the day he died. I am shocked and appalled that no mention was made of my father in your story. That omission is an insult not only to his memory but to veterans everywhere. I look forward to receiving a public apology at your earliest convenience.

Yours indignantly,

Abel Wackaugh, Proprietor, Abel Wackaugh's Hair Styling and Hardware.

*   *   *

Dear Sir:

Concerning your story re: opening of the safe—was there anything in it? We all want to know!

Andrew McAndrew and family.

*   *   *

Parrot Involved in Safe Caper at Famous B&B
by Altona Winkler

Alleged reports that a wall safe, hidden behind a portrait in the library of a local bed and breakfast, and which had remained sealed for almost 50 years, was finally opened with the assistance of a parrot, have been confirmed.

Caedmon Harkness, who is under 60, in an exclusive interview with *The Rumour*, confirmed that it was the bird, Mrs. Rochester, 86 if she's a day, who told him the combination that allowed daylight to finally illumine the darkened vault. Reached at his home, a thatched school bus currently parked in the yard of the Bachelor Brothers' Bed and Breakfast, Mr. Harkness told *The Rumour* about the exact circumstances that led to the event:

The Rumour: What happened?
Harkness: I was doing some chores in the library and had removed the portrait that hangs above the fireplace.
The Rumour: This would be the portrait behind which is concealed the safe?
Harkness: Yes. It's a portrait of a lady with a greyhound and a parrot.
The Rumour: Why had you removed the portrait?
Harkness: In order to clean it. You can do it very easily you know, with just a bit of window cleaning solution and a toothbrush.
The Rumour: Is that a fact?
Harkness: It is.
The Rumour: That's amazing
Harkness: The world is full of wonders.
The Rumour: Isn't it just! Where were we?
Harkness: Cleaning solution and toothbrush. I was carefully removing the grime that had built up over the years—
The Rumour: On the portrait?
Harkness: Yes. Mrs. Rochester was in the room with me, and—
The Rumour: You are referring to Mrs. Rochester, who is herself a parrot and lives at the Bachelor Brothers' Bed and Breakfast?
Harkness: Exactly. Mrs. Rochester was in the room with me, sitting on a ledge—

The Rumour: Excuse me. It is alleged she was sitting?

Harkness: No. It was a ledge she was sitting upon, near the fireplace, between a vase and an antique clock. She was humming quietly to herself. "Do You Know the Way to San José?" was the tune, I think. All at once, she stopped, gave a kind of bark, and spoke a sequence of three numbers.

The Rumour: And those are?

Harkness: It would be indiscreet of me to reveal that, I think.

The Rumour: Oh, you can tell me.

Harkness: For security reasons, I think I'd rather not.

The Rumour: Come on!

Harkness: No.

The Rumour: Oh, have it your own way then!

*   *   *

Dear Sir:

Concerning the involvement of a parrot in the opening of a long-shut safe, I feel it was irresponsible in the extreme of your reporter not to have mentioned that parrots are carriers of disease and can do human beings harm in other ways, too. My aunt once lost the tip of her nose to a parrot, at a hat fitting. The bird was called Titian, and he belonged to the milliner, who allowed him to roam freely around her shop. In a completely unprovoked attack, brought on evidently by his aversion to a particular arrangement of fruit on the chapeau my aunt was considering, he clamped his beak down hard on her person and the damage was done. "There was blood everywhere," my aunt would say, years afterward, when describing what occurred. She was a woman gifted with an unusual turn of phrase.

The event was both painful and disfiguring and was in no way mitigated by the shopwoman's offer to make my aunt a balaclava that would be both stylish and concealing. Please ensure that in the future your coverage of the news is more sensitive both to the possibility that such mishaps might occur, as well as to the feelings of those who have suffered them and who do not care to have the embers of such sad memories fanned once more into flame.

Thank you. Veronica Hough, M.A.

* * *

Dear Sir:
I was curious to learn that window cleaning solution can be used to renew paintings. Does this apply just to oil paintings, or are water colours and pastels also susceptible? Also, which grade of toothbrush is best suited to this purpose? Is there any way a water pick can be brought into play? You might be interested to learn that kitty litter can be employed very effectively to remove oil stains from lampshades. Looking forward to your reply, or to any assistance your readers may be able to offer, I remain,
    Miss Tilly Getzhier, Home Economist (retired).

* * *

Sir:
Was there or was there not anything in the goddam safe?
    Andrew McAndrew and family.

* * *

A Happy Resurrection: Remembering Solomon
An editorial by J. MacDonald Bellweather II,
adapted from a sermon he delivered at
the Church of God the Technician and Marketer,
founded in 1993 by J. MacDonald Bellweather II

In 1947, two Bedouin shepherd boys accidentally unearthed the cache of papyrus which we now know as the Dead Sea Scrolls, and in so doing unwittingly changed the whole complexion of Biblical scholarship. It is too early to tell if the discovery late last week of almost a hundred works by Solomon Solomon will have the same global impact. It is our opinion and our hope that it very well might, and that one of the finest and most unjustly neglected poetic talents of this or any other time will finally be led in from the nether world and into the sun, to receive the glory, laud and honour it so richly deserves.

Make no mistake about it. We cannot overestimate the importance of this find. In one fell swoop, treasured works that were thought to be lost forever have been restored to us for our delectation, including the mysteriously coded fragments that are almost certainly the working draft of the fabled companion volume to his ground-breaking textbook, *Hygiene for Boys: Good Clean Verse for Growing Minds*.

And now that the initial shock and euphoria of the discovery are beginning to subside, we must ensure that the name of Solomon Solomon is no longer allowed to linger in the subfusc shadows of obscurity. Rather, his *oeuvre*—which is his legacy not just to those of us who are pleased to call this island and this valley our home but a benefice deeded to all mankind—must be ushered into the golden, glorious light of day. Let us call upon God the Technician and Marketer to give us the strength and courage to see that we have here the means not just to rehabilitate the name of the poet but of transforming this sleepy little backwater into a shrine to which the whole world will want to beat a hasty path. Who would not want to come to breathe the same air and view the same hills as the man who wrote, in *Hygiene for Boys*:

> When you find a pimple, lads,
> You musn't make fuss,
> Although I know you're eager, boys,
> To see that gush of pus.
> Leave the nasty welt alone—
> Don't give the thing a squeeze.
> And if temptation proves too great,
> Then wipe the mirror, please.

Who, indeed? It is up to each of us to do his part, with the assistance of God the Technician and Marketer, to see that Solomon Solomon achieves the place he merits in the Pantheon with the greats. It is up to each of us to see that this island, and this valley, take their place alongside the Lake District, Lesbos and Père Lachaise Cemetery as places of literary pilgrimage.

Therefore, it gives me great pleasure to announce today, before you all, and in the presence of the great GTM, that I am personally undertaking the publication of a commemorative edition of the newly found poetry of Solomon Solomon. This seems only apt, as it was in *The Occasional Rumour* that the bard first published his verse, over a period of some 35 years. To this end, I have engaged the editorial services of Dr. Bardal Finbar, whose academic work on Solomon will be known to some of you, to crack the code devised by the crafty poet, no doubt to befuddle the Philistines. I furthermore suggest that we, as a community, pull together to create the Solomon Solomon Award for Improving Verse. We must strike a medal that bears his likeness. We must raise money in order to endow a prize fund. We must invite poets around the world to submit their finest verse for judging. With good planning, and with the smiling assistance of God the Technician and Marketer, I envision a day when there will be Solomon Solomon festivals, a Solomon Solomon stamp, a Solomon Solomon theme park! Praise be! I have a dream! I feel in my heart that it shall be so! Here endeth the lesson.

* * *

Dear Sir,
Will there be water slides?
    Delaney Grouper, age 8.

* * *

Sir,
Solomon Solomon was a chain-smoking drunk and a lecher. Surely you could find a more suitable object of veneration than a man who would wander the streets with his shoelaces undone, his tie askew, his shirt spattered with who knows what residue from who knows how many dinners, not even trying to conceal the fact that he was packing a flask of sweet sherry in his pocket and with breath that was powerful enough to light a barbecue! I was in my father's office the day he made an indecent proposition to the whole of the steno pool. I have it on reliable authority that he thought nothing of relieving himself in alleyways in broad daylight. I was never able to prove it, but I'm sure it was he who hanged my cat. His stupid cigarette foil ball was a blight on the landscape, and in my humble

opinion that blast of lightning was the best thing that ever happened to this valley.

Yours in astonishment, Edmund Ninian.

* * *

Dear Sir,

Thank you for your efforts on behalf of Solomon Solomon. How well I remember him! What a kindly, gentle soul, with his twinkling eyes surrounded by a web of fine lines, and his tumble of snowy hair, and his lovely tobacco smell! Some of the happiest hours my brother and I spent in our childhoods were at his house in the woods. We would stop there after school, and he would teach us bird calls. Sometimes, if we were very good, he would let us stick a piece of foil on his ball! We used to save our parents' cigarette foil to take to him.

Oh, how he loved children! Nothing gave him greater pleasure than dressing up as Father Christmas and passing out presents at the hall. And although he never spoke of his work among the sick, it was well-known that he would sit by their beds and read to them from his own writing, sometimes for hours at a stretch. Often they would beg him to stop, for fear that he would tire himself out. But he would persevere, just to bring joy to others. He was St. Francis and Wordsworth rolled into one. He was a genius.

Yours with all my compliments and best wishes and pledges of support, Petronella Mellon.

* * *

"Lord," said June only this morning, when I dropped into The Well of Loneliness for a visit and a much needed caffeine infusion. My self-induced early rising was beginning to catch up with me. "Solomon Solomon, Solomon Solomon, Solomon Solomon! If this keeps up, we might have to name the baby Sheba."

She patted the swell of her tummy, which is starting to look like the back end of a lute. She hiked up her sweatshirt and showed me the new and protuberant thrust. I was at a loss for words, I must confess, rather in the way you might be if someone showed you a painting you just didn't understand, but about which you felt you had to say some something approbatory.

"That's a very nice vein," I said, pointing to the blue highway that snaked its way over the growing hill. "In fact, Solomon Solomon might very well have had you in mind when he wrote his poem, 'Lady in Waiting':

> If camels pass through needles' eyes and rich men enter heaven,
> You are surely playing host to some exotic leaven.
> If geese will group in gaggles and if witches like a coven,
> You are truly lovely when the bun is in the oven."

"Yeeesh. You made that up," said Rae.

"I'm afraid not. It's one of the Solomon poems I remember from all those years ago, when he published in *The Rumour*. A photographic memory isn't always a blessing."

"Evidently not. Your brain must be crawling with snippets from *Hygiene for Boys*."

"Sure. I think almost any boy who grew up and went to school here could rhyme you off most of the book. It was a required text. Why, even now when I'm in the shower or the bath I can't stop myself from chanting:

> Scrub a dub dub!
> A boy in the tub,
> Whether he stands or sits,
> Ought to remember
> To launder his member
> And lather up both of his pits!"

"Surely not."

"It was very effective! Once learned, never forgotten."

"I'm not sure I want little Martina to hear any of this," said June, clapping her hands over the waxing moon of her tummy. "You grew up with this stuff?"

"Sure. Solomon Solomon's musings influenced a whole generation of valley men."

"One more reason to give thanks for being a dyke," said Rae.

77

"Are you going to the planning meeting for the commemoration celebration?" June asked, returning to her knitting. She's crafting a little jumper that has the word "Womyn" worked into the pattern.

"I'm afraid I have to, if only to act as a voice of moderation. If Mac is going to be at the helm, you can count on things getting out of hand."

"Spare us!" said Rae, as she whacked the dripping grounds out of the espresso filters. "A literary prize is one thing, but I can't say I'm thrilled about the idea of a theme park. And do they really mean to rebuild that cigarette foil ball?"

"Oh, yes! Plans are well underway."

"Virgil," asked June, "has anyone figured out how those manuscripts landed in that safe in the first place?"

"Ah," I answered, "now there's the real and abiding mystery of the thing. Who put them there, when and why? Fear not, my dears. As facts come to light, I'm sure you'll read about them in *The Rumour*. I have to nip. Bardal Finbar is arriving this afternoon to examine the evidence, and I still have to pick up the mail."

"Any more missives from Polly Perch?" asked Rae.

"Not so much as a whimper. I think we've thrown her off our traces. What a nightmare that would have been! Speaking of nightmares, I had the strangest dream this morning."

And then I told them of the vision that had so tickled my predawn fancy.

"Palm! *Pomme*! Get it?"

The puzzled silence with which they greeted the punch line was sobering.

"Perhaps you had to be there," I said, weakly, as I took my leave and headed for the communal mailbox to harvest the usual crop of bills, magazines, inquiries, and unsolicited pleas and promises. "You may already have won . . ." said the tantalizing script on one envelope, which I didn't even trouble to open before consigning it to the trash. For what more did I need? It was a beautiful morning. The sun was making his stately passage overhead. The trees were heavy with birds. My two hands bore all their familiar lines and traces. In the truck, I turned on the radio and listened to a polka. I sang along, "Pom pom pom! Pom pom pom!" all the way home.

Edith Patterson's Food for Gods

Mix thoroughly:
  12 graham crackers, rolled fine
  1 cup brown sugar
  1 tsp. baking powder

Add:
  1 cup chopped dates
  1 cup chopped walnuts
  2 large eggs, well beaten

Press into a buttered cake pan, 8" x 8". Bake 30 minutes at 325 degrees F. Ice with butter icing.

Hello, dear men. Here is the recipe, as promised. Frankly, I find it hard to believe the gods would be interested in such simple fare. Surely they'd rather tuck into something more ambrosial than this! I send it along with my thanks for all the kindness you showed the women of the South Wind Reading Circle on our very first retreat.

We've been meeting once a month in each other's homes for over fifteen years. We've talked about a weekend getaway for the longest time but have never been able to organize jobs, husbands and children in such a way as to make it possible. I can scarcely believe we've finally managed it, and I'll think twice before I ever again volunteer to choreograph such a complicated dance. I felt like an admiral in a wartime strategy room, sticking tacks into a map to mark the positions of all the necessary players. There were days when I'd be nearly reduced to tears on the phone. Everything would be in place. Then Cindy's daughter's soccer team would make it to the city final, or Lorna's mother would get an appointment with an elusive rheumatologist, or Heather's husband would be called out of town to mediate a settlement, and we'd be back to square one. I was on pins and needles until the moment the ferry left the dock and there was no turning back. You could see a look of collective relief settle over everyone's face once we were underway. Not even the dreadful breakfast we had in the cafeteria—everything swimming in some sweet yellow goo that was meant to be Hollandaise—could squelch the mounting joy. It was happening! We'd escaped! No blood had been spilled. The world was still spinning. If anyone worried that an oven had been left on, she kept it to herself.

Oh dear! I sound so uncharitable! It's true the retreat required more organizational work than I'd have ever thought possible. But no effort would have been too great to expend on these friends, who have saved my life more often than I can say.

When I became a full-time mother, almost twenty years ago now, I thought I was the most privileged of women; privileged because choosing to be an at-home mom was exactly that—a *choice*. It was one of several options available to me. I was lucky. My husband was well-compensated for his work as a high school principal. There was no pressing financial necessity dictating that I abandon my babies to the uncertain rigours of daycare and hurry back to the so-called "work force." Electing to stay put with the kids (we had two in rapid succession) was more a source of relief than of trepidation, and I never felt my self-esteem was in need of bolstering or validation by a pay cheque.

I smile now when I remember how I saw motherhood as a kind of escape. I'd read about Margaret Drabble, who had somehow managed to have her babies, tend to their needs, and write her novels, all at the same time. I imagined I would do likewise, imagined that during those long unstructured hours of the afternoon when the children were down for their naps, or at night when they were in their cribs and entertaining visions of sugarplums, I would sit at my typewriter and spin out funny, ironic, slightly disaffected stories about modern domestic life. I have an almost completed first chapter tucked away in a bureau drawer. Every so often, when I'm looking for a missing earring or vaccination certificate, I'll come across it and force myself to sit on the bed and read about the wisecracking Alexandra, my heroine, who had a glamorous job as a documentary filmmaker and who looked with wry and superior detachment on the world around her. I never know whether to laugh or cry. Usually, I do both.

Some day, I'd like to meet Margaret Drabble and ask her how she was able to convince her children to nap at the same time; or to nap at all, come to that. I'd like to find out if childbirth changed her chemical balance so that she became clinically cheerful and energetic, or if the Quaker boarding school she attended somehow left her with sufficient inner reserves that she was able to write through the oppression of the diaper pail with its malodorous breath. Was she untroubled by chapped nipples, by spills and stains, by living rooms that never looked like anything other than temples to Fisher Price? Did she ever find herself calling her husband away from an important meeting so that she could deliver herself of a rant about the toothpaste blob he'd left in the bathroom sink? Was she ever so antagonized by a coffee cup ring on a dining room table that she emptied the better part of a can of furniture polish onto it, making herself ill by inhaling the lemon-scented particles of mist? And then did she just sit right back down and hammer out another chapter of *The Millstone* or *Jerusalem the Golden*?

One day, my daughter had a blue-faced screaming fit in the frozen meats department of Safeway. While I was trying to calm her, I lost sight of my son, who used this unguarded moment to dismantle an impressive and towering display of bean tins. Can connected with skull, and blood gushed everywhere. I scooped him up off the floor and clutched him to my shoulder. Holding my daughter—who was still in the throes of her tantrum—under my other arm like a squirming football, I made for the door.

At the entrance to the supermarket, there was a community events bulletin board. I can only suppose that the shock of all that had just transpired had induced in me a state of preternatural calm. How else would I have had the wherewithal to pause for a moment before exiting, scan the board, and somehow, in spite of my many encumbrances, remove the notice that had been placed there by a woman who wanted to start a reading circle? All I know is that when my son was being stitched up at the hospital emergency and my daughter was sniffing beside me, and I reached into my purse for a Kleenex, there it was. "Like to read? Need a break from the house and the kids?" I called as soon as we got home.

"That's good news," said my mother, when she learned I was joining a book club. "I've been telling you that you need some kind of distraction. No one can stay at home with a couple of kids all day and still feel like she owns her own mind. I think I might have gone mad when you and your sister were little, if it hadn't been for the ucw."

For the whole of my young childhood, my mother was a stalwart of the United Church Women, Circle 3, Sunnymount United Church. She was the recording secretary of their circle for ten years and dutifully filled steno book after steno book with neat shorthand records of the meetings they held in living rooms around the neighbourhood. When the ladies (they called themselves ladies, in spite of the conspicuous "W" on their letterhead) congregated at our home, I would sit on the periphery of the group and listen as they planned pageants and banquets, or arranged for a slide show by a visiting missionary who had actually seen and *touched* a leper. Tea was served, of course. There were dainties, too: a slice of some kind. Butter tart square. Matrimonial Cake. Food for Gods.

There would always come a point in the meeting, usually just after the orange pekoe tea was poured into bone china cups and the dainties distributed on elegant plates, that my mother closed her steno book and the conversation drifted away from matters that were strictly church or ucw business and veered off in the more dangerous direction of domestic perils and pleasures. Colic, braces, piano lessons, hockey, baby sitters, bridge, husbands: all were fair game, and it almost always came round to husbands. Their irritating ways were examined, dissected and turned over. One by one, these women brought forward their mates and held them up for comparison, praise, analysis and outright mockery.

"He's a doctor. A *doctor*! Don't you think after ten years of university he'd have learned how to flush a toilet?"

"I'm telling you, he's going to wear me out. Wear me out! I don't know what to do."

"He told me that he couldn't use a Player's tobacco tin for his washers. Player's tobacco tins are for screws, he said. He needs a MacDonald's tobacco tin for his washers."

"Does Harold back you up, Bernice? With the kids, I mean. When you've told them no for the umpteenth time, will he support you? Or does he just turn up the hockey game and pretend that none of you are there? Because that's what Gary does, and I'm just about ready to throw that darn boob tube out the window."

I remember all these women by name. Bernice Schneller. Grace Hamilton. Winnifred Thorvaldson. Bobbie Simpson. Mickey Dubinksi. Edith Patterson. I remember them as they were then, fully ten years younger than I am now. I see each of their faces every time I open up the cookbook they compiled in 1963, as a Circle 3 fundraiser. I see Bernice with her laugh lines, Grace with her beauty mark, Winnifred and Bobbie who spent so much time together they had started to dress and talk like sisters. I see Mickey, whose eyebrows joined above her nose, and who favoured gypsy-style jewelry and who was the first of the group to go back to school. She went to art college, graduated, left her husband (who was wearing her out), and one day got on a Greyhound for New York. Nobody ever saw or heard of her again. And I will never forget Edith Patterson, who made Food for Gods.

Edith fascinated me, with her blond hair, her porcelain skin and her baby doll good looks. She was so petite she had difficulty finding clothes in her size at the Bay, or at Eaton's, or at other department stores, and so preferred to shop at Little Miss Pretty, which carried mostly fashions for young teenagers. Somehow, she managed to pull it off. She always looked *à la mode* with her leopardskin tights and her man's white shirt hanging down to her knees, and never invited the whispered rebuke: "Mutton dressed like lamb." Edith would curl her legs up under her on the couch and chain smoke during the meetings. She rarely said anything, except to sometimes send off a zinger that would end a conversation that had gone on too long, or to issue a snorty laugh of contempt at an idea that everyone but its presenter could see was flawed at root. Bullets of smoke shot from her nostrils. Her gaze would travel around the room, and it was impossible not to feel that she was passing silent judgment on everyone present, issuing blanket dismissals as she looked from face to face, squinting through a mentholated haze. Sometimes she would wink at me, or half roll her eyes, taking me into her confidence, sending me a clear and silent message: "Isn't this the dumbest thing?" She was certainly the most exotic minister's wife anyone at Sunnymount United Church had ever seen or heard of.

Edith and my mother were the co-editors of the cookbook. They worked at our house rather than at the manse where Edith said there were too many distractions. Representatives of the church finance or maintenance or Christian life committees were forever dropping in unannounced, expecting her input on issues about which she didn't care in the slightest. Troubled parishioners might call at any time of day or night looking for her husband. If he was absent, they expected her to be their wailing wall. It was a relief to her to get away, to bring her portable typewriter to our house and transcribe the prized recipes handed over to them by the Circle 3 ladies. She and my mother sat at opposite ends of the kitchen table and clacked away, my mother with the assured rapidity of someone who graduated at the top of her class in secretarial school, Edith with two hesitant fingers and frequent mutterings of "damn," and an ashtray at her side that would be brimming with butts by the end of the session.

"I don't see how she can type at all with those nails of hers," Mother would say to my father when he returned from driving Edith home. The two women had taken to working late into the evening as the printer's deadline drew near. It was often after 10 by the time they called it a night. It must have been on one of those Good Samaritan jaunts between our place and the manse, just six blocks away, that my father and Edith came to whatever arrangement people come to when they decide to have an affair. I try not to think about it, but I can hardly keep myself from imagining the two of them, parked in the deserted lot behind Little Miss Pretty, performing all the necessary contortions in the back seat of our Chrysler. I imagine Edith's long and perfect nails clawing at the shirt my mother had ironed.

"Your father won't be living with us any more," was the tactful way my mother informed my sister and me of his eventual, inevitable desertion. She was unwilling to offer any other details, but it didn't take us long to know the score. News of this magnitude travels fast and wide in so tightly knit a community.

No one could fail to note the irony when the cookbook was released, and Edith Patterson's Food For Gods appeared on the same page as my mother's recipe for My Husband's Favourite Angel Food Cake. I overheard her telling Bobbie on the phone, "Now, he can have his cake and Edith too." Tragedy had a way of sharpening her wit.

Edith's only other contribution to the cookbook was a recipe for something called Skillet Balls. "I wonder if that's her pet name for him," Mother sneered one night, when Circle 3 had assembled in our living room. There was a moment of stunned silence, followed by the most raucous laughter I'd ever heard from these decorous, church-going ladies. You could feel the sense of release in the air. And the anger. That night, they garroted men as never before.

Edith was not seen at church again. Mother spared us the embarrassment of attending Sunday School for the rest of that season, although she compelled us to go back again in the fall. We didn't want to. We were petrified by the snickers and jeers and contemptuous looks we knew were in store for us. We knew we'd be treated as though we were somehow culpable. "You can't hide from it forever," she told us. And she was right. Mother was braver than we. She never once stopped attending services at the United Church, and her connection with the UCW ladies became stronger than ever. They rallied round. Some even brought casseroles to the house, as though there had been a funeral.

"Thank you, Bernice. This looks delicious."

"It's in the book," she answered, then blushed, wondering if this might have been a *faux pas*.

Eventually, my parents patched things up and Father returned home. They lived together without further rupture until he died three years ago. It was never as easy between them, though, as it had been in the days before Edith lured him away with her Pretty Miss wiles and her promises of Food For Gods.

"Of course it's never easy," my mother has told me when I've complained to her during rocky moments in my own marriage.

"Of course it's never easy," echo the women in the South Wind

Reading Circle, as we set down our Marge Piercy, or Anaïs Nin, or Alice Munro, and dig into whatever slice or cake or plate of cookies has been produced for the occasion. When we first started getting together, back in 1979, we all agreed there wouldn't be a food component to our monthly get-togethers. We all of us remembered seeing our mothers panic before bridge parties or church group meetings. We all remembered how competitive they became. We wanted none of that. We wanted to meet for the sake of discussion alone. We wanted to "feed the mind." Can you believe it? We actually said that. "We're here to feed the mind." There was never an official edict to amend the no food stricture. It just slipped away. Slowly, bit by bit and bite by bite, it eroded. Now, we look forward to feeding the body, too— as you may have noticed when we descended like ravenous locusts on your house!

We take turns picking our books. The one I chose for our first go round, all those years ago, when I was a smart young woman going crazy at home, was Doris Lessing's *The Summer Before the Dark*. It's about a woman who loses control of her life when its underpinnings—her husband and children—leave her for a summer, and she is cast adrift. How I longed for a crack at her madness, rather than the lunacy I'd chosen for myself! When I said that out loud, slowly and nervously, to a room full of relative strangers, in my very own home, with its nice furniture and trimmed lawn, and my considerate husband reading to my two beautiful children in another room, I was astonished to find that everyone knew exactly what I meant. Exactly! I can't tell you what a relief it was to me. I wasn't as nuts as I'd let myself believe. I still had a mind. And I could still speak it. Nor can I tell you how often I've found relief and solace with those women since then. We've seen each other through illness, birth, death, divorce. We've cheered each other's joys and successes, too: in love, in work, in family, in the simple business of getting through. We're the South Wind Reading Circle. We love each other. We should really get away more often. And we've never once had Food for Gods at any of our meetings.

All the best to you both, and to Caedmon and Altona too!

Love, Jane Armstrong, Victoria, B.C.

Media Alert

For immediate release to all outlets

The Organizing Committee of the Solomon Solomon Commemoration Celebrations is pleased to announced the establishment of the Solomon Solomon Prize for Improving Verse. Solomon Solomon was himself a poet who was concerned first and foremost in his writing with advancing the cause of moral rectitude, especially among male youths.

The Committee invites the submission of couplets, quatrains, sonnets, etc., which are celebratory of right living and which emphasize both the high artistic standards and the societal values Solomon Solomon held so dear. The winner will be chosen by a panel of eminently qualified judges and will be presented with a cheque for $500, as well as a unique folk art medal bearing the likeness of Solomon Solomon. The medal will be crafted by the accomplished hagiographer and bread dough artist Caedmon Harkness. The winning poem will be published in *The Occasional Rumour*, the bard's own journalistic *alma mater*.

Entries must be received by September 15. The awards ceremony will take place on October 31, the anniversary of the poet's death, at the soon-to-be renovated Solomon Solomon House.

Please direct all inquiries to J. MacDonald Bellweather II, Chairman, Organizing Committee of the Solomon Solomon Commemoration Celebration.

-30-

Memo: From the desk of

Memo: From the desk of Polly Perch, Editor-in- Chief, *Interference*
To: Moffat Lindisfarne, Executive Assistant to the Editor-in-Chief, *Interference*

Sorry, Lindisfarne, but it will take more than a little hissy fit by the photocopier and a faked-up note from your mother to make me believe that you really need a week of paid stress leave. Your predecessor, as you may recall, never received such pampering, even after he threatened to unman himself with the paper shredder and was subsequently committed. I rue the day I coaxed him in off the ledge. Especially since I found out he was the one who wrote "Cruella Lives" all over my parking stall.

Now listen, Lindisfarne. Before you lock yourself in a cubicle in the men's room and start spouting out words that rhyme with "ditch" and "punt," let me tell you that your hard work on behalf of *Interference* has not gone unnoticed. Your "Celebrity Condo(m)s" feature demonstrated sheer brilliance! Imagine having both the inspiration and the gall to masquerade as a housecleaner and thus penetrate the inner sanctums of some of our most talked-about movers and groovers in the worlds of entertainment and business. Imagine having the nerve to conceal a miniature camera in your dustbuster and to take snaps not only of their private quarters but also of their birth control devices! Not many would have done that, Lindisfarne. But you did. That issue was our hottest seller ever!

Every good boy deserves a favour, I've always said. And as you've been a very good boy, and as you *are*, truth to tell, looking a little frayed around the margins, I've decided to take you on vacation with me. Picture it, Lindisfarne! A rustic B & B on a pretty little island off the west coast of Canada! Mountains and rills! Muffins and sausages! Oh, what fun! Why, it'll hardly feel like work at all. Call and make a reservation under your name. Bring your camera and something to read. And remember—if you book your ticket now, you'll be able to pay for it with your frequent flyer points.

How vexing are the bristles

> How vexing are the bristles in my nose and in my ears,
> I see them and I curse my wretched luck.
> I know it would be prudent to remove them, but I fear
> I simply haven't got the needed pluck.

Thus saith the bard. Although I wasn't there to witness the froth and bubble of the creative moment in full ferment, I'd wager that flawed gem was visited on Solomon Solomon when he was in the throes of a cosmetic crisis. Many readers will look at it askance, rolling their eyes at its self-indulgent triviality. They would be well within their rights to point out how, in a world riven by privation and by the grievous atrocities we foist on one another, it is unseemly to use the power of poetry to amplify such supercilious concerns as a surfeit of nose hair. I take their point. At the same time, I have to wonder if there is any man "of a certain age," however charitable and service-driven a fellow he may be, who will stand up and admit that he hasn't at one time shared the terrible loathing pinpointed by Solomon. Is there anywhere alive a man who hasn't cowered before his shaving mirror, using rarely exploited facial muscles to dilate his nostrils and peer up into the moist caverns of his own nose; who hasn't withered inwardly at the sight of a small forest growing where no forest grew before, aghast, like Macbeth witnessing the arrival of Birnam Wood in Dunsinane?

I think not. And I'm persuaded that all men in their middle years have wondered what foul trick of biology makes their ears so attractive to the wiry scouring pads that take over the aural canals, like cuckoos pirating an attractive nest.

Of course, not all men are equally afflicted. Virgil, for instance, has only the downiest dusting of fuzz. You'd never even notice it, unless the sun was angled the right way.

"Excess of testosterone! Lucky me!" giggles Altona when she tickles my lobes as a prelude either to romance or to a facial.

Once a week or so, I am the happy recipient of one of her customized home beauty treatments. What good fortune, I always think, to have fallen into the tender hands of a lover who is also a licensed esthetician. What a rare thing it is in a life to find one's fate linked with that of someone who really understands what it is to moisturize and who furthermore has her finger on the frantic pulse of cosmetics merchandising. Hardly a week goes by that Altona doesn't take delivery of a shipment of creams and unguents that revivify, lift, elasticize, blast away blemishes, effect a wholesale erasure of lines. Latterly, I have noticed that the labels of many of these miniature pots are inscribed with the virtuous disclaimer: "Not tested on animals."

"Then let me be the guinea pig!" I trill, when she trots in with a new crate of hydrating goo, for want of which some white rat is unnecessarily wrinkled. Oh, I bless the day Altona turned up on our stoop with her saleswoman's case full of beauty products and stuck her foot in the door. I'll never forget how, on that morning of our first meeting, she sat opposite me in our kitchen and stared at my face in a practised and penetrating way, as though bent on memorizing every crease and fissure, divining from them the life events that had brought about their tracing. While she made her diagnosis, she spoke quietly to herself, in terms of gentle affirmation, as if going through a mental check list preparatory to beginning reconstruction.

"Hmmm-mmmm. Yes. Yes. Mmmmmm. Oh, yes. I see. Right. Uh-huh. Oh dear!"

"Oh dear?" I gulped, my heart double shifting with anxiety at what she might have garnered.

She took my hand and patted it gently.

"Not to worry," she murmured, reassuringly. Her teeth were white and her breath was minty. "The pores are always with us."

She took a long hard look at my nails, then muttered something that made me shriek aloud and leap up onto my chair like a timid *hausfrau* alarmed by a mouse.

"Madam! We've only just met!" I blustered, staring down at her, my voice rigid with indignation.

"I only said," she answered, peering up into my nostrils and making a mental note, "that I can't wait to see these when they're buffed."

I had misapprised her innocent remark, born of professional concern, as "I can't wait to see you in the buff."

"And I bet you can't wait to see me in my Freudian slip," was what she whispered in my whiskered ear when I had made my confession and she had finished laughing. Then she slapped a hot towel on my face, and there was no looking back.

On my birthday, Altona gave me—along with the batteries required for its operation—a nifty personal care utensil called the Fuzz-B-Gone. It is the most cunning thing I have ever seen. It's shaped like a tiny missile, and its whole purpose in life is to prune away those filaments that clog the ears and nose. In order that the sink will be innocent of trimmings, postoperatively, thoughtful and fastidious engineers have also built a little vacuum into the Fuzz-B-Gone, so that it sucks while it chops. It is truly awe-inspiring, a real testament to the inventiveness of the human spirit. The one liability is that it lacks an adequate muffler. I don't even want to think about the long-term deleterious effects. I know for a certainty that for some hours afterward, I am prone to auditory misconstruings.

"Do you have a lap dog?" I heard Dr. Bardal Finbar ask Virgil, only this afternoon. There were nine of us, all told, in the kitchen. Mrs. Rochester and Paolo, who are becoming thick as thieves, were playing a game of what looked to be soccer with a gooseberry on the linoleum. Waffle lay on the window ledge, half napping, and watching them with her one open eye. Caedmon was puttering at the sink, experimenting with the several cleansers we have on hand, trying to determine which was best equipped to blast away stains, yet still leave his hands silky smooth. Francesca clung to the rim of his baseball cap. Altona was doing an experiment of her own, using my face as her laboratory. She has been reading recently about how common foodstuffs can be used as beauty aids, and had slathered me from brow to chin with an egg-white solution (free range, of course), which had been mixed with thinly diced avocado. I looked very much as though I had been visited by some new and awful virus. We were sitting at the kitchen table, timing how long it would take the ointment to harden and watching Dr. Finbar and Virgil sort through the newly discovered Solomon Solomon manuscripts: wrinkled scraps of paper, fudgsicle wrappers and a blank school scribbler.

In the last week, Dr. Finbar has organized the poems into three categories: *The Rubaiyat*, miscellaneous verses and the poems written in a complex code that are believed to be the legendary companion volume to *Hygiene for Boys*. It was these arcane fragments to which he was applying his attention today. He tapped with a fevered urgency, transcribing Solomon's brain-teasing cuneiform from the fudgsicle wrappers on which the bard had set them down. It was hard and exacting work, since the texts made no sense whatsoever:

> ,r,nrttsu pudnsu piusu idy,su pymsu r;vjdwisu
> idy,su pymsu trddtr[tsu pitusu ithrtsu ppysu r;vjnsu

Virgil handed them to him, morsel by morsel, after passing an iron gently over the most wrinkled of the papers. He had borrowed a pair of white gloves from the local bell-ringing group and wore them so as not to damage anything that might prove useful to the world of scholarship.

> it[omnsu odsu s suesu ppysu tsomfsu
> bo;rusu iptjis,su pgsu ryjsy tsomnsu

In answer to Virgil's polite question about the tiny computer to which he was consigning all this evidence, Finbar launched into a lengthy exposition about the power of his RAM. He sounded like a proud farmer, explaining why his sheep all wear silly grins. And then, out of nowhere, came his canine query.

"Do you have a lap dog?"

Altona slapped my hand in an admonitory way when I sucked in my breath and lurched forward.

"Don't move!" she barked. "You'll wreck everything!"

I looked at her, amazed, for I had fully expected her to burst into clamorous tears. She has done so every time the word "dog" has been mentioned, in whatever context, ever since the sad disappearance and supposed demise of her own Pekingese, Valentine. Hair of the dog, dog-tired, dog-eared, dog star, dog days, dog in the manger: any of these usually sent her right over the edge.

It happened early in December of last year. Altona had gone to Las Vegas, where it happened that a conference of romance writers was taking place at exactly the same time, and in the same hotel, as a big international convocation of beauty consultants.

"Has my name written all over it," she chuckled, when she came by the house with the brochures and told me about her impending trip. "And I've always wanted to see Wayne Newton!"

Up to that point, we had only ever encountered two significant stumbling blocks in our relationship. One was that we were of two distinct minds about Wayne Newton. The other was Mrs. Rochester's aversion to the presence of Valentine in her home. Our parrot decided early on that she would draw a line in the sand and take the sternest of punitive actions every time the dog crossed over it. She devised all manner of devious ways to torment the poor pooch. She would hang from the chandeliers, waiting for the perfect opportunity to drop down like a hawk and deliver a resounding nip. She would bark like a rabid rottweiler, a stunt from which our carpets suffered, as it always made poor Valentine forget his housetraining. She learned to mimic Altona's "come here" whistle and drove the poor creature mad by flitting from room to room, summoning him, then disappearing to yet another part of the house, where she repeated the same stunt. She assailed him with hailstones of biblical scholarship. "Flee! Save yourself! Be like a wild ass in the desert!" she would bellow, and then giggle, *sotto voce*, "Jeremiah 48.6."

Little wonder that Valentine, with his bulging eyes and his sad, adenoidal wheezing, seemed to be in a constant state of existential torment. To be sure, he did his best to have his revenge. He would bark resoundingly when he saw his antagonist, and growl and nip at the air around her. But he was hopelessly outclassed by our nasty old harridan. He never stood a chance.

It was perfectly clear to all concerned that it would never be possible for us to act as baby sitters for Valentine. And so, when she went to her twin conferences in Nevada, Altona chose to take her furry chum along, rather than consign him to sure despair at the B&B or to the uncertain rigours of a kennel.

As it turned out, the hotel was playing host not only to the estheticians and the novelists but to a confab of exotic pet fanciers. They were there with their ferrets and their ocelots, their tarantulas and their scorpions, their leopards and their boa constrictors.

"Oh, God! It was so awful!" Altona told me on the phone, when the sedatives the house doctor had administered had finally taken effect. "I'd just come back from seeing Wayne Newton. Some of the girls were going to play the slot machines and invited me to join them, but I told them no, no, I had my Valentine to take care of, I had to take him for a walk. I went back to my room, opened the door, and there, smack dab in the centre of the bed, was this huge, huge, boa constrictor! It was as big around as a fire hose, with a gigantic lump, like a knot, in its middle. It was just about—just about—"

She burst again into convulsive sobs and excused herself while she put me on hold. I listened to Wayne Newton sing "Red Roses for a Blue Lady" while I waited for her to come back on the line, already certain that I could guess the punch line.

We had to wait till Altona came home to get the whole story. Evidently, she turned into a raging Medea when she saw the bulging serpent on her bedspread. She started pelting it with little sample jars of vanishing cream. It was too bloated to move or to seek egress by way of the vent through which it had presumably slithered into her room in the first place. Some of the pots smashed against the wall, some of them bounced off the bed and rolled over the carpet. At least one beaned the murderer right between the eyes, rather putting the lie to its "not tested on animals" reassurances, and dispatched the boa to meet its maker. A notice was posted on the bulletin board in the lobby advising that a lost snake had been recovered, but the owner never did come forward, and Altona declined the hotel management's offer to slice the creature open to see if the contents of its gut were in any way recuperable. She preferred to cling to the possibility, however remote, that the sad lump within was not in fact her beloved dog but a small suitcase the snake had absorbed somewhere *en route* to her room, and that Valentine had been pirated away by a lonely chorus girl, who would pamper him and tie jaunty red ribbons in his hair.

"He shall bruise your head, and you shall bruise his heel," muttered a self-satisfied Mrs. Rochester when she heard the news. "Genesis 3.15."

This was why I found Dr. Finbar's innocent, odd *non sequitur* so agitating, and why it excited my involuntary forward motion. I was readying myself to take my beloved in my arms and comfort her. After all, the memory of how she sobbed convulsively for the better part of Christmas Day when I—rather insensitively I fear—gave her the gift of a feathered boa, is still fresh in my mind.

"A lap top?" Virgil answered. "No, no. I'm old-fashioned, I'm afraid. I still prefer to write with pen."

All of which makes me question whether or not I should keep using the Fuzz-B-Gone, or whether I should investigate electrolysis, or some quieter means of hair traffic control. The phone rang, and I lurched again, making to rise to answer it. Altona seized me by the shoulders and shoved me back into my chair.

"Sit!" she yelped, much as she might have to Valentine, and I wondered for an instant if I were being made to play a surrogate's role. "Caedmon can answer the phone." And indeed, he had gone off to do just that, with Paolo and Mrs. Rochester scooting along behind.

tsomdnsu strtsu rtrejsu pitsu o;;desu strtsu ,o;;rf,su
sdrdhsu ogsu ;perffsu ppysu io;fnsu

"How curious," said Dr. Finbar, "that Solomon would have used fudgsicle wrappers for his manuscripts."

"Not so odd, really," answered Virgil, "when you remember his penchant for collecting cigarette foil papers. That sort of gathering must have been a fetish for him. And remember, too, how very poor he was. Hector and I walked by his hut on our way to school, and we often saw fudgsicle wrappers hanging from his clothesline."

95

"You mean he laundered them?"

"Evidently. Look how pristine they are. Wouldn't you expect a fudgsicle wrapper to be dirty and sticky?"

"Quite right," said Dr. Finbar with an admiring glance at my brother, who has no formal academic training but whose literary instincts are naturally acute. "But how did he come by so many wrappers? There are thousands of them!"

"Ah. That's a story. Solomon Solomon subsisted on little other than cigarettes, fudgsicles and orange pekoe tea, supplemented from time to time with a sip of sweet sherry. It was not unusual for him to go through half a dozen fudgsicles on any given day. Even so, he wrote so voluminously, so compulsively, that his own diet could never furnish him with as much paper as he required to sustain his poetical habit. I don't know how it happened, but over time it became a tradition among school children to leave their wrappers outside his house. Hector and I did this. So did all our friends. So did subsequent generations. It was passed on, like a schoolyard game. He kept a wooden box outside for that very purpose."

Caedmon came back from the phone with his rooster under his arm. He rubbed its wattles, lovingly.

"A Mr. Lindisfarne," he said, "He and his wife have booked in for next week."

Mrs. Rochester fluttered into the room and came to light atop the food processor. "Sit at my right hand, till I make your enemies your footstool!" she announced, gravely. "Psalm 110."

"He sounded quite pleasant," Caedmon continued. "Very chatty, certainly. He had all kinds of questions. He said they'd heard the weasel spotting was good at this time of year."

"Weasel spotting?" said Virgil, furrowing his brow. "Are you sure it isn't some kind of weird euphemism? Did they sound like honeymooners?"

Altona poked at the mask on my face. "Still a little tacky," she announced. "Excuse me for speaking my mind, but I have to say that this Solomon Solomon sounds like a right lunatic. That stuff about the cigarette foil ball gives me the creeps. And what on earth did he do with all the sticks from the fudgsicles?"

"Hmmmphhhhgrreexsstrwaaaaarrrrr," I started to answer, as I

was feeling rather left out of the conversation. The mask had hardened sufficiently that mouth movement was out of the question. Altona shot me a warning glance.

"You screw that up now," she said, coolly, "and you're cut off. You'll be lying alone in bed reading *Lysistrata*."

"Used them as kindling, mostly," answered Virgil, "although some he saved for crafts projects. Here and there around the valley are Solomon Solomon fudgsicle stick lamp shades. And we ourselves have a huge fudgsicle stick parrot cage in the attic that he made and presented to Mother. It's quite lovely, actually. I recall the day he brought it over. She accepted the gift, so as not to give offence, but Mother would never have dreamed of putting Mrs. Rochester in a cage. And she didn't want to do anything to encourage Solomon in his pursuit of her."

"Ah, yes!" exclaimed Dr. Finbar. "The great tragedy of his life! The depressive fuel that fired his creative engines! His unrequited love for your mother."

st,gi;jsu rdditrd[tsu ohjy,su rtyrcsu
idyjsu ppfsu tsomdnsu smfsu o;;desu ryhsu jitytsu

He hunched his shoulders up around his ears and grunted, "By gum, but I'm stiff."

"I don't wonder," said Virgil. "You've been hunched over that computer for the last six hours. Maybe Caedmon will give you an acupressure treatment."

"Gladly," said Caedmon, who set down his rooster and positioned himself behind the aching academic. Finbar groaned with pleasure and relief as our resident hagiographer and massage therapist manipulated the knots in his neck. As he worked, Caedmon hummed "Mio Babbino Caro" and looked in a blank kind of way down at the amber effulgence of the screen.

All at once, he left off his rubbing and with a happy exclamation of "*Ecco!*" leaned over the Solomon scholar and began to talk and type at the same time.

"When I learned to touch-type in school, we were taught to keep our index fingers centred over the F and the J on the keyboard. My fingers were forever sliding one over, to the G and the K. What I wound up with, of course, was plain gibberish, rather like what you're working with now. What would happen if you shifted the centre of the keyboard over to the left?"

We all of us clustered around the screen to watch what he was doing. He typed:

Onihay Oitsay
Memberray oysbay ouyay ustmay otnay elchsquay
Ustmay otnay ressrepray ouryay urgreay ootay elchbay.

We stared at it in silence for several minutes. Those of us who could move our lips mouthed these peculiar syllables over and over. Then, from the vicinity of the food processor, there came a raucous cry.

"Ixnay! Ixnay!"

Mrs. Rochester was flapping her wings, and shouting into the air.

"Ixnay! Ixnay!" she bellowed again.

We looked back to the screen. Finbar gave a gasp.

"My God! Oh, my God, but he was a devious one! Not one code, but two! We've got it! We've got it!"

"Hooray!" we all shouted, to greet the collective dawning of epiphany. "Oorayhay!" we carolled again, even me with my encumbered face. The mandibular action was enough to jar the moorings of the ripened egg white and avocado concoction. It slipped off in one miraculous swoop, like a green-flecked snakeskin. It hung suspended in the air for a second or two, a ghost, uncertain about what direction to take. It was unnerving to see the mask, which bore the clear contours of my face, cave in on itself and flutter to the floor; and more unsettling still when Paolo dashed across the room and gobbled it up.

"Quick!" said Altona, "have a look!"

Eager for me to take in the full effect of her handiwork, she grabbed her compact. In her haste to show me my rejuvenated self, she smashed the mirror against the side of the heavy vessel in which she'd mixed up the mask. The glass webbed out and fell from its frame into the bowl, just as neatly as the eggs had tumbled from their shells.

"Damn!" said Altona. "Whose luck is that out the window? Mine or yours?"

"Time will tell, I guess."

I looked into the bowl and gazed down at my splintered reflection. Maybe it was because of the fracturing, or maybe it was because of the residual egg white goo that covered the shards, but I had the distinct impression that I looked at least seven years older than I had only an hour before.

Entry: I was very interested to read

I was very interested to read in my local paper the news that you are looking for improving verse and offering a cash prize for same. I wish to commend your efforts in this regard and submit my own humble offering, along with a self-addressed, stamped envelope.

The poem, I think, speaks for itself. I would say by way of preamble only that I have been distressed for some time by the evident moral decline among today's young people and think that we can only reclaim the ground we have lost to the invidious influences of television, pornography, bilingualism in the schools, and the general laxity of modern parenting techniques by returning to the disciplinarian child-rearing sensibilities of yesteryear.

Hubert Jarlath, Ottawa.

Spare the Rod

Will someone tell me how the kids have come to be so bad?
They're rude to one another, and they're rude to Mom and Dad.
They're lazy and they're surly and they've got a lot of gall,
They like to hold up liquor stores and hang around the mall.

They do not care for reason, they are chippy and they're rude,
And some of them, I fear to say, are sometimes even lewd!
So, here's the best solution to their brassy, sassy talk:
Just take them to the village square and clap them all in stocks!

Great-Grandma Hattie's Egg Shampoo for Hair

Take ¼ pound of white Castile soap, the white of 1 egg and 4 pints of soft water. Beat up the egg white, and after dissolving the soap in 1 pint of soft water, fold in the beaten white, then add the remaining 3 pints of water. Keep in a covered jar when not using.

Ahoy there, laddies! Just a short note to say thanks a bundle for letting me stay on an extra night. I'm sorry it caused such a battle royal with that couple of johnny-come-latelies. I feel badly they had to sleep on the daybed in the library, especially when I could so easily have moved down there myself. Probably, I ought to have insisted on it more strenuously. But at the same time, I can't help but feel they got what was coming to them. What was their name? Lindisfab? Lundisfar? Something like that. After all, they might have thought to phone you to say they wouldn't be arriving until after midnight. Your brochure does state very clearly that reservations must be claimed by 6, unless a prior arrangement is made. You were perfectly reasonable in your assumption that they had made other plans and not notified you. Anyway, in my very Canadian way, I feel as though I were in some way responsible for that unfortunate altercation, and I do apologize. I hope Mrs. Lindyfax, or whatever the hell she's called, also had the decency to apologize once she had cooled down. Geez Louise! Can that woman swear a blue streak!

On a cheerier note, I include, mostly for Altona, Great-Grandma Hattie's formula for egg shampoo for hair. Great-Grandma Hattie will be 105 on her next birthday, in two months' time. She has lived in the same small apartment in the same senior citizens' complex for forty years. She moved in the very day she turned sixty-five, not because she was infirm or immobile or in any way in need of day to day assistance but simply because she was eligible. She was also sick of looking after the big house in which she had lived alone since her husband's death, and she wanted to have ready access to bridge partners. She does the *New York Times* crossword each and every day before lunch, and she hasn't lost a Scrabble game for over ten years. Her appetite is leonine, and she has the eyes and the ears of good hunting dog. She is, in short, one of those amazing old ladies you read about in the paper. And you can count on it, come her birthday, you *will* read about her in the paper. She makes sure of that.

I have come to believe that Great-Grandma Hattie owes her easy longevity, in part, to the great pleasure she derives from misleading journalists as she ricochets down the long corridor of the years. It all started on her ninetieth birthday. One of the nursing staff alerted the community newspaper, which frequently runs "good news" stories about golden-agers who are scaling ever loftier pinnacles. Great-Grandma Hattie sent me the clipping:

> The spunky nonagenarian attributes her good health and high spirits to the Cuban cigar she smokes every night after dinner. "It's a habit I picked up when I was working as an agent in postwar Havana," she explained. Asked if she liked the odd drink, she twinkled, "I never say no to a wee nip, my lad! And by the way, what are you doing on Saturday night?"

"Oh, pish-posh! What harm can it do?" she asked when I called her to see if she had gone right off the rails. "I just thought I'd give them something interesting to write about instead of the usual drivel about teas and corsages."

As it turned out, Great-Grandma Hattie's brief foray into the uncharted territory of her fictive past had jarred some unwholesome longing loose. With each successive birthday, her stories have become more and more bizarre, and she has been accorded more and more attention, as both her age and her improbably concocted reputation grow apace.

Showing the congratulatory telegram she received from the Queen, the 92-year-old great-grandmother smilingly recollected the summer she spent teaching Princesses Elizabeth and Margaret the finer points of skeet shooting.

At 96, she is still bright and chipper, and full of stories about her pioneering work as a lobster farmer off the coast of Maine.

Now 99, she looks back on her career in tennis with a wry fondness that never lapses into soggy nostalgia.

She's 102, but her hair is thick and full and falls in a silver cascade over her shoulders. "I owe it all to my egg shampoo," she told a curious reporter. "The recipe has been in the family for generations, and I wouldn't sell it for a million dollars. Do you mind if I smoke?"

One day, not so very long after this last story hit the wire services, she called me up and said, "Kevin, dear. I wonder if you'd do me a favour?"

"Let me guess. You want me to return your long and silver cascade wig to the costume rental?"

"No," she replied, rather coolly. "I want you to go the library and look through some old cookery books and see if you can come up with a recipe for an egg shampoo."

"Why, Grandma Hattie," I chortled, "why would you give up your tried and true recipe after all these successful years?"

"Listen here, young man. You do as your great-granny says. There might just be something in this for you. I've been getting dozens of phone calls from pharmaceutical and cosmetic companies wanting to buy my formula. Now, I just need to figure out how to make the shampoo. I'm sure there must be a recipe somewhere. So be a dear, will you?"

I went down to the library and very quickly found, in a book of old household formulas, what has since become Great-Grandma Hattie's Egg Shampoo.

"Oh, mercy!" she laughed when she'd read it. "Can you imagine anyone dumping that gloop on her head? Hee-hee!"

She passed it on to her lawyer, who sold an option on the formula to a large multinational concern. After her lawyer's fees were deducted from the take, she was left with just over ten thousand dollars and the promise of much more to come in the event they decided, after testing, to produce and market the stuff: an offer, by the way, which has not so far been forthcoming. She threw herself a tremendous party on her next birthday (the 103rd) and everyone from the seniors' complex came. The press, of course, was in attendance.

Resplendent in a Balenciaga dressing gown from the '50s, and a hand-quilted jacket, she lounged on her divan and recalled how she drank her first glass of champagne with Archduke Ferdinand, the very night before his fateful ride through the streets of Sarajevo. "Poor Ferdie," she said, wistfully, and leaned forward to accept a proffered light for her cigar.

Great-Grandma Hattie did not forget her promise and gave me a cheque for a thousand dollars. I wish I could say I proved principled enough to turn it over to a worthwhile charity. In fact, I put it in a term deposit and bought a ticket to Maui a few days before she clicked over 104.

"It wasn't the same without you," she pouted when I returned, tanned and rested and blissfully ignorant of all that had transpired in my absence. "Promise me you'll be here for my 105th! After all—it could just be my last birthday . . ."

I have two months of suspense ahead of me. There's a gleam in her eye I don't much like. The other day she asked, "If you wanted to sell the rights to your story to a major television network, which one would you pick?" In the event that I need to plan a fast escape, could I have the daybed?

All the best, Kevin Dermot, St. John's.

ALTONA

I had almost given up

I had almost given up on men when I met the one I'm watching now. He is lying beside me in my bed, dead to the world, curled up like a comma. Which is only an "m" removed from coma. His hair is a tangle. His thumb is stuck deep in his mouth. He's making a contented teat-sucking smack. It's just one of his nighttime sounds. He chuckles. He groans. He whistles. Sometimes, he pops. He talks nonsense. "Where are the cowboys? The ballet's about to begin!" "No! No! No! Don't polish the plumber! No need! No need!"

Sometimes, it's hard for me to look at him in the morning when he's awake and cheerful. When he's drinking coffee, or preening in front of the mirror. Cock of the walk. It's hard for me to look at him and not laugh out loud, loving him as much as I do and knowing what I know. Of course, I could never tell him. Men aren't equipped to handle such news. And anyway, what would it accomplish if I said it? If I said it out loud?

"You suck your thumb at night."

He would never believe that I was being impartial, that I was passing on information for its own sake. He'd think I was poking fun or teasing. Even if he laughed it off, I know he'd be a wreck. He'd find himself bothered at noon but unable to say why. I wouldn't want to plant some needless worry in the bright light of day, wouldn't want to run the risk that its roots would spread and break through the concrete casing of his sleep. Thunder crashes, the earth trembles, alarms sound, the wind howls, the panes rattle: nothing can prod him toward wakefulness. So much the better, I say. If I wake before dawn, I can do so with impunity. Sometimes I give in to a girlish whim and paint his toenails. He protests, but deep in his heart, I know he loves it.

"And this is the one that had roast beef!" I whispered to myself yesterday morning as I decorated his little piggies with a bright new shade I just got in. It's called Pistachio.

"What if the fellows see!" he wailed, when he woke and saw my handiwork.

"How are they going to see? You'll be wearing your Wellington boots! This will just give you something to smile about when I take the picture. You'll look enigmatic. The Mona Hector. It's good to have a secret!"

My sweetie is one of the brave members of the valley's volunteer fire brigade. Virgil, Abel Wackaugh and Caedmon are all part of the crew. J. MacDonald Bellweather II—my boss—is the chief. Thanks mostly to good luck and careful observation of safety rules by all concerned, the volunteers have never actually been called upon to extinguish a fire. Apart from the incendiary bolt that destroyed the Solomon Solomon house, the only blaze in living memory occurred when Abel set his soldering iron down in a pile of sawdust, and his work shed went up. He was too embarrassed to call for aid, and just let it burn to the ground.

"Needed a new shed, anyway," he said, philosophically, when I brought him some aloe vera cream for the slight burn he'd sustained on his ankle.

The picture-taking, to which the toe painting was a prelude, was Mac's idea. His plan was to raise an endowment for the reconstruction of the Solomon Solomon house by producing a calendar featuring beefcake photographs of our local firefighting talent.

"Saw one like it in the city once! Lots of fine specimens of manhood standing about the station. Washing the truck. Sliding down the pole. Petting the Dalmatian. You know. Some without their shirts on. Just the thing to set the ladies' pulses to racing! Good, clean, honest fun, really. Very moral. Solomon would approve. No reason why we can't do the same thing here. You'll take the photos, of course."

Yesterday afternoon, a hot August day, the members of the brigade got together in the garden of the bed and breakfast. They were primed to pose.

"Mommy," asked one little girl, who was paddling with her mother in the wading pool, "why are those men wearing red suspenders?"

This classic accessory is as close as our brigade comes to having a uniform. Otherwise, they are free to wear anything they feel is well-suited to the stamping out of flames. They are inventive, that's for sure. It's always a surprise when they turn up to march in the Canada Day parade.

"This won't take very long will it?" asked Virgil, who was a reluctant participant at best. He was looking very natty in his big yellow hipwaders, and his overalls, and the construction worker's hardhat that he found one day discarded in a ditch when he was out picking blackberries. "It's a very busy time here! There are beds to change and linens to launder and sinks and tubs to scrub and shelves to dust, people checking in, people checking out—"

"Hush, man!" Mac barked. "It will all wait. This a day when practicality must give way to art! Surely your guests understand that!"

He thwacked his suspenders, which made a loud snapping report against the latex coveralls he'd spotted while browsing through an "adults only" mail order catalogue that came, he assured me, unsolicited in the post.

"Most guests would," said Hector. He checked his left bicep to see that the serpent tattoo he had applied from a decal was holding up. He was a vision in jeans and Wellington boots and a Stetson. He was shirtless. I noticed he had touched up the white hairs on his chest. He was doing quite a nice job of sucking in his gut. He didn't even let it slip when Abel poked him and made a totally uncalled-for joke about haggis. "It's just that we have an especially demanding couple with us right now—"

"Careful! Careful!" Caedmon whispered an alert. "Here they come! Lindisfarnes at 6 o'clock."

Hector, Virgil, and Caedmon shuddered all together, as if they had stepped into an elevator inhabited by a bad smell. The obnoxious couple, decked out in whites from head to toe, like bwanas on a safari, bore down on us. They had the look of voracious piranha slavering at the sight of a group of innocently bathing wildebeests.

"Oh, Moffat! Look! Barefoot boys with cheeks of tan! We're back from weasel spotting in just the nick of time! It's a party! How very, very festive!" crowed Mrs. Lindisfarne from her wheelchair, as her husband huffed and puffed to shove her across the green.

"That goddam wheelchair," Virgil muttered under his breath, betraying the depth of his upset by resorting, as he rarely does, to a profanity, "is going to destroy our lawn!"

"How insensitive, man!" Mac bristled.

"Insensitive, hell!" said Hector, coming to his brother's defence. "She doesn't need it! You should see her scamper to the breakfast table. She just likes him to push her around."

And indeed, at that very moment, as if on cue, she leapt from the chair and cantered over the grass.

"Oh! Let me take a closer look at you all! Let me drink it in! My goodness me. It's just like a Village People concert out here today!"

"Who are the Village People?" asked Mac, *sotto voce*.

"Beats me," said Caedmon.

"Aren't you sweet," she cooed at Abel, who was wearing a yellow plaid lumberjack shirt and amply patched blue jeans. She flicked the little whirligig on top of his blue and green beanie with her blood-coloured, well-lacquered nails and giggled girlishly. "Now, who's going to tell me what's going on?"

"Oh! That is just the *best*," she chortled when the plan had been explained to her. "Would you mind very much if Moffat took a few pictures of you as well? It would mean so much to us to be able to show people back east how you all live out here!"

"Well, I suppose if you really want—" Mac began.

"Excellent! Perhaps you wouldn't mind if I made a suggestion or two about positioning? It's just that I know so well what works for our slide shows. And I think you could use some make-up. Just a teensy-weensy bit here and there. Moffat! Hand me that case!"

"She never goes anywhere without it," her husband simpered. He handed her what appeared to be a fishing tackle box. It proved, when she flipped open the lid, to be brimming with cosmetic supplies.

"May I help?" I asked. I didn't think this was inappropriate. After all, I do know something about the business. Her only answer was to roll back her lips in a tight smile and bare her teeth.

"You'll thank me for this later," she said as she rouged Caedmon's cheeks.

"Hold still!" she commanded Abel, attaching false eyelashes with a practised hand. I bit my tongue when she applied some blush to my Hector's nipples. I don't think of myself as a jealous person. But the smirk on his face didn't come from thinking about his painted toenails.

"Rosy buds!" she twittered when she was done, and then attacked Virgil with her eyeliner. Her husband followed in her wake, waving a powder puff. He undid a few of the firefighters' shirt buttons here and there, as he deemed necessary.

"There! We're all ready for our little photo shoot! This is going to be fabulous. Fabulous! Moffat! Camera! Now! Shall we have some individual shots as well as some group pictures? Oh, yes, I think so. Hector, let's have you first. Come on, now, flex those arms for us! Oh, that's good. That's perfect! Work with us, baby. Work with us! You're a natural. You ought to be in pictures. Oh, yes. You have a kind of Buster Keaton magnetism about you. Now, let's have a picture of you and your brother. Come along, Virgil. No, no! Too far apart. Cosy up a little. That's right! Put your arm around his shoulder. Good! Perfect! Now, keep that loving mood, and we'll bring Caedmon into it. That's good. Oh, you're a natural. Yes indeedy! Moffat! We can't see enough chest on Caedmon! Buttons! Good. Good. Now, you other two. Let's see if we can do a pyramid shot! On your knees! No, no, Moffat! Not you! Caedmon, Abel and Mac! You'll be the base. Now, let's see. I think I want Hector up on top. Give him a chance to show off that manly chest. Hmmmmmmm. We need two people for the second storey. Damn! We're one short! You there!"

"Me?" I asked.

"Yes. You with the camera. What's your name? Atonement, isn't it? You'll have to do. You get up there with Virgil. Atta girl. Good! Now, Hector! Up! Up! Up on top! Ride 'em cowboy! Yeehaw!"

There was a time, years before, when I desperately wanted to have a baby. It was a real longing. It was an animal hunger. It was hormonal, I guess. I knew I couldn't just give in to the impulse. But it was a struggle not to. When the baby lust was in full flower, I'd sit on a crowded bus, staring at the crotches of men and fantasizing about how any one of them, regardless of suitability or qualification, could help me fulfil my destiny as a woman. I'd find myself moving my lips, forming the words of a direct proposition. At moments like this I would close my eyes and repeat a mantra I'd made up. "Poverty, diapers, bees. Poverty, diapers, bees." Only in this way was I able to stop my ears against the tick-tock of the biological clock.

Poverty and diapers need no explaining. As to the bees, I am the fourth generation of women in my family to be so phobic about bees that I become wild with hysteria whenever I see one. I learned this behaviour from my mother, who got it from my grandmother, who picked it up from my great-grandmother. Lord only knows how far it might go back. I found dumb solace in knowing there would be one less person afflicted with this paralysing fear if I didn't bring a daughter into the world. I am the end of the line. It will die with me. It's a kindness to all humanity. As I'm sure the firemen must now agree.

Hector had scaled the two levels of the human pyramid and was just about to clamber onto my back, when a fat round bee flew into view and hovered before me. He was round. He was genial. He was wearing a smart striped suit. Paroxysm followed.

Exactly what happened, I put together only later, thanks to the eyewitness reports of the several other guests who had stopped their croquet game to watch these six unlikely, fleshy building blocks ape the triumph of Egypt. In short, what seems to have transpired is that I unleashed a banshee wail. I started in to flail and grab. Hector began to teeter and fall. I clutched at his big Wellington boots, and in my eagerness to lay hand on any weapon, yanked them both off, and began to bat at the air. The sensible bee was long gone. Caedmon, alarmed, made to rise. Virgil did likewise. The boot connected with Caedmon's fine, long nose, then carried on through on its arc and caught Virgil squarely under the chin. They both of them lurched face forward, colliding like two angry bighorn sheep on a mountainside. They clutched their respective foreheads and fell, crashing down on their colleagues who had been so firm a foundation. We all of us wound up in a kicking, moaning tangle on the lawn.

"Oh, Moffat! Look! I haven't seen such fun since those Twister parties back at Wellesley! And what pretty toes! Get the toes, Moffat! Be sure you get the toes!"

"This little pig went to market," I said, earlier tonight, as I was removing the Pistachio paint from my wounded boyfriend's feet.

109

"And this little pig stayed home!"

"I bloody well wish the Lindisfarnes had followed his example. What cheek! What an insufferable pair! That woman!"

"To say nothing of her ferret of a husband," I added, rising in defence of my sex. "This little pig had roast beef," I continued, swabbing the colourful nail with acetone.

"I can't imagine what that calendar will look like."

"Me neither."

I didn't have the heart to tell him just then that I'd forgotten to load my camera.

"And this little pig had none."

"By golly but I'm bushed."

"Ready for sleep?"

"Hmmmmmmmm."

"Hmmmmmmmm."

I held his foot in my right hand and pressed with my left on a special acupressure point. I've never known it to fail. Does he even know I do this? Has he ever made the connection? Cause and effect? I hope not. After all, a girl has to hold onto a least a couple of secrets.

"And this little piggy," I continued, "went—"

"Oui! Oui! Oui! Oui!"

"All the way home."

We were recently the objects

We were recently the objects of a government-sponsored phone survey. For want of anything better to do, a subcommittee of federally sanctioned number crunchers has decided to gather as many crumbs of innkeeping intelligence as they can muster.

The statistician called from Ottawa and peppered me with questions about our role in what she insisted on calling the "hospitality industry." I did my best to answer her quantitative and qualitative queries; but over the whole course of our interview, I found myself inhabited by a growing aversion to that phrase, "the hospitality industry." Now, as then, when I roll the words around on my tongue and savour their separate essences, I can find nothing in their flavours that is in anyway complementary. Hospitality. Industry. Nope. It just doesn't work. Not for me, anyway.

I appreciate that this lexical coupling is convenient for people whose sad work it is to try to convince the public that truth can be wrung from statistics. But I can't shake the feeling that it does a disservice to those of us who till these honourable fields. Hospitality is not a tool and die operation. It is not boiler repair. You can't insert tab A into slot B and come up with hospitality. In short, hospitality is not an industry. It is an art. A gift not universally bestowed. And not everyone can dispense it convincingly. It's easy enough to know when someone is simply going through the motions, to know when what is meant to pass for generosity is in fact superficial pleasantry, straining and labouring under the yoke of obligation. Nor are we all comfortable as recipients of hospitality. We sometimes have guests for whom the fact that this is our home, full of the visible watermarks of our long years of living here, proves an impediment to relaxation. They feel alien and invasive. They move through these rooms on tiptoe, like dancers *en pointe*. They whisper apologies for imagined slights. For running the water. For breathing the air. Heaven forfend they should hiccup or belch. Then there are the others who have a proprietary attitude to the space around them. They are perfectly at home and make free with all we have to offer them, filling the bureaus with their undergarments, rearranging the furniture in their rooms, pulling books from shelves, playing the piano, stoking the fireplace, digging through cutlery drawers for cork screws, leaving dirty dishes in the sink. Or better still, washing them. And while I like all of our guests, regardless of their idiosyncrasies, I must say that those who are quick and ready vessels for hospitality make it easier on themselves and on us.

Hospitality may not be an industry. But it does require industriousness. There is always something that needs doing. Sheets to bleach. Dishes to wash. Dust to disperse. It would be all too easy to be consumed by the ongoing needs of the house. To maintain a certain equilibrium and cleave to what is left of my mental health, I make it a point to take an hour each day for the solitary and pleasant business of practising the bassoon. Even this summer, with the impending Solomon Solomon festivities adding to the pressures of a full house, I have persisted in bumbling along with my bassoonery. I retire, as is my habit, to the pantry off our kitchen, which is a small and resonant room, with Mrs. Rochester as my dependable audience. Sometimes, if our guests are using the kitchen, they too will be privy to my music making.

Just now, we are playing host to a genial threesome who are friends of long standing; and while it is always fun to have a houseful of strangers who get to know one another over the course of a week or so, it is rather more restful for us, as hosts, to have on hand tried and true combinations who are already well acquainted with each other's quirks and foibles. A coterie devoted to studying Marcel Proust, a book club, a writers' support group: such well-established squads come with all their connections and histories and jokes and secret phraseologies in tow, and require no cosseting.

The trio we now have in residence are using their time here to collaborate on a group project, and the room in which they have chosen to work is the kitchen. This morning, directly the breakfast things were cleared away, they arranged themselves around the table and began piecing together a quilt they are making in memory of a man called Mark.

They have a basket full of fragments that remind them of his living. There is a photograph taken of him at his last Christmas: presents and smiling faces around a hospital bed. There are the bits and pieces of happy times. Subway tokens from a trip to Paris. Ticket stubs from a Broadway show. His business card. Swatches of fabric from jeans, from shirts. A birthday card, drawn by his niece, age five. A cigarette pack. His friends took this miscellany of souvenirs and incorporated them into a lovely and touching collage. I watched them at it all day, as I passed through the kitchen chasing after my own industrious and hospitable tail. There was nothing maudlin about their undertaking. They hooted with laughter. They joked. They talked quite frankly about his shortcomings, and how they had been amplified by his dying. It was plain he was someone for whom they deeply cared. As I was hauling my bassoon into the pantry, they were debating the best adhesive to use to make a compact disc stick to the quilt. I looked at it, quizzically.

"Madonna," explained one of the friends. "He loved Madonna."

"I don't suppose you could play 'Material Girl' on the bassoon?" asked another.

I agreed that it might have been a nice touch, but that it was not among the musical possibilities available to me.

"What are you going to put in the middle?" I asked. The various oddments had been arranged as a border, a frame for some feature item still to come.

"Yet to be decided," said the woman in the group. "I do calligraphy, and we thought we'd find some kind of text. A poem. Mark would probably have wanted 'Like a Virgin.' But there are limits."

I thought for a moment, set down my bassoon, excused myself, and went to the library. I returned with my favourite poetry anthology, *Come Hither*, edited by Walter de la Mare. As an anthologist, he cast a very wide net. Whenever I require a poem to match a mood, I can always count on *Come Hither*.

"Maybe you'll find something in this," I suggested.

I retired to the pantry and gave my attention over to Vivaldi. The red-haired priest wrote lovingly for the bassoon: concertos and sonatas that were first performed by the girls in the school where he was employed. I can only suppose that there must have been some young thing who was deft of finger and firm of lip, because he made no concessions to an absence of virtuosity. When I emerged an hour later, quite tuckered from my exertions, the three friends looked up from their work and smiled. The calligrapher was just coming to the end of her work. Her beautiful script was the perfect vessel for the anonymous words they'd chosen as a memorial.

> I have lived and I have loved
> I have waked and I have slept
> I have sung and I have danced
> I have smiled and I have wept
> I have won and wasted treasure
> I have had my fill of pleasure

And all these things were weariness
And some of them were dreariness.
And all these things, but two things
Were emptiness and pain:
And Love, it was the best of them
And Sleep, worth all the rest of them.

"You don't think it's too sentimental?" asked one of the men.

I didn't hesitate to answer that I did not. I wish I could understand how and why sentiment and sentimentality have fallen into such deep disregard. When did "sentimental" become a pejorative barb? I do not at all share the notion that a piece of music, or a poem, or a film that bypasses the brain and aims straight for the heart, and canvasses for an emotional rather than an intellectual response, should automatically be heaped with scorn. I think it is symptomatic of a sad and dangerous impoverishment of spirit.

We live in a world that values objectivity and detachment above all else. Everywhere we turn, we see demonstrations of the brutalities of which we are capable. If we do not cultivate a distance, either through cynicism, or aloofness, or analysis, we risk opening wide the door to the chain-rattling spectres of responsibility, involvement and complicity. And that would be too much to bear. Inasmuch as sentiment might subvert the necessity of holding ourselves at a safe remove, we have come to the firm, if tacit, agreement that we will both damn and dam sentimentality.

There are not many ways in which I am a maverick. But this is one. I won't abandon sentiment. Oh, no. Not yet. I am grateful for every sign that the mysterious and essential germ it pleases me to call my soul retains some lambency. It hasn't been so tumbled by the passage of tumultuous days that its coarse and receptive edges are worn away, leaving nothing but a round, cold stone. My tear ducts have not yet become overgrown. Indeed, as I proceed along the shady avenues of this, my fifth decade, I find I am crying with less and less provocation.

Keats will do it to me. So will parts of Ecclesiastes. And music makes me long for a lachrymatory. There are certain singers especially who set my salty waterworks to overbrimming. Gigli. Baker.

Flagstad. Stratas. Piaf. And I dread the day I grow so callous that I am inured to the emotive tug of Callas. That rough and ragged powerhouse of a voice! That two-ended candle, burning bright! *Un bel di* she sang on the radio only today, and my eyes turned into pitchers.

"Here," said Rae, "have a Kleenex. It's the new kind, with lotion. I think it's just about the greatest product innovation since they started making those panty liners with wings. I must remember to call up the Nobel people and nominate them for a prize."

"In what category?" I snuffled. "Chemistry? Peace?"

"Literature, I think. These things are pure poetry. Two-ply, what's more."

We were in Rae and June's truck. I had left the house with the mail in mind, and made a pit stop at The Well of Loneliness just as the two women were hanging their "Gone with the Wind" sign on the door. With very little arm twisting, they convinced me to accompany them to the cemetery for a late afternoon doggy walk. Their old golden retriever, Toklas, was already sitting in state in the back of the pickup, like a dowager duchess waiting on the arrival of her chauffeur.

"Should you be doing this in your condition?" I asked June as we jounced along the rutted road that leads up the hill to the lovely parklike expanse where the nonsentient serve as sentinels.

"Hell, sure," she answered, petting the cresting swell of her middle. "She's well-insulated down there. And I figure it's all to the good. Little Martina will never get seasick. Will you, honey?"

"Has she started to knock once for yes and twice for no?" I asked.

"Nyuck, nyuck."

A staunch advocate of prenatal education, June likes to make sure the foetus is acknowledged in every conversation. It's her feeling that the eventual child's language skills will be enhanced if she hears her name used in conjunction with complete sentences, which have in turn been enriched by the inclusion of colourful vocabulary. Sometimes, I wonder if the poor little shrimp ever gets a moment's peace to simply kick back, ride the tide, and twiddle her vestigial, homuncular thumbs. In addition to investing in her future linguistic stock, June is making sure her daughter-in-the-making has a head start on numeracy. Every morning, Martina has a mathematics tutorial, which involves her mother-to-be tapping numbers on her midriff as she speaks them aloud. One. Whack. Two. Whack whack. One, whack, plus two, whack whack, equals three: whack whack whack.

"If she comes out with a burning desire to take up the timpani, we'll know why," Rae says, wryly.

Music is also part of little Martina's amniotic ambiance. June has purchased several tapes of classical music that are meant to induce in the wiggling worm a sense of calm and purpose; and which, postnatally, can be played crib-side to remind the infant of the warm, wet paradise of the womb. These tend to be the restful slow movements of baroque and classical concertos: Vivaldi, Corelli, Bach. I recall how, a few years back, exactly the same repertoire was reported to help plants grow. And in fact, I've noticed that the philodendron that hangs over the cash register at The Well is coming along swimmingly.

"She adores Mozart," June said. I snuffled into my lotion-laden tissue while she cranked up the volume on Maria's *Madama Butterfly*. "But I think this is her first Puccini."

We reached the cemetery and stayed in the cab of the truck to hear the doomed and deluded Cio Cio San finish her foolish, optimistic aria. June swayed back and forth to the lush and tuneful melody, crooning along, thumping time. Toklas lumbered over the back of the truck and began to sniff about the cemetery while we waited in the cab for the music to reach its gorgeous climax.

"Oh dear," I wailed, snivelling shamelessly and honking like a northbound goose, unable to control myself even for the sake of the attentive Martina. "I hope this won't put her off opera for good."

"Nah," said June, opening her door and clambering down. "She loved it. She was right there for the whole thing, kicking away like a Rockette. She'll turn out to be one smart cookie, I can promise you that."

June began to perform a series of tai chi exercises prescribed for ladies in waiting. Rae and I moved to one of the benches that look out over the shallow bowl of our valley, and sat with our backs to the ranks of memorial stones and mausoleums. Night, that merriest of widows, was creeping over the edges of the world. We could see the most diaphanous of her several black veils. We watched an eagle, slowly circling, working out the end of her shift. We heard an owl clocking in for night patrol, ready to ensure that complacency wouldn't intrude on the lives of small and scurrying creatures.

"Bats!" said Rae, as a few swift smudges wrote their signatures in front of us. A solitary skunk ambled out of the bushes on the margins of the graveyard, regarded us solemnly, and continued on her insect-grubbing way. Rae looked about anxiously for Toklas, who was absorbed in her own project at a safe distance downwind.

I felt the intricate web of connectedness tighten between us as we sat there, watching: one barren woman and one bachelor man, our arms folded over our respective chests, our two hearts dictating their separate memos, content in our bodies with all their inadequacies and unrealized potentials, content in the lull of the moment. Happy. Happy. Somewhere in the valley, there were children playing at hide-and-seek. Every so often, the sound of their voices would doppler elegantly up the hill.

"Ready or not! Here I come!"

"Cheater cheater pumpkin eater!"

"Liar liar pants on fire!"

"Allee allee in come free-ohhhhh, free-ohhhh, free-ohhhh!"

A shudder shook me. Sudden. As if a cold front had passed through. I looked around to see where Toklas was walking, wondering if she had just passed over my one-day grave.

"You all right?" asked Rae, who misses nothing.

I nodded, although I was not, in the strictest sense, "all right." But I let it slide. I would need too many words to explain that I had been seized just then by a visceral understanding of how nothing is as simple as it seems, and that there is always more to a game than the game itself. Even the giggles that drifted up to us from that innocent round of hide-and-seek masked a darker purpose. Those children who were counting and running and squeezing themselves into hidden nooks and crannies were also rehearsing for the sad and complex play called Dying. Some of the actors who were already well-acquainted with their parts were speaking their muffled lines only a few feet from where we sat.

"98. 99. 100! Ready or not! You must be caught!"

The voice was shrill with warning and excitement. "You must be caught!" Truer words were never spoken. After all, what do we do with our lives, any of us, regardless of place or station, but wait out the count, hiding as best we can, looking over our shoulders, scampering home whenever we dare, flushed each time with the pride of accomplishment at getting there? But one day, we are sure to be nabbed. Oh, yes. Oh, yes. One day, we will be It.

"Free-ohhhhh, free-ohhhhh, free-ohhhhhh! Allee Allee in come free!"

I stood up and stretched, raised my hand to my brow to shield my eyes against what little was left of the late August sun, and took in the whole sweep of the valley. Damn! Why had this invasive and irritating niggling muscled its way into my awareness just now? I gave my foot a stamp, as if I were trying to waken a somnolent leg, though in fact it was a shameful and childish kick of frustration, born of the dispelling of my settled happiness by some bullying reality.

"Can you see your house?" asked Rae.

I nodded. There it was. A golden window or two glinting through the trees. The ancestral home, with its wraparound porch and its cupola attic, its parquet floors and its big country kitchen with the checkerboard tile, its wide entrance way and majestic staircase and the dark panelled library with its silly portraits and its books, books, books. Our little fortress against—well, against what, exactly? Against the world and all its ugliness, against everything that was rising and boiling beyond the illusory protection of those slight hills? Here was night, invading the valley of the shadow, and reeking of cheap perfume. I shook again.

"Free-oooooooohhhhhhhhhh!"

Those children. At some deep, deep level they understood very well what their game was hinting at. And in a few hours, its real meaning would surface in their unguarded dreams. I stepped back away from the bench and onto the grass made green by bones, extended my arms, inhaled deeply, and began to twirl. Slowly at first, then faster and faster, I spun and whirled, dervishing, challenging the upright dictates of my own axis, then flung myself to the ground between two graves and watched the plots thicken and blur. Beneath me, I could feel the world pounding along at real speed on its muscular, determined legs.

June wavered into focus above me. I could just make out her face above the blossoming orb of her tummy. Rae joined her. An interested Toklas licked my chops.

"Exactly," asked Rae, "what the hell was that all about?"

Prone victim of vertigo that I was, I could only laugh by way of answering. High, high up in the deepening blue, Widow Night was trying on her jewels.

I pointed skyward.

"Star light," I began, "star bright, first star I see tonight."

"I wish I may, I wish I might," we all continued together, "have the wish I make tonight."

"Virgil," June asked, as we chugged back down the hill and home, "what was your wish?"

"I can't believe you'd ask him!" said Rae.

"I'll never tell," I answered.

"I'll tell you mine, then. I wished that when Martina decides to make her entrance, you'll be there and play the bassoon during the delivery."

A fermata, rich with incredulity.

"What?"

"It's so important that a baby's first exposure to the outside world be as gentle as possible. Soft lights. Music. I've been planning on taking some of my tapes in, but I really think a live performance would be better. Would you do that?"

"Why Virgil," said Rae when a few minutes of silence had elapsed, "I don't believe I've ever seen human flesh go quite that shade of pale."

"Oh. Oh. Oh. Oh, June. I'm . . . I'm . . . well . . . I'm—"

"Scared shitless?"

"You might say so."

"I hoped you'd be honoured. After all, it's a significant event in my life, and especially in Martina's. And when else will you get a chance to see a baby come into the world?"

"Oh, I'm honoured. Of course! And surprised! I'm sure you can appreciate how very surprised I am. It's not an inconsiderable thing to ask."

"I know. But you're not an inconsiderable friend. Think about it, why don't you? You've got more than three months. And it'll give you a reason to keep practising."

Here was something to chew on, that was certain. Other than my own birth, the memory of which is lost to me, the only biologically significant event I've witnessed was the bloody emergence of Waffle's kittens all those years ago. And even that was almost too much for me to bear. I had to put my head between my knees. I couldn't imagine how I might cope with the noise and gore of a human advent. It made my thighs hurt just imagining it. We drove back toward The Well in silence. As we passed by the community mailbox, I remembered that I hadn't accomplished the mission I'd had in mind when I set out from home, and flagged a stop.

"Anything of note?" asked Rae, as I climbed back up with my fistful of mail.

"Oh, hell! I can't believe it! Look! It's a copy of *Interference*! Will that woman never stop hounding us? I thought she'd given up."

"Let me see," said Rae.

I more than willingly handed it over.

"Keep it, please," I huffed. Rae leafed through the glossy pages of Polly Perch's vile and vitriolic volume. She opened up a perfumed strip, and a cloying smell filled the truck. Then there was a terrible sucking in of breath.

"Oh Jesus!" whispered Rae, in a fit of unaccustomed reverence. "Oh sweet Jesus and Mary and Joseph."

"What? What?" clamoured June, dangerously averting her eyes from the road.

"What? What?" I parroted, like Little Sir Echo.

"Oh, Virgil!"

"For heaven's sake," I spluttered, "What? What? What is it?"

"Oh Virgil! You've been outed!"

"Outed?"

June slammed on the brakes and grabbed the magazine. I sat there in the gathering darkness, trying my best to remember my wish. As if it could be an anchor. A touchstone. But it was gone, gone, gone. A cool breeze slipped through the open window, bearing on its back the distant cry of the night's last game.

"Ready or not! You must be caught! Caught! Caught!"

My Mother's Bread and Butter Pickles

Take 25 medium cukes (sliced fairly thick). Let stand in water and salt (³/4 cup salt to 8 cups water) overnight. Next day, wash and drain. Cook 2 large onions, sliced thin, 10 minutes in clear water.

To make syrup, combine:

4 cups vinegar	*4 tsp. celery seed*
4 cups white sugar	*4 tsp. mustard seed*
1 tsp. turmeric	*¹/4 tsp. alum*

Bring syrup mixture to boil with cooked onions, which have been drained. Put cucumbers in syrup, stirring over heat until they start to change colour. Bottle and seal.

Yo! It's your buddy, Billy Boy, with a cordial hello to everyone at the Bachelor Brothers' Bed and Breakfast. I wonder if you'll capitalize on your new celebrity by amending your letterhead to read "as seen in *Interference* magazine." *Quelle chance, alors!* I'm writing this from the landscape of my birth, the prairies. I've come to roost for a golden, autumnal week or two in the house where I grew up and where my parents still live, and keep company with ghosts.

"Too bad," said my father when I came through the door, after almost a year away, "that you weren't here yesterday. You could have watched me sand your teeth marks from the window ledge."

Dad is a past master of the odd opening gambit.

"Teeth marks?" I asked, setting down my valise.

"You were so sweet," said my mother, eyeing me up and down. I could tell she was itching to get her hands on my jeans so she could launder them and iron in razor-sharp creases. "You used to haul yourself up to the kitchen window, hang onto the frame, look out at the back yard, and have a good old chew."

"When I was teething?"

I thought the question was rhetorical.

"Oh, no! You had all your teeth. I think you just liked the taste of the wood and the varnish. We used to call you our little beaver. So cute!"

I ran my hand over the smooth surface of the ledge from which my dental traces had been so recently expunged. I felt a small and unreasonable sadness at this cavalier erasure of the evidence that once I passed this way. You can go home again, easily enough. But as time goes by, you just can't count on finding the same old souvenirs.

"Well, after all," I chided myself as I hiked my baggage up the stairs, "it's their house, not some sacred reliquary. Why shouldn't they devote their declining years to removing blemishes from around the windows?"

Cleaving to a perspective as tempered and as grownup as this is not easy when you're back under the roof that sheltered your childhood. When I opened the door to my old room, I came within a hair's breadth of giving in to a full-scale pout. Nothing was the same! What was mine was gone. The familiar crannies and corners were jammed with alien stuff.

"Different, isn't it?" said my father, who had followed me up. "We just didn't know where else to put the old furniture when we remodelled."

Ghosts, ghosts. There is nothing in the outward aspect of this well-kept postwar house, white with green trim, on a quiet crescent in the middle of an unremarkable suburb, that would hint at haunting. And yet, everywhere I turn, I see protoplasmic shreds of who and what went before. Out of the corner of my eye, I might see my older brother, now two years dead, and with whom I shared the room that is now the *de facto* attic and dumping ground for household dross, saunter round the corner at the top of the stairs. My grandmother's face peers out of the steam rising from the kettle. Sometimes, I even see my much younger self, bent over what was my desk, wrestling with the angel of French irregular verbs, or standing at the south-facing window, staring through the frost flowers, repeating the word "California" over and over, like a spell. Such unlooked for visitations are not confined to domestic surroundings. The whole city seems full of revenants. For instance, I saw the adolescent me loom out of a storefront when I was downtown, walking along Portage Avenue, past the place where the Mardi Gras used to be.

No one who grew up in Winnipeg in the '50s and the '60s could fail to appreciate the significance, the deep resonance, of that name. *The Mardi Gras*. The Mardi Gras was a place of shame. The Mardi Gras was a whispered name. The Mardi Gras was the restaurant where the fruits went. We'd jeer, "You belong at the Mardi Gras," in the same taunting way we'd say, "You belong in Selkirk," which was the site of a large mental hospital. Oh, the Mardi Gras! It was nowhere you wanted to go. It was nowhere you cared to know. And of course, I was fascinated by it. It was a magnet that both attracted and repelled. Inside the Mardi Gras, I knew, I would find the key to open the door to many mysteries. And all I required to lay my hands on it was what I absolutely didn't possess: the courage to step inside. For what if someone saw and told? What if someone looked and guessed? How could I bear the shame? What would the neighbours think? Oh no. Oh no. It would be easier to clear out. It would be easier to get out of town. And that, in the end, was what I did.

As I hurried on by a few days back, my mind fixed on some mission, I saw myself mirrored in the window of the mall that stands where the restaurant once was. Even though I long ago sprinkled the ashes of the self-loathing that had made the Mardi Gras an impossibility, I found myself once again held in the grip of those old familiars, worry and shame. They took me by the shoulders and shook me when I stumbled on my own ghost, so young, so frightened, standing beneath the motley harlequins that once hung from the Mardi Gras sign, looking furtively in the door, too scared to make a baby step without asking mother-may-I, fearing to be seen, wanting to see, but seeing nothing but my own watery reflection in the glass, totally transparent, revealing every longing and every beat of my quickened heart.

"I'm off to the lumber yard," my father bellowed up the stairs, not half an hour ago.

"Great," I shouted. "Pick me up a two-by-four!"

"Stud grade?" he called back.

Well! Lucky me, huh? My folks have become easy enough with my choices that they can acknowledge them with jokes. I never imagined it would be this way. Telling my parents about the gay facts of my life was one of the hardest things I ever had to do. This seems ridiculous now, years later. What worried me? That they'd scream, rant and carry on operatically about the grandchildren who were not to be? That they'd summon lawyers and change their wills? That they would stagger through their days, heavy with disappointment? That they might blame each other?

"This would never have happened if you hadn't worked late!"

"You shouldn't have let him listen to all those Broadway musicals!"

Of course. That was exactly what I worried about. Such things happened. They happen still, believe it or not. As it turned out, they took the news with enviable nonchalance. Whatever unhappiness or puzzlement they felt, they kept to themselves, which is a time-honoured tradition in our family. Frankly, I found it unsettling. For years, I'd girded my loins for the big explosive moment. When it came, there was hardly a whimper, never mind a bang. A reflective pause, a wistful smile, and a gentle "As long as you're happy, dear."

My mother, who is an optimist by nature, might even have felt something like relief. I imagine her pouring a cup of tea, resting her chin in her hand and thinking, "Hmmmmm. Aren't gays fond of interior design and the decorative arts? I think I read that somewhere. Well, good! Then he can have the Blue Mikado!"

The Blue Mikado, and its eventual disposition, was on her mind just about then. This dinner service was produced by Royal Doulton: blue and white china, patterned with stylized scenes of pre-industrial Japan. Women in kimonos pass over a bridge that spans a little pond in which a young boy fishes among the reeds that grow in the shadow of an old pagoda. My grandmother started buying the stuff in the '40s. My mother and her sister, ever on the alert for birthday and Christmas gift possibilities, added to her set.

She accumulated a basic service of eight dinner plates and side plates, eight cups and saucers, a cake plate, a stack of trivets, and a couple of candlesticks. Soup bowls, cream and sugar containers, gravy boats and ladles: these and other oddments must surely have been available, but were never acquired. War, marriage, fashion, loss of brand loyalty: something got in the way. When my mother and aunt married and left home, Grandma was on her own and not much inclined to entertain; the Blue Mikado was put away. I never saw it during the whole of my growing up, although I heard it spoken of, and always reverently. When time and dissolution did their work, the whole set, snug in its box, came to my mother. This was in the late '70s, just when I was starting to make public declarations, as described above.

"I've decided you should have the Blue Mikado," my mother said to me, not long after I'd told her the Big News. I was sufficiently steeped in the Blue Mikado myth to understand that an honour and blessing were being conferred; and I also intuited that this legacy wasn't yet ripe for passing. I'd have to wait for the Blue Mikado.

That was seventeen years ago. "One day, I must give you that Blue Mikado," my mother would say when I went go back to Winnipeg for a visit. "I've taken the Blue Mikado out of storage," she said a couple of years back. But I never clapped eyes on the stuff until this visit.

"Here," she said, shortly after my arrival, presenting me with what appeared to be three pizza delivery containers. "I've packed these for you to take back. These are some of the plates from the Blue Mikado." She opened one of the boxes, and I looked at the miraculous, kitschy, lovely pattern for the first time.

"I used to drive your grandmother crazy by lining up my peas along that little bridge," she said with a chuckle that was wry and in no way nostalgic.

Then this is how it starts: life's grim, necessary installment plan. The letting go, for which she's decided she's ready. The handing on, for which I'm primed. Half a dozen plates and all those pieces yet to come, with their fragile possibilities and the troubling imperative of preserving a continuum. It's as inevitable as dinner, isn't it?

Dinner here comes at 6 on the dot, and my mom has been spoiling me with home cooking. Maybe because this whole visit has had a "passing of the legacy" subtext to it, and because I've been eating with so many ghosts, I found myself hungering after the foods of my childhood. I spent a few evenings going through her old cookbooks and recipe cards, copying out my favourites. Bully Pudding. Cheese Dreams. Self-Saucing Fudge Cake. Double Snackers. And the Bread and Butter Pickles, for which I have appended the simple instructions.

Mom hasn't made them in years. I think she must have decided, very sensibly, that life is too short and the supermarket too close to bother with the whole sticky rigmarole of home preserving. But if you are fond of pickles, I recommend these to you. When I was a child and had the constitution of a goat, I would stand by the fridge with a jar of Bread and Butters in one hand and a fork in the other, shovelling them down. Oh, Lord. When I get up now and walk through the kitchen (just redone, by the way, and very handsome), I wouldn't be astonished to see myself there, fourteen years old, translucent and hazy around the edges, illumined by the 40-watt glow, feeding one of my several old hungers.

A wind has just come up out of the northwest, and a big black battery of clouds is thundering in like invading tanks. I can hear the chime outside, going ballistic, registering the passing of everything that's invisible but real in the air. Goodbye, goodbye. Perhaps I'll come for a visit before Christmas, if the two great limiters of space and time allow. Of course, I'll want you to autograph my copy of *Interference*. Oo la la! You boys! For now, I've got just enough time before dinner (pork chops, cunningly cooked up with cream of mushroom soup) to take this to the letter box. If I'm lucky, I'll get there before the weather does whatever foul thing it's preparing for, erupting like a genie from a bottle, bringing with him all those surprises we thought were safely bottled and sealed.

I am yr. fond B.

P.S. I am enclosing some cigarette foil for the "Rebuild Solomon's Ball" endeavour. Don't ask where I got it. I'm supposed to be quitting.

Entry: I see you are on the lookout

I see you are on the lookout for improving verse. I am submitting for your consideration the following poem. Its twenty-four lines fell full-formed from my head after my son had six of his friends over for his tenth birthday party. Even if I don't win, will it be possible to buy a commemorative medal? I collect such things. I look forward to hearing from you!

Joan Petroc, West Paradise, Nova Scotia.

Little boys from near and far, from this and every nation,
Let us sit for just a bit and speak of mastication.
Every cow who's in the field, content and brown and mooing,
Knows that after grazing there's a cud that she'll be chewing.
And that's because she knows full well how there can be no
 question
That mashing up her food improves her mood and her digestion.

And similarly lions, when they're on the veldt and gnawing,
Chewing in the sun while all the carrion birds are cawing,
Know that munching sets in motion salivary action,
Which is cool, since pools of drool are tools of satisfaction.
This is nature's way, and so of course I'm well contented
Every time you show you know why molars were invented.

And sure as Ebeneezer Scrooge was famous as a miser,
I'm pleased as punch you bunch can munch and crunch with your
 incisors.
However, you are different from the beasts. Because you're human,

You can learn to close your mouths and keep the spit and spume in.
So, when you sit a table with your parents, friends and siblings,
Do not open wide your chops and show us what you're nibbling.

No one needs a guided tour, and none of us can bear it
When you gnash the nasty hash of chocolate, peas and carrots.
Eat your food and make good use of all your pearly fixtures.
Clean your plate. Don't demonstrate the half-ingested mixtures.
Thanks for your attention, and I'm sorry for this nagging.
It comes to this: I'm 36, and none too fond of gagging.

On this frabjous day I won

On this frabjous day I won an unexpected victory and made the wounded welkin ring with raucous cries of praise and thanksgiving. Glory be! Hallelujah! Laud creation! Hot damn! Given that no historian will consider my accomplishment worthy of attention, and as I am certain it will rate not even a footnote in the eventual annals of these, our perilous times, I will set down the news here. Perhaps some future curiosity seeker will read it and be coaxed haltingly to the understanding that the thunderous, flesh-tearing, terrain-sundering doings of the generals and industrialists are not what power the turning of the planet, but rather the dull, quotidian and largely overlooked progressions of ordinary pilgrims.

Know ye then that on this day, at precisely 11:27 A.M., with the sun in Virgo, underneath a cobalt sky unsullied by cirrus or cumulus mottling, with the stillness of nearly noon settling on the changing trees, and with only God, Mrs. Rochester and Paolo as my witnesses, I, Hector, achieved that which has eluded me for nigh on forty years. I learned to hula hoop.

By gum! If only we had a bar, I'd have bought drinks for the house. As it was, I had to be content with treating myself to a solitary glass of sherry. Well, maybe I had two. Small ones, though. *Dio!* Even now I can hardly believe it has happened! If you were to open the catalogue of my private shames, you would find "defeated by hula hoop" very near the top of the list. It cedes precedence only to the time I cheated to win the fifth grade spelling bee.

I wish I could say just why I have been so consistently unsuccessful in the repeated efforts I have made over the decades to keep one of these wretched things aloft; at least, to keep it aloft in the conventional way by whirling it about my middle. Early on in my association with Altona, I was able to prevent one from falling to earth for almost ten minutes in a more *outré* fashion, by way of proving a point and winning a bet. There's no need to go into the particulars here and now, however.

Had the hula hoop had only one vogue, had it slipped in and out of fashion, I would certainly not have been so troubled by this singular centrifugal ineptitude. However, it has insisted on making comeback after comeback as new generations and subgenerations discover it afresh. Every couple of years, some visiting child will drag a hoop along, as if to taunt me. Sometimes, when a "what the hell" spirit has seized me, and hoping against hoop that something will have changed since my last excursion, I'll ask to borrow the toy and, quite literally, give it a whirl. The results have never varied. I stand with feet planted firmly on the ground, put the ring over my head, lower it until it is on a parallel plane with my navel, give it a clockwise spin, then begin to shake and gyrate for all I'm worth. And always, in mere seconds, it will prove some Newtonian theorem by slipping quickly down over my waist, my thighs, my knees, my shins and ankles, until finally it lies, ignominious, at my feet. What could possibly be more diminishing?

"No, no!" its pint-size guardian will chime. "Do it like this!" And then give a very convincing show of how it is, in fact, possible to thumb one's nose at that grave old dictator, gravity.

"Every motion tells a story!" laughed Altona, the one time she tried to show me how it was done. "Just let yourself go!" But not even putting "Hot Night in Waikiki and other Hawaiian Hula Hits" on the stereo was an effective teaching aid.

"You just have to find your own centre," a grandmotherly physics teacher once told me, as she turned herself into a human gyroscope and kept not one but two bright yellow hoops in the air at a time.

"The hips! The hips! Leave the chest out of it!"

"Try to pretend you're stirring a pot with your belly button!"

"Clench your butt!"

"Bend your knees!"

"Pretend you're giving birth!"

Oh, I've had more advice than I would have thought possible, and none of it has made a difference. So, what can explain today's triumph, the recreational apotheosis of which I sing? All I can say for sure is that late this morning, when I was snipping some snapdragons and pansies to brighten up the kitchen, I spotted the red and taunting round of one of the devilish contrivances, abandoned under the chestnut tree. At first, I tried to ignore the saucy O. But every time I looked toward it, it appeared to rise up and throw my past defeats back at me, hurling them through its own vacant centre. Blank and inanimate though it was, it nonetheless seemed to pass judgment. It was assigning me a grade. A big fat zero. Anger welled.

I looked around. I was all alone, save for Mrs. Rochester and Paolo. Virgil was lying in his room holding a cold compress to his head, as he has done most days since the arrival of that infernal *Interference* magazine. Caedmon was locked away, putting the final touches on the prototype of the Solomon Solomon memorial medal. Our guests (only four in residence just now, thanks be to God) were looking to their individual knitting. Mrs. Rochester was perched on Violetta, alternately watching her coxcombed companion scratch after bugs and studying her own reflection in the side mirror. She bobbed and muttered, as if she were puzzling over the caveat that "objects are closer than they appear." When she saw me set down my scissors and bouquet and move to pick up the hula hoop, she cackled aloud and quoted from the ninety-first Psalm.

"A thousand may fall at your side, ten thousand at your right hand; but it will not come near you!"

I flashed her a pertinent finger and stooped to conquer. Half-remembering some words of advice I'd gleaned years ago from a book called something like *Zen and the Art of Carving Radish Roses*, I imagined a fresh and fragrant wind blowing through my head. I saw how I was one with the hollow plastic ring and with the empty space inside the hoop's circumference. A warm wash of understanding flowed over me like a tropical wave: I was one with the earth beneath me, one with the sky above, and one with the spin itself. The gentle breeze acquired a voice and chanted a plainsong hymn: "I am the spin and the spin is me. I love the spin and the spin loves me."

I held the hula hoop above my head, feeling how it pulsed with energy and benevolence. *Is me! Loves me!* I lowered it as I have done so often before, full of a certainty that came from a place beyond knowing: a certainty that we had already achieved a glorious *entente* and that the actual whirling was no longer the point. It was already taking place. Making it visible was nothing more than a demonstration, a crass but necessary proof. *Is me! Loves me!* As I placed the ring over my own body, rather like Napoleon crowning himself emperor, I understood that I had come to nothing less than a wedding at which I was to be both the bride and the groom of the teeming cosmos. I was void and without form. *Is!* I was moving like a mist over still waters. *Loves!* I was the word, unencumbered by flesh. *Is!* I was Saturn, acquiring his jewels. *Loves!* I filled my lungs with morning air and my heart with gladness and then I spun. *Is! Is! Loves! Loves!* The air rang loud with my clarion call of triumph.

"Wheeeeeeeeeeeeeeeeee!"

"Oh sing to the Lord a new song, sing to the Lord all the earth!" cried Mrs. Rochester when she beheld the wondrous sight.

Golly! It was some fun, I can tell you that! As soon as I had shed my godlike demeanour and taken on human form again, I scampered into the house and skipped up the stairs, bursting with the need to tell my loving twin my astonishing news. I imagined he would find it a tonic; that it might dispel the lingering miasma that has shrouded him these last several weeks. I found him lying on his cot, with the curtains drawn against the day's evangelistic summon to cheerfulness. Waffle, who has decided she will demonstrate codependent behaviour during his bout of despondency, was stretched across his eyes, like a furry light guard. He didn't even trouble to lift her off when I burst through the door and shouted out all that had occurred. I hadn't been so excited since the day I had the revelation about how Evian spelled backward is naive.

"Oh. That's nice," was as much of a reaction as Virgil could muster.

"For the love of Mike—whoever he was—snap out of it! It's not so bad. A scum-bucket magazine like that! No one takes it seriously."

His only answer was a fluttering sigh that had all the oomph of wind in dry grass. My brother has always been somewhat inclined toward depressive fits. When he was a child, the most minor episode could set him off. I recall how once a robin beaned herself on the window of our room. She did herself no injury, but that night, Virgil woke me with his sobbing.

"What's wrong?"

"The bird. The robin," he gurgled.

"The bird flew away. We saw it."

"I know. But what if she had fallen all the way to the ground and broken her wing? What if she couldn't move? What if a cat came along and killed her? And what if she had babies in a nest and they were waiting for her to bring them a worm, and they were crying and crying and she never came because she couldn't come because she was dead, because she'd hit our window and the cat got her—and then what would happen to those babies when their mother never came home?"

For days afterward, he was inconsolable and gnawed on the bitter bone of abandonment anxiety. Now when I look back on this and other warning childhood incidents, I regret there was no one nearby with the insight to encourage Virgil to channel his warped imaginings into something constructive, like writing fiction. He has always had the novelist's inclination to take hold of a situation and turn it over and over in his hands, examining it for all its hidden possibilities. The question "what if?" hangs at the forefront of his mind. In and of itself, this is an admirable impulse. But there are times when a questioning nature, working hand in hand with what I can only suppose is a brain-centred chemical imbalance, can provoke episodes like the one I was now witnessing.

It's sad watching my brother hang on the cross of sordid circumstance. It's frustrating, too, because he exacerbates the situation by maintaining close contact with the source of his torment. As though possessed by the perverse need to drive the nails in deeper, he keeps the offending issue of Interference on his bedside table, open to the two-page spread of photographs that shows us capering and prancing upon the lawn, all dudded up in our firefighting finery.

"Bachelors in Paradise!" is the simpering headline that runs atop the half-dozen glossy photos. In the spirit of "a picture is worth a thousand words," there is very little text, save for the captions and a breathless introductory paragraph, which was branded onto my brain with a single reading.

> Come with us to meet Hector and Virgil and some of their fascinating friends at a bachelor party on an island paradise! Hector and Virgil, who run a bed and breakfast in their charmingly decrepit house, and who have long referred to themselves as "brothers," like nothing better than to have dress-up parties with their chums! They call their exclusive club "the Volunteer Fire Brigade!" Only one girl is allowed to play! And we're not sure just how "real" that girl is! When the Volunteer Fire Brigade gets together on their island paradise, anything is possible! Come on, baby! Light my fire! Then do your best to put it out! I dare you!

The night Virgil arrived home with the magazine, he was pale but lucid. The shock had not yet set in. Rae and June helped him into the house and arranged him on the couch in the library. I happened to be nearby, playing Scrabble with Caedmon and two of our more courageous or foolhardy guests. As anyone who knows me can attest, I will wring every brain cell and bend every rule in order to win at Scrabble. Ironically, I had just set down the tiles to spell out "perfidy" on a triple word score when the troubled threesome came into the room. It was all I could do to wrench myself away from the evident dismay of my competitors to make the necessary inquiries of the stricken. Caedmon came with me.

"Sure are a lot of exclamation points," was our hired hand's admirably contained reaction after he had sized up the muckraker's spillage.

Snide comments about sloppy editing practices did nothing to assuage Virgil. "I should have known," he said, sucking back his third single malt scotch. A measure of his discontent was that he was mispronouncing "Glenlivet" as "Glenlivid."

"Should have known what?" asked Rae.

"Those so-called Lindisfarnes! Ha! How could we have been so gullible as to be taken in by those wolves in sheep's clothing," he croaked, grabbing back the magazine and staring at it in stark disbelief. "What insolence! What unmitigated nerve! What—what—what—"

"Perfidy?" I suggested, for once having *le mot juste* on the tip of my tongue.

"Exactly! Look! Look at these pictures! And the text! The text! Of all the sleaze-bag, underhanded, sniping, nasty, carping, insinuating—"

He began to splutter and wheeze. I pried his fingers from the magazine and sat down to assess the damage. I'm afraid it doesn't speak very well of me that I looked at the pictures of me first. My blush-enhanced nipples were as pink as dime store mints. My Stetson was askew. My suspenders were awry. My Wellington boots were cast off to one side. I lay supine, spread out on the lawn, with Abel leaning suggestively into my face, his knee on my sternum. Altona's head was caught between my knees. My pistachio-tinted toenails were as bright as Christmas lights.

Why did the fireman paint his toenails!

The other photographs and cutlines were just as bad. There was J. Mac in his latex coveralls, holding a garden hose at an unfortunate angle and sporting an expression of almost religious ecstasy.

Too hot to handle!

Caedmon had been convinced to scale the Maypole we'd erected in a corner of the yard, years and years ago when a vernal mood was on us. The vile worm Moffat had photographed him staring down at the ground, a look of abject terror on his face.

Help! This little kitten can't get down!

Nor did Virgil fare well. He stood in front of Violetta, an axe clutched in his hands, in a ready-for-action pose. He glared out from under his hardhat with what was meant to be fierce determination but read more like "serial killer in the bud." Paolo was pecking at his feet, evidently unconcerned by the proximity of a nutbar with a lethal weapon.

Unable to find a goose who lays golden eggs, Captain Virgil decides a cock-a-dude'll do!

No one who wandered into Polly Perch's snare escaped unscathed.

"It's as transparent as it is suggestive," said June, "and puerile, too. Don't fret. No one will really believe you're turning the valley into Fire Island West."

"I couldn't care less about that! Hell's bells! People can think what they like. What bothers me is the feeling that I'm sliding down the cutting edge of the decay of our civilization. If this is what goes on out there," Virgil declaimed, gesturing toward the world beyond the valley, "then what is the point of going on? We're all of us done for! Perfidy, thy name is Polly!"

"My spirit is broken, my days are extinct, the grave is ready for me," lamented Mrs. Rochester, calling upon the Book of Job (17.1) to sum up the mood of the assembly. And after that, Virgil's decline was precipitous.

"Maybe pharmaceuticals are the answer," suggested Altona this afternoon. We were sitting on the front porch glider, each of us nursing a gin and tonic. Anyone might be forgiven for thinking, given what I've revealed about myself, that I'm rather too fond of a drink in the middle of the day. Nothing could be further from the truth! I am merely practical and loath to throw anything away if it can be finished before its usefulness has passed. As the end of the hot weather G&T season is nearly upon us, and as the tonic won't overwinter, we are simply trying to circumvent the sin of wastefulness. Every now and then, one has to force oneself.

"What? I should put Prozac in his cocoa?"

"Depression is nothing to joke about!"

"If it goes on much longer, I might start to worry. But I suspect he'll come around pretty soon. I hope so, anyway. The Solomon Solomon festivities won't be easy on any of us. I never imagined the day would come that I'd be serving on so many committees."

Altona nodded. She had just come from covering one of many planning meetings for the big day of celebration. Most tempers are by now somewhat frayed. Others have come completely unravelled.

It would seem that Solomon, even dead, is as divisive a force as he was when he walked among us, smoking incessantly and scribbling verses on fudgsicle wrappers. Everyone, regardless of whether they actually knew the man, has an opinion that needs airing.

"Who said what?" I asked.

"Oh, dear. I don't think I have the energy to go into it now. You can read the full and gory account in *The Rumour* tomorrow."

"Ah. Forgive me for saying so, but you seem a little down yourself."

"Oh, it's nothing, really. I'm still hurting from the suggestion that I could be mistaken for a drag queen. Not that I have anything against drag queens, of course. I've seen some beauties in my time."

I crunched my ice and gave her a questioning look.

"I'll tell you all about it. Someday."

Altona is a woman of untapped depths, and that's for sure. She heaved a deep sigh. "I still wish we could sue the bastards!"

Taking libel action against *Interference* was Mac's idea. We talked him out of it by stressing how the embarrassment would only be prolonged if we waxed litigious. I think it just pleased him to bluster on about "class action suits."

"Even this shall pass away," I said, doing my best to be chipper.

"You sound like a dietitian," she snarked.

A woman scorned is unlikely to find a rattling apothegm useful as a balm, and I should have learned that by now. More drastic action was required to extricate her from this funk. I leaned over and took a thin tendril of her ash blond hair in my fingers, leaned closer still and whispered in her ear, "Hey, lady. Wanna see a trick you've never seen before?"

"Oh, I guess so."

"You won't be sorry! Wait there!"

And I ran to the back of the house, where I'd left the hula hoop under the chestnut. I ran with wing-powered heels, hardly able to keep myself from laughing out loud at imagining the look on Altona's face when she saw me engulfed by the wonderful spin of the hoop that had so far been impervious to my considerable charms. She would laugh and clap and smother me with kisses and lavish compliments.

I reached the backyard just in time to see Caedmon, who was cutting the grass with our little tractor lawn mower—Paolo perched on the front like a mute figurehead—take aim for the green around the chestnut tree. There was a terrible crunching sound as the efficient blades decimated the hula hoop and sent bits of it flying all over the yard, like the dragon's teeth Cadmus sows in the myth. I was given pause to think, for the first time, that Caedmon is remarkably close to Cadmus, phonetically speaking. I wondered if Altona would find that amusing.

En route back to the front porch, I passed through the kitchen to pick up three oranges, hoping that I might learn how to juggle them in the time it took me to walk down the hallway and that I could pass this off as my amazing, mood-altering stunt.

"There you are!" she carolled when I returned to the porch, feeling quite dejected myself. "There was a special delivery package for Virgil while you were gone. Very official looking. I took it up to him."

"Oh-oh. I hope it's nothing that will send him over the edge. He's had such a lot of bad luck with the mail."

"Maybe you should go up and check," she said.

But before I had reached the bottom of the staircase, I heard a tremendous whoop and holler. Virgil, dressed in his pajamas, was dancing on the landing, waving an envelope and shouting, "Vengeance! Sweet, sweet vengeance! Justice! Oh happy, happy justice! My prayers have all been worthwhile. Oh! Oh! Oh wonderful, wondrous world!"

He leapt into the air, clicked his bare heels together, clambered onto the banister, slid merrily down, did a jaunty jig out to the porch, bussed Altona loudly on the cheek, and proceeded to turn cartwheels across the grass.

"I didn't know you could do cartwheels," I said, when he finally crawled back to the porch.

"Never have before in my life," he panted. "Oh, it is a day of miracles! The Lord works in mysterious ways, and help comes from strange sources. Here! Take a gander."

And he handed over the envelope and all it contained, then sprawled on the porch at our feet, huffing and happy, like a terrier with his nose down a rat hole. I passed him an orange and opened the package to see what glories it might contain.

"Ladies and gentlemen," he crowed, "the fun is about to begin!"

Clippings from *The Occasional Rumour*

Dear Sir:

On behalf of the ever-increasing membership of Save Our Weasels (SOW), I am taking this opportunity to register our protest against the plan to rebuild the Solomon Solomon house. It is our contention that the derelict dwelling be left as it is and be designated a nature preserve, inasmuch as the largely burned out shell has come to be the favoured breeding site of the valley's once burgeoning weasel population.

Thirty years ago, the lithe and supple creatures ran thick on the ground. Loss of habitat drove these beloved sons and daughters of Gaia to seek greener pastures. Solomon Solomon himself lamented their loss in his poem, "Whither, Weasel? Whither?"

> Whither, weasel? Whither?
> Are you going hence to wither,
> While we blither and we dither?
> Tell us,
> Whither, weasel? Whither?

Efforts by concerned conservationists to reintroduce the weasel to the valley met with very little success until after Solomon's unfortunate demise and the fiery razing of his hut. It would surely have pleased the bard to learn that the charred remnants of his simple home proved, for reasons that science has never been able to clearly delineate, to have what can only be described as an aphrodisiac effect on the few weasels who had elected to stay put. Hardly had the smoke cleared when they began to congregate beneath the blackened rafters and to breed with a hitherto unimagined ferocity.

We agree in principle with efforts to rehabilitate the reputation of Solomon Solomon, but we will not sit idly by and watch the weasel be pushed once again to the brink of local extinction. We are here to Save Our Weasels, and we will take every measure available to us under the law to ensure that they prosper and thrive.

Norbert Ninnoc.

cc. *International Bulletin of Weasel Spotting*

* * *

Sir,

My family and I are very much hoping that, as part of the Solomon Solomon Commemoration Day festivities, there will be tours of the safe. Can you please advise if such activities are planned? If not, why not? Thank you.

Andrew McAndrew and family.

* * *

Solomon Solomon: A Dream of Reconciliation
An editorial by J. MacDonald Bellweather II,
adapted from a sermon he delivered at
the Church of God the Technician and Marketer

My good friends, I come before you today with my heart laden and heavy and full of grief. And the source of my present distress is none other than the cause of one of my most abiding joys. I refer to our great poet and moralist, Solomon Solomon.

I know full well there are those among you who scoff to hear me append such an honorific to his name. I know there are those among you who look at the surface record of the man's life, who study the most superficial aspects of his biography, and raise a clamour of protest. "Moralist?" you gasp, unable to conceal your stupefaction. And it is true that Solomon led a life that was not, in any outward aspect, upstanding and fine. It is true that he was

139

given to excesses. Stories of public drunkenness, rumours of lechery, whispered allegations of improprieties with livestock: all these reprehensible behaviours have been exhumed from the dank grave of the past and presented for dissection.

I stand before you today, in the presence of God the Technician and Marketer, to tell you that presentation to the contrary, Solomon Solomon was a deeply moral man. For morality is not always manifest in action or outward display. This was a man who knew what it was not only to struggle with his baser impulses, but to lose to them, time and time again.

When the needs of the spirit and the acts of the flesh are so much at odds, there can only be only one outcome. And that, my friends, is a terrible divisiveness of being, with its slavering attendants, Tension and Remorse. These were Solomon Solomon's two constant companions. And tragic though it be to tell, it was thanks to those that Solomon Solomon made art. It was to placate and redeem his soul that Solomon Solomon poured into his writing both his recognition that a proper life is a moral life, and his acknowledgments of his own shortcomings. As he wrote, feelingly and unforgettably, in *Hygiene for Boys:*

> As decent men are far and few,
> Do as I say, not as I do.
> And when, good lads, you go to play,
> Shun what I do, do what I say.

Which of us, my friends, can cast that first stone? Who among us can stand and say that he or she is without sin? I say to you that when we honour the Bard, we honour Everyman. When we commemorate our valley's laureate, we commemorate one who knew the meaning of struggle and failure, but who never lost sight of the living, moving spirit of God the Technician and Marketer, who is both immutable and ever changing. Hallelujah! May the great GTM be praised!

VIRGIL

Sometimes, while I'm blithely puttering

Sometimes while I'm blithely puttering, dumbly building each new day's straw house—heedless of the fact that it must fall to the lupine blusterings of night—I'll be taken forcibly, and all at once, by a demonstration of the transcendent beauty of the ordinary. At moments like this, I am filled with such a sense of peace and of purpose that the insignificant thudding of my heart becomes a hymn. I'll look from the window on a grey afternoon to see how the sun has broken through; that its one broad beam has been fractured and strung across the clouds like harp strings. I'll walk into the library and find one of our visitors snoozing in a wing-backed chair, her book fallen to the floor, her glasses akimbo, and observe how her reading is feeding her dreams, see how her eyes are darting back and forth under their concealing lids. Her dog is also asleep, but running, chasing pell-mell after a rodent of his own inventing.

Or sometimes I will look over at my brother, Hector, or at Altona, while one or the other is in a moment of fierce and unguarded concentration: plotting a Scrabble move, or separating a white from a yolk. In that one revealing instant, the proof of time's passing settles upon them as easily, as silently and as painlessly as a piece of silk slips through a golden ring. The first slight trace of a new line appears around an eye. A liver spot begins to develop on the back of a hand. These are among the bittersweet inevitabilities that come with the package plan we buy into when we arrive on the planet. Not even two people as devoted to astringents and facial packs as Hector and Altona can hide forever. Or even for long.

I am discreet about these observations, of course. I don't make a point of calling attention to the birth of a blemish or the deepening of a wrinkle. No one likes to have his nose rubbed in the fact of his ageing. Me, least of all. In fact, I owe these reflections to revelations regarding my reflection, visited on me only this morning.

I was out in the yard, dealing with the fallout from our chestnut tree. A big and vagrant wind had whistled through, shaken its leaves from their moorings, then left them lying all over the lawn, rather than ushering them out of the valley. I decided that as long as I was out of doors, I would do some more tidying up after nature and scrub away the mottled bird droppings from our sundial. The sundial is one component of a frankly peculiar sculpture that was bestowed on us by Altona. It came to her from her ex-husband as part of her divorce settlement, and was taking up space in her garage that could be better filled, she felt, by crates of cosmetics.

It is certainly unique. There cannot be, in this world, so very many combination bird bath / sundials crafted to look like a miniature volcanic island. The mountain rises from a sandy beach and stands just over five feet in height. About a foot from the summit, the volcano forms a plateau, which accommodates a deep depression. This is the bird bath portion of the structure. The peak rises up again from the basin, and the sundial is installed on the summit. In a particularly imaginative stroke, and to honour the literary nature of this place, Altona herself chose two texts from Donne to incorporate into this masterpiece. Pebbles arranged around the beach remind us that "No Man Is an Island." And encircling the summit, ranged about the sundial itself, mosaic tiles spell out "Busie old foole, unruly sunne, why dost thou thus?"

One of the children who visited us recently and who was of time-telling age asked me the hour in plain view of our kitchen clock. I gestured upward, and she shook her head. "I only read digital," she told me, sneering at the archaic sweep of our trusty timepiece's hands. I was appalled in the moment but have since come to feel some kinship with her; for I am as at sea with the sundial's antique technology as she is with antedated analog time telling. I can't for the life of me wring any sense from the spill of the shadows. And when daylight savings time has to be calculated into the mix, I am utterly at sixes and sevens.

You will gather that I feel a certain ambiguity about the sundial. The birds, however, are unanimous in their approval. They perch upon it before and after they've had their baths. They preen, they flutter, they dive, and they poop, poop, poop. This morning, I scoured long and hard to clean away the souvenirs of their ablutive rituals, then removed the feathers and twigs and other jetsam from the bath itself. As the water settled down, it took on a clear and glassy quality. I leaned over to gaze at my reflection, forgetting momentarily one of the cardinal rules of gravity and mid-life flesh—that the one has a devastating effect on the other. When I leaned over, the back of my face fell forward to meet the front, creating a kind of hangdog look that put me in mind of a basset hound called Chuckles, who was one this past summer's visitors. Chuckles bayed at the slightest provocation; and the frightful sight of my sagging visage provoked me to let out a howl even Chuckles would have admired.

I recovered quickly and looked around to see if anyone had witnessed the episode. There was only Waffle, sitting in the kitchen window over the sink. She was sniffing the narcissus which has only just come into its heady seasonal flower. It was such an arresting sight—the window-framed cat and the flower forced from its bulb, and so apt that my attention should be drawn to a narcissus at that moment—that I was wrenched from misery to calm. I thought of how the clock that ticked inside me also ticked inside the bulb at the base of the flower that even then was hypnotizing the cat with its sweet and waxy smell; and it ticked too, in the bulbs we had so recently bedded in our garden. Tulips. Daffodils. Crocuses. Each one huddled around its own ticking heart, nursing its own perfect moment, knowing in its every silent cell that soon enough, the time will be right.

"Soon enough," sighed June on the phone, when last I called her up to check in. "Soon enough, and I just can't wait for the invasion of the body snatchers to be over and done. My shoes don't fit. I couldn't get through a revolving door without using a crowbar. I feel like my every organ has been squished into a space the size of an eggcup. And on the rare nights I can actually sleep, I have these wild dreams. Last night, for instance, I got on a double-decker bus. The driver was a baby. The conductor was a baby. Every passenger was a baby. They all looked the same, and every one of them was telling me in some telepathic way that it was mine and I had to look after it, but I knew that only one of them could be and I had to make the right choice."

"What did you do?"

"Asked for a transfer and got off at the next stop. I seem to be losing my memory, too. I just can't keep the spelling for 'hemorrhoid' in my head."

"This is a problem?"

"I hope you never know. And frankly, I'm getting sick of Vivaldi. I'm starting to wonder if little Martina wouldn't like a hit of Coltrane."

The Solomon Solomon celebrations are ripening, too. More than enough foil has been collected to reconstruct the giant ball. Assembly begins next week, and it will be unveiled at the sod-turning ceremonies on October 31. Funds are pouring in for the refurbishing of the house. The submission deadline for improving verse has come and gone. In terms of volume, the contest proved a tremendous success. Almost 10,000 poems were received. A whole range of subjects and concerns were made manifest. Scolding sonnets adjuring dog owners to pick up after their pets. Vilifying villanelles abhorring the rudeness of shop clerks. Simpering sestinas set down in praise of temperance. If anything like unity is to be found in this tremendous hodgepodge, it is that almost every single verse is unbelievably bad. I do not envy the judge, who arrives tomorrow to begin her sage deliberations.

"Celebrated Journalist to Judge Poetry Contest!" ran the banner headline in *The Rumour*. There was considerable astonishment that someone of the stature of Polly Perch, editrix of the celebrated *Interference* magazine, could be seduced into taking time from her busy schedule to come to a backwater like this to serve as the arbiter of a mountain of poetry written almost entirely by amateurs.

"However did you manage it?" people ask me, when they see me on the street; for it has become generally known that it was I who extended so quixotic an invitation.

"Ask, and it shall be given," I reply, with a smug and self-contented grin.

For days after I received them, I clutched to my heart the letter and photographs that enabled me to persuade Polly Perch to return to us, this time playing herself. I could scarcely believe my good luck!

Dear Virgil:

I know you will remember me, and I fear that it will not be with gladness that you now read my name. I am Moffat Lindisfarne, who arrived late one night at your B&B, in the company of my so-called wife. You will no doubt have surmised that the putative Mrs. Lindisfarne was none other than that celebrated toxin of the journalistic world, the noxious Polly Perch. The mere mention of her name is enough to make me break in to a cold sweat, and I am pleased to report that I have severed my connection with her and with her miserable excuse for a magazine. I can offer no excuse for my own complicitous behaviour, save to say that I have always been too inclined to value style over substance, and that I fell victim, for a sad while, to the glittering spell cast by the demimonde to which she had access and of which I was, however peripherally and for however short a time, a part. But even a toad as grovelling as I has his limits of endurance.

The weight of my past sins and indiscretions is heavy on my shoulders. I have much to do to redeem myself. Tomorrow morning I am off to Central Africa to work for a month among the lepers. When I return, I shall try to find some more honourable inkwell for my nib. My soul is undergoing so rapid a burnishing, I feel myself changing even as I write. Already, I have shed the need I once felt for securing anything as tawdry as vengeance. However, in the event you and your brother may not have attained so lofty a spiritual pinnacle, I am enclosing some photographs you may find useful in pursuing a constructive course of action. It seems a charitable thing to do.

Goodbye. I send you every good wish and hope we may meet again under more appealing circumstances. Until then, I beg your forgiveness and ask for your prayers and remain your servant,

Moffat Lindisfarne.

"Oh, my. Oh, my," was all Hector could sputter when I showed him what had been delivered into our hands.

"Surely," said Altona, when she had read Moffat's letter and examined his enclosures, "that is not a real goat!"

Dear Ms. Perch:

Thank you ever so much for your kindness in sending us a copy of your magazine. You can imagine how thrilled we were to find ourselves featured therein. All the members of our volunteer fire brigade join me in thanking you for your kind consideration.

Inasmuch as one good turn deserves another, I thought you might be interested in publishing some photos that have recently come our way. We have already had a strong expression of interest from your colleagues at Pry Magazine, who are very eager to have them for an upcoming issue. However, given that we have established so strong a connection with Interference, we felt we should give you the right of first refusal. We would require no cash outlay for these very charming snapshots, for which we also possess the negatives; however, we would like to discuss with you the possibility of "payment in kind." You see, we are having this poetry contest—quite small, really—and we are in need of a judge . . .

Oh, Polly Perch! Soon she'll be on her way! I can hardly wait to see her again. The look on her face will add years to my life. Which makes me glad, as life is so very grand! If only it could go on forever!

May we recommend?
Virgil's books for baby Martina's first five years

You might wonder why a barren old bachelor such as I imagines himself qualified to suggest books that will please youngsters. However, I will say in my own defence that I am not without some experience in this regard. From time to time, I have volunteered to read aloud to the children of grownup guests who seem frazzled and worn out from the exertions of a day of active parenting, and who could benefit from a quiet half-hour away from the needs and demands of their offspring. Mothers and fathers look on me as a saint, but I don't think I'd be so forthcoming if I didn't think it was fun. I go at it with great gusto, allowing the inner ham to come to the surface. These are the books which I have never known to fail with the under-five set, and are among the stories I look forward to sharing with little Martina.

Ballad of the Blue Bonnet, **Robert Priest, illustrated by Debi Perna**
An endearingly alliterative and cumulative rhyme about a blue bonnet that gets passed from baby to baby and town to town in "the baby-go-round." This is great fun to read aloud, and babies love nothing better than stories about babies.

The Elephant and the Bad Baby, **Elfrida Vipont, illustrated by Raymond Briggs**
When a co-operative elephant meets a bad and manipulative baby, what else can they do but go "Rumpeta, rumpeta, rumpeta, all down the road!" This is not a story for the shy. It is subversive and

sly and requires a high level of dramatic involvement. Raymond Briggs's drawings are full of life and drive.

Gingerbread Man, traditional

There are a number of different picture book versions of this nursery story, but the one I like was illustrated by Paul Galdone. I love the cumulative nature of the story, the way it builds and builds, with the rude little rogue gingerbread man taunting everyone he meets, until at last he comes to the fox who ferries him over the Styx. It's important for adults to find something in children's stories to like and believe in, and I find this fable about as convincing a lesson in inevitability as has ever been set down on paper.

Goodnight Moon, Margaret Wise Brown

The perfect "goodnight book," especially for a very young child. A baby rabbit is getting ready for bed. His (or is it her?) granny sings this soothing, gentle, pretty little lullaby, a countdown to sleep. The only challenge for the grownup reading aloud is to remain awake until you've pronounced the amen: "Goodnight noises everywhere."

Gorky Rises, William Steig

Any child who has ever played scientist by mixing together unlikely liquids into a potion, and any child who has ever dreamed of flying—all of which is to say, any child at all—will be a willing participant in the story of what happens when a junior frog called Gorky swills his home-made brew and rises. And rises. And rises. Here, as in his many other books for young people, William Steig creates a loony, surreal universe that is wry rather than threatening; sophisticated, but in no way forbidding. Both grownups and children will find much to amuse them here.

Green Eggs and Ham, Dr. Seuss

Dr. Seuss is not without his detractors. There are those who say his many, many books—which were written as much with the beginning reader in mind as they were for reading aloud—are formulaic and silly. They may well be. Certainly, there are some that are better than others. But so what? For the most part they are fun, and children love them. Eudora Welty, in her memoir *One Writer's Beginnings*, tells of how she read incessantly as a child: books that were good, bad or indifferent. This, she says, was a blessing; for how else do you acquire taste, if not through wide-ranging experience? What's important in the moment is to satisfy the longing to read. The rest comes later.

Mr. Gumpy's Outing, John Burningham

Goofy and genial Mr. Gumpy is heading out for a boat ride. He runs afoul of livestock and children when he tries to accommodate them all as passengers. They ignore his pleas to not muck about and squabble, and disaster ensues. It all works out well in the end, though. Here are many opportunities for animal sounds and good-natured carrying on.

Red Is Best, Kathy Stinson, illustrated by Robin Baird Lewis

One does one's best not to buy into or to encourage sex stereotypes. However, I have noticed that little girls particularly love this book about a fussy dresser with a marked colour preference. It's a simple, engaging and persuasive story. You can expect that after reading it, your child will start clamouring for red pajamas. And that will be just the beginning. You might want to have some red socks on hand for the morning.

When We Were Very Young, A. A. Milne

This, along with any good edition of *Mother Goose*, is the perfect way to introduce children to poetry. "The King's Breakfast" and "Jonathan Jo," "Disobedience" and "Halfway Down," and all the other poems that are such close kin to Pooh were staples of my own childhood. I think they've lost none of their fanciful punch. I've spoken to some parents who think they are "too English," but I've never known a child to make the same complaint.

Where the Wild Things Are, Maurice Sendak

I wish this well-loved book had been available to me when I was a tad. The story of Max, who is always on top of things and who is never at a loss; who goes to the land where the Wild Things are, roars his terrible roar and cows the Wild Things, then leads them all in a wild rumpus, is now feeding the dreams of the children of the children who first heard it, over thirty years ago.

Dusting makes me happy

Dusting makes me happy. It always has. When I was a little boy, I would beg my mother to cede that household chore to me. I must have been an odd sight: a preternaturally tall and gangly child with moppish hair, a rag dangling from my back pocket, clutching a feather duster with the kind of reverence a priest might accord a monstrance, moving solemnly about the house, from room to room. While other boys were out playing baseball or trading marbles, dust became both my hobby and solace. Tops of door frames and lampshades, hard to reach crevices in the kitchen, the insect mortuary of the inner window sill: nothing escaped my scrutiny. On summer mornings, I would lie in bed and watch the many motes jive in the broad beam of the transient sun. I welcomed them, gladly. They meant I had my work cut out for me. They were my *raison d'être*, my impetus to rise and greet the day.

Then, as now, dusting engendered in me a pervasive, meditative calm. As I stood with a Toby jug in hand, bringing my whole attention to the slow and purposeful business of expunging a fine and sooty layer, I would float the question: *What is dust and whence has it come?* And sometimes, from the depths of my stillness, a small voice would answer:

> Chaff, born on the wind from Samarkand. Sand, risen from the baked expanse of the Gobi. Ancient skin and dander from Eden, pollen from Babylon's hanging gardens, fragments of pyramids, shattered bones, beaten feathers, pulverized tusks

from Hannibal's elephants. This is all the world, and more besides. This is you, my little friend. This is you.

It was rather a Blakean vision to be visited on one so young, and it did not leave me untouched. It made me aware that I belonged to a world larger than the one circumscribed by my room and my duster. It made me see how the whole universe could fit inside a Toby jug. And it instilled in me early on the conviction that I would be better served by intuition and by listening to the dictates of my gut than by allowing myself to be swayed by a barrage of cold facts. Learn this by the age of seven, and not even the Jesuits can get to you. Take this in early on, and you are blessed with the knowledge that you need only be true to yourself to be liberated from the terrible prospect of falling into error. Mistakes are simply not possible, for every seeming blunder is just another step along the scenic and circuitous path you're following to wherever it is you're going.

The sum of my failures is my present happiness. Had I not settled on the ill-conceived career move of becoming a thatcher; had I not given in to the whim of making bread dough saint's medals; had I not acquired a broken-down school bus, a mute rooster and a sad lizard; I would never have come to this place, where there is no end to the dusting and where the rooms are electric with voices and rich with tangible invisibilities. Children who come here are more inclined to sense it than are the grownups.

"Who's the lady in the overalls?" one little boy asked me, not so very long ago. I was cleaning his room, which happened to be the very room Hector and Virgil's mother occupied for the seventy-odd years of her living. Mother, as I, too have come to call her, was a powerful woman. While the whole house remains rich with her presence, it is nowhere more potent than within the confines of the small cell she called her own.

"We left it untouched after her death," Virgil told me on my initiatory tour of the premises. "Boys love staying here."

And I can see how they might. Her chemistry set is there, its test tubes and Bunsen burners and jars of explosive powders ready for action. Her Meccano collection, which is vast, is stored in a tea chest. The model planes she loved to build hang from the ceiling. Her football pennants still decorate the walls, as do her astronomy and anatomy charts. Her complete sets of the Hardy Boys and Tom Swift books, the only fiction she was inclined to read, have been lovingly maintained. There is a ship in a bottle, boxes of shells and minerals, an impressive assortment of plastic dinosaurs, and a stuffed and snarling weasel mounted on a twisted branch.

"Road kill, poor thing," said Virgil. "It was one of Mother's only adventures into taxidermy. Be careful. Its teeth have lost none of their bite."

Indeed, I was in the midst of dusting the weasel, cautiously polishing its choppers and nails, when the little boy, who was building a Meccano replica of a ship's conning tower, asked his unsettling question.

"You saw a lady in overalls?" I asked, looking around me.

"Sure. Just now. She was standing right there beside you. She's gone now."

"Where'd she go?"

"Through the wall."

He reported this with the nonchalance of an eight-year old for whom the divide between this world and the next has not yet hardened. There was no doubt in my mind what—or more exactly whom—he had seen. Every so often, when I am putzing around her room, and my mind has been lulled by dusting into a state of heightened psychic receptivity, and the alpha waves are rising from my skull like heat from asphalt, I will see a hazy, protoplasmic something standing by the chemistry table or examining the propeller on a model Spitfire. I blink and it's gone. But I know full well that this is Mother. Mrs. Rochester is a reliable barometer by which to measure the shifting pressures in the room when her mistress's shade passes through. She puffs up her chest, flaps her wings, and quotes King David.

"Thy rod and thy staff are with me!" she will intone.

Mrs. Rochester happened to be accompanying me on my rounds that morning. I looked to where she sat, perched on one of the Marie Curie bookends. She had spread her every feather and grown to twice her size. Her small, ringed eyes were flashing. She danced a jig, spun round in a circle, threw back her head and cackled with unalloyed glee.

"She walks! She walks! She walks!"

And then, there was a sharp and jabbing pain, and a terrible yelp: my own. I had allowed the index finger of my right hand to come to rest on the pointed spears in the weasel's grim and open mouth. I looked down to see that the jaws, for the first time in over twenty years, were clamped shut, and a trickle of red seeped from a corner of the wretched thing's lips. Do not ask how. It happened. It happened.

"Who's that laughing?" asked the little boy, as I fought back tears and pried my finger free. I strained my ears, but caught only my own strangled sobs. I didn't need to hear the malevolent chuckle to understand its source.

"Accident with the electric can opener," I say to anyone who asks how my finger came by its cowl of gauze. The truth would just take too much telling. So, I'll keep my counsel, and heal, and wait. Something big is about to happen, that much I know. And I feel certain that we'll none of us be untouched by whatever waits for us, just around a not too distant corner.

October 24: The day's mail

To the Proprietors, Bachelor Brothers' Bed and Breakfast:

The wife and I have been married for thirty-five years and the magic has plumb gone out of our relationship. I hope you don't mind my speaking frankly like this. Sylvia—she's the wife—and I have tried just about everything to rekindle that old spark. We've gone to "recommitment classes" at the church. We've purchased videos that come in discreet brown wrappers from a P.O. box in New Jersey. We've sought private counseling. We've spent a fortune on scented oils. But nothing has really done the trick. The situation is desperate, and we're ready to sign on for just about anything to put us back on track.

Last night, at the supermarket, we picked up this magazine

called *Interference* and it fell right open to the story about the goings-on at your B&B.

"Look at that," said the wife, "aren't they cute? I've always had a thing for firemen."

Was I surprised or what? That was the first I'd ever heard her mention such an interest! It both amazes and reassures me that you can live with someone for so many years and still not know everything about her. Anyway, we wondered if we might come up there to one of your "adults only costume weekends." Do we need to bring our own gear? Or do you provide everything? And is that same lady who's in the magazine one of your regular facilitators? I like the look of her. The wife has a particular fancy for the guy with the painted toes.

I'd be grateful for a brochure or anything else you can send me, at your earliest possible convenience.

Raphael Canterbury, Beaverton, Oregon.

*   *   *

Dear Sirs:

We at the Pentecostal Assembly of Yaweh the Vengeful have been extremely heartened to read about your Improving Verse contest. Thank you for your efforts to coax young people down the path of righteousness!

It is my happy duty, as Director of the Youth Wing of the Assembly, to inform you that you are on the shortlist for this year's "Isaac on the Rock" Award for Achievement. Congratulations! This handsome statue, which depicts Abraham about to slaughter his son, is given to mature members of the community who have shown a keen interest in the spiritual development of young people.

As you can surely appreciate, our administrative costs are very high. We would therefore be very grateful for any donation you might be able to make. May we suggest that $500 would an appropriate gift? Be assured that you will remain on our shortlist, regardless of whether or not you are able to comply with this request.

Yours most truly, Hilary Lobur, Greaseburn, Alberta.

*   *   *

From the Desk of Dr. Bardal Finbar

Professor, Bellweather Endowed Chair of Solomon Solomon Studies

My Dear Hector and Virgil:

It's Yeats I'll invoke, rather than our beloved Solomon, to begin this short note. All is changed, changed utterly. There is much I have to tell you, but news of such magnitude I can impart only in person, confidentially, and face to face.

Were it not for an extremely hectic teaching schedule and an appointment on Monday with a laser specialist who promises she can remove my plantar warts for good, I would make my way to you without delay to assuage the curiosity this communication must have wakened in you both. As you know, the terms of my agreement with Mr. Bellweather, who has funded my research into the life and times of Solomon, stipulate that the decoded poems be kept under wraps until the day of the celebrations. It is his wish that Solomon's companion volume to *Hygiene for Boys* be unveiled in front of the whole community and that no one's surprise be diluted by prior knowledge of what is contained therein. I appreciate the generosity of the impulse. However, now that I know what I know, I am compelled to say that I regard this as a highly imprudent course of action; sufficiently imprudent that I am willing to renege on the confidentiality clause of my contract and expand the web of knowledge to include the two of you and Caedmon, too.

Damn! Damn! Damn! This is as frustrating for me as it must be for you! For the nonce, I must ask you to take me at my word. When I have told you what I have to tell, you will understand both my reluctance to explain myself fully here, and my conviction that you three be made privy to the secrets of Solomon.

I am due to arrive early on the morning of the 31st for the commemoration festivities. I will do my utmost to put into port a day in advance to fill you in, so that you will be able to bolster yourselves against the real possibility that things will go dreadfully, dreadfully wrong. I beg your indulgence and look forward to seeing you before the week is out.

All the best, Bardal Finbar, Ph.D.

Exclusive preview from the strictly embargoed manuscript
Tight Jeans for Boys:
Probing Poems for Pubescent Punks

Honi Soit

Remember, boys! You must not squelch,
Must not repress the urge to belch.
Burping is a way to drain
Evil humours of the brain.
Brains are where our wills are milled.
Gases, if allowed to build,
Harmful pressures might exert:
Thus do brains and wills get hurt.

Listen therefore not to those
Prudes who strike an upright pose,
And who claim you rock their boat
When a belch lifts from your throat.
Let them not your light make dim,
Damning nature's sweetest hymn!
Open, therefore, wide your lips!
Hold back nothing! Let 'er rip!

Solomon Solomon Commemoration Day:
Schedule of Events

8:00 A.M.—Pancake Breakfast at The Well of Loneliness. Dramatized reading of Solomon Solomon's whimsical "Never Will I Waffle, Dear One, When It Comes to You!"

9:00 A.M.—Morning service at the Church of God the Technician and Marketer, J. MacDonald Bellweather II, Celebrant. Sermon topic: "*Quo Vadis*, Solomon?" The Junior Choir will present Solomon's rarely performed cantata, written in 1951 for the World Chiropodist Association: "Paul Bunion and the Alien Corn."

9:45 A.M.—Costume Parade to the site of the Solomon Solomon house. J. MacDonald Bellweather II, Honorary Marshal.

10:15 A.M.—Treasure Hunt and Three-Legged Race.

11:00 A.M.—Recitation Contest Finals. Altona Winkler, Journalist and Licensed Esthetician, Adjudicator. Five young finalists will give memorized renderings of selections from *Hygiene for Boys*.

11:30 A.M.—Unveiling of the Solomon Solomon Medal, designed by the celebrated bread dough artist and hagiographer Caedmon Harkness.

11:45 A.M.—Unveiling of the reconstructed cigarette foil ball. Abel Wackaugh, Project Engineer, to officiate.

11:55 A.M.—Announcement of the winner of the Solomon Solomon Prize for Improving Verse. Polly Perch, Judge.

Noon—First Public Reading from the sequel to *Hygiene for Boys* by the winner of the Recitation Contest. Introductory remarks by Dr. Bardal Finbar, internationally renowned Solomonist.

12:15 P.M.—Turning of the sod for the Solomon Solomon House. J. MacDonald Bellweather II, Sod Turner.

12:30 P.M.—Picnic and Morris Dancing Instruction by the Valley Morris Men, J. MacDonald Bellweather II, Director.

2:00 P.M.—Unveiling of the plans for the proposed Solomon Solomon Theme Park.

2:30 P.M.—Tours of the safe at the Bachelor Brothers' Bed and Breakfast.

A dishwasher is a splendid thing

A dishwasher is a splendid thing. Ours is a very recent addition to our menagerie of appliances, and I can hardly credit there was a time when I was resistant to the idea of allowing one over the threshold of the kitchen. Even after we opened our house to friendly strangers of a literary bent and consequently increased our time at the sink tenfold, we persisted in clinging to the old ways: attacking plate and flatware with scouring pads and bristly brushes and rags that hung over the faucet, limply and shamelessly flaunting their tattered fetidness.

"You don't have a dishwasher?" our guests would ask, reeling with disbelief, as if they'd stumbled upon a clutch of Luddites who probably carted their clothes to the river to beat them clean on a handy rock.

"No wonder you go through so much hand cream," Altona would admonish whenever she came by and found us standing once again at a sudsy basin. "You boys need to get with the century and buy yourselves a dishwasher!"

Although in my heart of hearts I knew this to be true, I would always fire back some feeble salvo. Too expensive, too noisy, too cumbersome, too much potential for unleashing a flood, too unreliable, too inclined to leave spots on the cutlery. For each of these, Altona had a ready riposte.

"Well, they're much too hard on delicate china!" I'd snort, with an air of finality.

"Delicate china? What delicate china?" Altona always scoffed at this purported *coup de grâce*, and with reason. For the most part, we rely on hardy, mismatched plates and bowls that even the most determined and accurate of skeet shooters would be hard pressed to reduce to shards, and on service station mugs that Mother collected over the years. Function over elegance has always been one of our abiding rules, here at the Bachelor Brothers' Bed and Breakfast.

Virgil was equally impervious to the labour-saving siren song of the dishwasher. I think we were so mutually inimical to the prospect because we knew that while it might lighten our load, it would also be an intrusion, for from early childhood on, the time we spent washing dishes was also a time of fraternal communion.

We couldn't have been much older than six or seven when Mother began to usher us into the tedious world of chores: making beds, cleaning toilets, raking leaves, and all the usual ho-hum initiatory rites that prepare a child to function as a responsible and uncomplaining adult in a world ruled by work. We performed our assigned tasks just as any other boys might, somewhat grudgingly and with a petulant lack of bravado. But dishwashing made us both glad. From the time we were old enough to reliably manage a saucer and a towel without dropping one or ripping the other, we were press-ganged into that service. For over forty years, the distribution of labour never varied. Mother washed. We dried and put away and wiped down the counters and the table. I think I never felt her loss more keenly than on the night after her death, when we faced for the first time the banal necessity of cleaning up without her. Our two minds met in the chill void of her absence, and we settled silently on the agreement that this responsibility should fall to the eldest. So it was that Virgil, who squirmed into the world twenty minutes before I followed on, donned Mother's rubber gloves and set in to scour. I spoke not a word but went straight to my work. Tears traced their paths on the rounds and contours of our cheeks.

Our weepy quietude, born of grieving and disbelief, was highly aberrant; for dishwashing in our household had always been a raucous business. The hours the three of us whiled away as we clustered at the sink were akin, I suppose, to the carefree evenings Victorian families might have spent gathered round the piano. It was a time of happy fellowship. Virgil would recite whatever poem he happened to be committing to memory. We would play "Guess the Scripture" with Mrs. Rochester. Mother would try to teach us the botanical names of plants and do her best to pass on her vast repertoire of rugby songs. Sometimes, if we begged, she would tell us yet again the story of our conception. We never tired of hearing how we owed our existence to her spontaneous copulation with an itinerant book salesman; never grew bored with her mimed re-enactment of how they had managed to consummate their brief affair under his broken-down truck.

In the years subsequent to her death, and especially since we took on the innkeeper's mantle, we two orphans could count on our time among the sullied dishes to throw us together, if only for an hour or so each day. These sessions became a way for us to keep in touch, to compare notes and strategies, to lay plans, to complain, and to joke, too. I think we both of us drew strength, or something like it, from such mundane excursions. In the early months of our B&B operation, before we got the hang of it, we were overwhelmed by the sheer volume of each day's tasks. Of necessity, these domestic exigencies had to be divvied up. I'll launder, you iron. You shop, I'll cook. You do the bathrooms, I'll do the bedrooms. And so on. Were it not for the predictable routine of one who washed and one who dried, in the same place and at the same time, we might very well have been reduced to haphazard encounters on the stairway as I scampered up with fresh sheets and a plunger, while Virgil hurried down with a faulty doorknob and towels for mending. A dishwasher was the last thing we wanted. But now, lo and behold, we have one.

It is late. I am writing this in the kitchen, half listening to the thing chug along. It is Caedmon we can thank for this: Caedmon, who came into our lives so unexpectedly and quietly and who, in his own sweet and unobtrusive way, has managed to change so much. There is nothing in his clownish and dishevelled outward aspect that suggests he might enjoy an easy *entente* with cogs, gears and flywheels. His amiable, vacant stare; the way he mumbles answers to questions no one else hears; his Italianate musings; his mute rooster and bright-eyed lizard; and his penchant for oversize cardigans: all contribute to the initial impression that he is impracticality incarnate. But we of all people should have learned how often a book belies its cover. To our great delight and benefit, Caedmon is one of those gifted people who speaks the arcane languages of mechanical and electronic devices. It is nothing to him to remove a switch plate, or open the hood of a car, stare for a moment or two at the Gordian tangle of wires and circuitry, and intuit what needs doing.

"*Ecco!*" he will mumble. "*Io vedo! Si, si, capisco!*"

Now, thanks to the dimmer switches he has installed throughout the house, we all have access to many interesting lighting moods and ambient effects. The chimney has been cleaned, the bathroom tiles regrouted, and the faulty washers replaced, so that sensitive souls are no longer kept from sleep by the torturous drip drip drip of rogue spigots. Every hinge on every door has been oiled, windows that were painted shut years back have been made operable, and a cat door has been installed, much to Waffle's delight. Caulking guns and staple guns and raspy files and drill bits in their pointy ranks have been acquired and arranged in a basement workshop. And his bread dough medals, bearing the images of saints both famous and obscure, hang from the walls and repose on window sills and ledges and plate railings throughout the house.

Here in the kitchen I can look around and see no fewer than five of these homespun artifacts. The great St. Blaise smiles down from above the doorway, holding his emblematic, iconic wool-comb. He beams out his canonic beneficence, and fends off viruses and fish bones and other subversive agents that can undermine the throat. The less celebrated but no less colourful St. Duthac rests atop the liquor cabinet, benignly offering support for hangover sufferers, just as he is reputed to have done in seventh-century Scotland. On the refrigerator, held fast by a magnet, is Duthac's Irish contemporary, Kevin, who was said to have sustained his whole community on the flesh of a single salmon, which was given to him as a gift by an otter. On the breadbox is the charming St. Zita, a servant girl from twelfth-century Lucca, who was employed by a family called the Fatinelli. Zita was forever losing herself in rapturous visions, and forgetting all about her household responsibilities. The Fatinelli were peeved, of course. But the angels, who loved her, came down from on high, and saved her bacon by baking her loaves. And dangling from a pretty red ribbon above the dishwasher is St. Christopher himself, the first of our saints and the patron of our house, the overseer of bachelors and travellers, both.

"See what I found," said Caedmon one afternoon, not so very long ago, as he backed his way into the kitchen with a dishwasher he had somehow hoisted onto a little red wagon.

"Found?" said Virgil and I at the same moment.

"Hoorah!" shouted Altona. We were all three of us sitting at the table, shelling peas.

"Abandoned on the side of the road. It's amazing what gets thrown away. I bet I can make it good as new."

"Oh Caedmon. I don't think so . . ." Virgil began. But Altona, who once took a night school class called "The Art of Persuasion" and whom we can thank, after all, for bringing us Caedmon in the first place, bulldozed right through and over our every objection and protest and left us gasping for air.

"Set 'er up, Caedmon, and let's see how she runs!" she cried, triumphant, when it was apparent that tradition was not strong enough to withstand the onslaught of technology; at least, not when she was the general in charge of the advance. Luckily, a very nice couple who were visiting from Nova Scotia rescued us when they came through the kitchen looking for a twosome to round out a game of Hearts. We retreated with them to the library. I'm glad we missed the ensuing excitement, and thankful that Caedmon had paid close attention during his volunteer fire brigade training. He knew just what sedative to apply to the flames that leapt from the wall directly the foundling was plugged in. Undaunted, he persevered in making the necessary repairs. And much to my surprise, I am glad he did.

Now, the dishwasher is cleaned and plumbed and fully installed and working ticketyboo. Virgil and I still have our time together, as we squabble genially over which berth is appropriate to which besmirched passenger. I am very pleased that Altona is not inclined to say "I told you so", as she could very well do in this case. Everything she promised is true. When the cycles have run their course, the dishes emerge looking refreshed and renewed, as if they'd just come back from a spa. But this is not the principal reason I've grown so attached to this machine. Oh no. Mostly, I love it for the songs it sings.

W. H. Auden, in a poem called "First Things First," describes a raging storm, and tells us that when he is half awake, or half sober, he can construe meaning from the roiling of the violent weather. Lying in his bed, he can distil sense from its random spill of consonants and vowels. This is just how I feel about the dishwasher. If I sit in the kitchen, as I'm sitting now, late at night, when I am the last one left awake, with only a modest glass of sherry and a small dish of poppycock for company; and if I close my eyes and listen with an open mind to this harvest gold wonder as it turns its small tides, I grow persuaded that I hear it chant simple choruses of antique nonsense songs. Behind the sturdy drone of its reconditioned motor I might hear, "No more, no more, be still, be still, restore, restore, until, until." Or "Chuckle, yip, hi, ho, come, stay, come, go." On this All Souls' Night, it seems to taunt me with, "Har-dee har, from afar, har-dee, har-dee, har-dee har." As I ponder all that has happened and all that I've seen, I can't help but wonder if the dishwasher isn't the agent for decoding some ribald message from the teasing gods. Har-dee har, indeed! The very prospect makes me quake. Decoding, as we've all so recently learned, is not without its perils.

I don't think I've ever seen J. MacDonald Bellweather II looking as well as he did yesterday morning when he stood before the assembled Commemoration Day multitude at the site of the Solomon Solomon house. He might have been fully a decade younger than his four score years. He was glowing with pride, riding the crest of a popular wave, never expecting for an instant that it was about to come crashing down and drench us all.

The day to that point had been a resounding success. Even the weather co-operated. The rain that is so common in our part of the world at this time of year, and which figured prominently in every forecast, chose to take a powder. The yellow sun beamed down. It was unseasonably warm. The pancake breakfast and the choir performance, the costume parade and the treasure hunt: all had drawn huge and enthusiastic crowds of young and old alike. The more formal part of the programme was held in the tree-flanked clearing that surrounds the site of Solomon's house. There was a small dais that served as the stage. To its right was the swaddled hulk of the reconstituted cigarette foil ball, ready for unveiling. To the left, and likewise concealed beneath what I recognized as a linen tablecloth from The Well of Loneliness, was an architect's model of the proposed Solomon Solomon house reconstruction and eventual theme park.

The recitations went swimmingly, and while each of the finalists in the contest acquitted himself brilliantly, there was no doubt in anyone's mind that Altona was spot-on when she named young Matthias Leodegar, age thirteen, as the winner. He was chosen for his reverent delivery of Solomon's stinging indictment of self-abuse, "Sow Ye Not What Can't Be Reaped." The audience burst into spontaneous applause when he reached the climax of the poem and chimed out in a voice that has not yet broken:

> Hear ye then, my comely lads, these sage and final lines:
> Keep your hands above your belts, and all will be just fine!

The crowd was equally well-disposed to Caedmon's commemorative bread dough medal with the graven image of Solomon.

"Gee," Altona whispered in my ear, "it looks like a self-portrait." And she was right. The solemn face of Solomon that stared down at us might well have belonged to Caedmon.

"Isn't that amazing," I whispered back. "I'd never noticed the resemblance till just now!"

There was little time to marvel at this coincidence, however. J.

Mac once again seized the microphone and called Abel Wackaugh forward to unveil the cigarette foil ball.

"That's a familiar looking sheet," I remarked, studying the pink, floral shroud that covered the structure.

"I should hope so," answered Altona. "You've slept on it often enough."

With great fanfare and considerable aplomb, Abel pulled back the draping veil to reveal the silver orb in all its glory. It caught the rays of the weakening sun and amplified them. It fairly pulsed before us. The applause was hearty and sustained.

Mac raised his hands to signal for silence. "Over 100,000 individual pieces went into the making of this ball," he explained, almost choking on the emotion of the moment. "Volunteers from up and down the valley laboured hard under Abel Wackaugh's direction to assemble it in time for today's celebrations. And well-wishers from around the world took the time and the trouble to send their foil our way. We must all hope and pray that these expressions of good will continue as plans move ahead for the development of the Solomon Solomon theme park. I think it can be truly said that our cause was advanced more than we will ever know with the Improving Verse contest, which attracted over 10,000 entries from all over the globe. For the last week our judge, the distinguished editrix Polly Perch, has been poring over the submissions, and only minutes ago she reached her decision as to the winner of the cheque for five hundred dollars and the Solomon Solomon commemorative medal. Miss Perch? Would you come forward?"

I turned to study Virgil, who was craning his neck to watch his adversary mount the stage. The corners of his mouth pointed northward in a self-satisfied smirk. Polly Perch, sporting a colourful turban and a stylish pant suit, looked remarkably fresh, considering all she'd been through. She nodded at Mac as she shoved him out of the way and took over the microphone.

"I wish I could say it's been a pleasure," she snarled. "but in my twenty-five years in the magazine business, I've never read such drivel!"

Ripples of laughter rose from the crowd. How grand, to be treated to such sophisticated big city humour! Polly gnashed her teeth with the ferocity of one who hates it when her motives are misapprised. With no ceremony to speak of, she announced that a Mrs. Lucy Plessington was the hands-down winner. Her poem was inspired by her husband, Mr. Plessington. Evidently, he collects the various bits and pieces, organic and otherwise, that at one time or another found lodging in his body but were surgically removed. He displays these grotesque mementos, lovingly preserved, on the mantel. Mrs. Plessington would rather he didn't. Her *chef d'oeuvre* was read aloud, with almost no stumbles, by the runner-up in the recitation contest, Rumon Birstan, age twelve.

Keep It to Yourself, My Dear, Just Keep It to Yourself

The ladies from my sewing circle came around today,
I saw them looking oddly at your jars.
"What on earth is this?" they asked, while viewing your display
Of oddments once installed beneath your scars.
At first I just demurred and said I simply didn't know,
But, oh, those dimpled darlings did insist.
And so I gave the whole accounting, blow by bloody blow,
I let them have the whole revolting list.

"These are Max's tonsils that were pulled when he was eight,
Here is his appendix! How it glows!
This contains his gallstones, here's his shrapnel on a plate,
Here are fungal warts from off his toes!"
I never got the chance, alas, to show your blackened nail,
The one you lost when hammer met with thumb.
The sewing circle ladies had, by this time, all grown pale!
Two fainted dead away, the rest went numb.

Of course it makes me happy that you have a hobby, dear,
I know I ought to take it with a smile.
I'm thrilled you face your surgeries without a trace of fear,
Because you know you'll supplement your pile.
But God, who gave us organs, meant that they should stay
     concealed,

Whether they're to flesh or flask consigned.
Take them all away, I pray! They're nasty and congealed!
In this one case, what's yours cannot be mine.

As young Birstan delivered himself of this decidedly improving and deservedly winning verse, I noticed Polly Perch slink off into the woods. Before she was swallowed by the trees, she turned to survey the crowd. She sought out Virgil and sent him a menacing stare that was chilling in its ferocity. I shivered and looked up at the sky. The sun was still spilling its golden fleece; but a cloud, no bigger than the hand of a man, was gathering on the horizon. I turned my attention again the stage, where Mac was speaking, flushed and florid with the headiness of the moment.

"And now," he bellowed from the podium, "we come to the moment we've all of us been waiting for! Unfortunately, Dr. Bardal Finbar is unable to be with us today. I regret to report that he fell victim to a carelessly misdirected laser beam while he was undergoing delicate surgery for the removal of his plantar warts. Happily, the doctors have assured him that he will walk again, and they also believe there will be no impediment to prevent him from fathering children. Should he choose to do so, of course! I'm sure you all join me in wishing him a speedy recovery. But on to happier things. May I call upon Matthias Leodegar to come forward and give the first reading from Solomon Solomon's companion volume to *Hygiene for Boys*!"

As Matthias made his way to the stage, Mac held up over his head a ribbon-wrapped box on which was written the stern warning "Under Embargo Till October 31." He looked like Moses, coming down from Sinai with the tablets.

"My friends, this is a pivotal moment not only in the life of our valley but also in the history of literature. No one save Dr. Finbar, who actually decoded Solomon's improving sequel, has seen what is in this box! We know only that there are four-and-twenty poems! Each one, we can be certain, is a gem!"

Mac pulled an envelope from under the ribbon. With trembling hand he broke the seal. "I have only one last order of business, and that is to tell you the title of this, the last book by the late and lamented poet Solomon Solomon."

He extracted a sheet of paper from the envelope and peered at it closely.

"The long-lost sequel to *Hygiene for Boys*, is—" and here, he frowned ever so slightly and hesitated for just an instant.

"The title is—"

Mac looked decidedly discomfited.

"Darn it all! I can't quite seem to make it out! Must get my eyes checked. Well! Let's not delay! I'll tell you all the title after! Matthias Leodegar, I will ask you to reach into this box and pull out any poem you like! Fate will decide which one we shall hear!"

Matthias, who has yet to shed his baby fat, and whose treble renderings of "You'll Never Walk Alone" never fail to bring a tear to the eye at any community concert, rustled around, chose his poem, stood before the microphone, and read.

Amour Propre

Mrs. Dorothy Parker, whom I recommend you read,
Called her budgie Onan, for he always spilled his seed.
And ever since his namesake in the Bible soiled the ground,
Finger-wagging strictures in the scriptures have been found
Counselling against such spillage in the noonday sun.
Pay them not the slightest mind, lads! Masturbation's fun!

Now, there are folks with outlooks that are puritan and bleak,
Folks who call it self-abuse and say it makes you weak,
Folks who say the practice is a ticking, potent bomb,
Sure to make you addled and grow hair upon your palms,
Folks who say your hand should never venture near your lap,
Say you must conserve each drop of nature's precious sap.

Lend an ear to Solomon, and he will set you right,
Put to rest the bleatings of the clinically uptight.
If you look me over, I can guarantee you'll find
My palms are smooth and blameless and I haven't yet gone blind.
The proof is in the pudding, and I'm very pleased to say
I practise what I'm preaching, and I practise every day.

Listen not, good fellows, to that tight-lipped, touch-not spiel!
Have they ever tried it? Don't they know how good if feels?
Would God up in His heaven have installed within our loins
All those tickly sensors if he meant us to enjoin
Against their stimulation? Sure as weasels root for grubs,
I feel quite sure he wouldn't! Aye, and therein lies the rub!

So, if the spirit moves you—and I rather think it might—
If you want, at noontime, or when you're in bed at night,
Or first thing in the morning, or when you get home from school,
Or when you're back from swimming in the teeming public pool,
Do not stop or hesitate! Go on! Strike up the band,
And strum your ukulele with a warm and open hand!

Once, in my childhood, I experienced a similar sense of breathing through thick gauze. Mother had only one decorative object that she truly valued, an earthenware cremation urn that her father had used as a cuspidor. As she was generally inclined to be scornful of anything like a sentimental attachment to a mere gewgaw, this marked fondness was most atypical. She never revealed exactly why it was so important to her, perhaps because she thought that doing so would betray a chink in her cynical armour. Whatever her reasons, the fact was that it was an object she treasured, and which she liked to keep on view. It sat on a low end table, by the couch in the library. I will never forget the day Virgil and I, at around the age of nine, were playing one of our favourite games, "Roundup." It was a rainy day and we were romping inside. As was our wont, I had taken on the role of the cowboy, and Virgil was the herd. I threw my lasso, as I had done hundreds of times before, expecting it would follow its usual pattern of falling flaccid on the ground, powerless to catch or snare anything. When, against every expectation, the looped rope dropped over the urn, I was so thrilled to have snagged any-thing at all that, without thinking, I drew the lariat tight, and pulled. The one or two seconds that separated the act from its inevitable consequence seemed to go on forever, ballooning out into space. In that short span of time I knew remorse, regret, sorrow, fear, anger, disappointment, horror, and even something like exultation that such a thing could ever happen at all, at all, at all.

That was the moment I remembered when Matthias came to the end of the poem, and a dreadful realization seeped up through the silence that greeted his last words. It was as though we were all waiting to exhale the breath we had collectively sucked in when we understood that Solomon Solomon's little joke, thirty years in the making, had finally been told. The punch line had been revealed. There ought to have been hisses and shouts of "Shame!" There ought to have been a general clamour of protest, and people shaking their fists in outrage. As it was, we were set upon by a pack of cataclysmic distractions. So much happened all at once and our attentions were drawn in so many different directions that it is a wonder we didn't bring on the first recorded case of collective whiplash.

The rigid silence that followed Matthias's reading was broken by a shrill and primitive cry. Every head jerked around to seek its source at the back of the crowd. It came again, the sound of a raucous crowing. Virgil, Altona and I all gripped one another in wonder and fear. For it was none other than Paolo, who had freed himself from Caedmon's arms and was standing atop the charred frame of Solomon's house. He puffed out his chest and threw back his comb and bellowed the loudest COCKADOODLEDOO anyone had ever heard. Mute no longer, he hurled out his pent-up song, over and over and over.

Like puppets controlled by one master string, we each of us followed his skyward stare, which was fixed on a cloud shaped remarkably like a clipper ship passing in front of the sun. In seconds, the noon went from bright to dark. The ship-cloud rumbled as its cannons were primed and loaded. And then there was a Zeus-like flash of light, a searing heat and a horrified cry. Jagged tentacles of lightning streaked down and found their intended target. For about the length of time it takes for a heart to turn over, the giant foil ball was surrounded by a glorious halo. Even before the acrid stink of its melting filled the air, even before the architect's model of the house and theme park burst into flames, the electric current ricocheted up and over the crowd, in a lofty, crackling arc, a twining braid of dangerous light. COCKADOODLEDOO! cried Paolo one last time, before an explosion of feather, beak and claw rained down on the fleeing crowd. No one who was there will ever forget it. No one who was there stopped to look back. No one who was there could wait to get home.

"All gone, all gone, all gone," croons the understanding dishwasher, as it comes to the end of its cycle. "Alone, alone, alone," it sings, as I come to the end of this page and the end of my sherry. "Go on, go on, go on," it murmurs, and that is good and sane advice. Sensible. For that is the only thing to be done. Go on to bed, go on to sleep, go on to the morning. The new day should have much to tell.

Dear Friends, I hardly know what to say

St. Oswald's Rehabilitative Podiatry Clinic

Dear friends,
I hardly know what to say. It was just as I feared. I blame myself in many ways, although in my defence I will say that I did try, and on more than one occasion, to alert Mr. Bellweather to the can of worms he was about to open.

"Mr. Bellweather," I begged, only days before the ceremony, "this is not what you think!"

"Even better than the first volume, is it? Wonderful news! Wonderful news! And to think they say the sequel never lives up to the original. Keep up the good work, son! Keep up the good work!"

When the hubris of the powerful and living meets the malice of the cunning and dead, what chance do the rest of us have?

My doctors tell me it will be at least another two weeks before I am fully mobile. I regret my inability to do the decent thing and turn over this notebook in person. You will recognize it as the school scribbler that was found in the safe, along with the fudgsicle wrappers and other miscellaneous fragments. If it seems cavalier of me to foist something so portentous as this on you through the mail, I must ask you to forgive me. I can no longer tolerate being the sole bearer of the burden of the intelligence it contains.

Before I go any further, let me reassure you that I am a trained and meticulous scholar. Indeed, I studied with no less an authority than the great palaeologist Dr. Edmund Mindred, who was careful to indoctrinate his students in the proper protocols for handling delicate primary source materials. However, even with all this buttressing against error, I somehow allowed myself to set the scribbler atop a radiator which is adjacent to my desk.

Dr. Mindred, were he alive to hear about it, would have me flogged. Direct heat, as you surely know, is the sworn enemy of paper. True, the scribbler itself was blank on its every page, and for all intents and purposes devoid of interest. True, the weather was still sufficiently balmy that the caretaker had not yet turned on the furnace, and the rad itself was stone cold. None of this mitigates or excuses my oversight. The notebook was part of the Solomon archive and ought to have been treated accordingly. I should have foreseen the possibility that a cold snap would settle in, that the caretaker would do his job, and that the heat would begin to rise. I was so absorbed in the work of translation that I paid no attention to the merry thumps and bangs of the steam in the pipes. The notebook remained in its perilous place for several days before I noticed it, its orange cover curling at the four corners, its paper getting more and more brittle by the minute. So aggrieved was my shriek when I realized my error that my neighbours came running to see who was doing me in. I seized the book. I opened it. The earth paused a second in its spinning.

When I was growing up, I was fascinated by spies and spying. In fact, now that I think of it, perhaps that's why I became a literary biographer. The two professions are not so very far removed. As a child, I read everything I could lay my hands on about espionage techniques. Although I've forgotten most of what I learned, I do recall an easy formula for invisible writing. You simply use lemon juice in place of ink. It dries without a trace and comes to light again only when heat is applied.

Now, I wonder if my carelessness *vis-à-vis* the scribbler isn't attributable to the subconscious suspicion that, like everything else connected to Solomon, there was more to these blank pages than met the eye. Of course, I sat down straight away to read the faint, sepia-toned script. I ought to have put the book down the second I garnered the personal nature of the message and the weight of its import. That I did not speaks volumes of my inadequacies as both a man and a friend. What can I say, except that I have been so consumed with piecing together the life of the Bard that I could not turn my back on the possibility of achieving closure. I had to know. And now that I do, I turn this record over to you, along with my apologies, and with my vows of future discretion. You have my word that I will never breathe a word of what I have learned.

I send you my every good wish, and my thanks for the card and the flowers.

All the best, Bardal Finbar, Ph.D.

What do you want all those lemons for?

November 2, 1959

"What do you want all those lemons for?" Abel Wackaugh asked me when he saw me carting three bags of the things down the road this afternoon.

"Invisible writing," I told him. "I've got a lot of invisible writing to do." There's nothing like the bald truth to dispel suspicion. No one ever believes it.

He guffawed. "You're a card, that's for darn sure. Say," he said, leaning in so close that I could smell the Vitalis on his scalp, "did you hear about what happened up at the Solomon place?"

He had the jumped-up eagerness of an inveterate gossip. Of course I'd heard. But since he was just about ready to explode with his need to tell all, I shook my head no. I'm glad I did. It was a very fine performance.

"And they say," he whispered, when he'd come to the end, "they say that the Devil himself was seen dancing around the burned-out house. Yes! They say that old Nick himself came up personally to take him straight to Hell. Do not pass go. Do not collect two hundred dollars."

"No!"

"Yup! That's what they say."

"Mercy!" My face was a marvel of contortion, and I clutched my hands to my breasts. "Mercy save us!" I actually crossed myself! I could hardly contain my laughter.

Solomon would be pleased. It's not even forty-eight hours since he was blown to smithereens and dispersed on the wind, and already he's become an epic. By the time you boys get around to finding these words, which I am confident will not happen till well after I've joined the ranks of the null and void, he'll have been transformed into a horn-browed god with miraculous powers to raise the dead and play the marimba at the same time. Either that, or he'll have been completely forgotten.

Now, there's every good chance that you'll never discover this notebook. And even if you do, it's unlikely that it would occur to you to perform the simple act of chemistry required to bring these words to light. Not that it much matters. If you never learn what I'm about to set down here, you'll be none the worse off. What will you have lost? You'll go through your days ignorant of a few family facts that are of little more than anecdotal interest, and which are beyond your power to change in any case. Knowing what I'm about to tell you won't alter the inevitable outcome of your living. Truth be told, I wouldn't have taken the time and trouble to wring these goddam lemons and write all this out had Solomon's hilarious exit not stirred the sense of fun in me. Now, cosy on up, and Mama will tell you a story.

Once upon a time there was a young woman who found herself in the family way. The father of her baby-to-be (babies-to-be, actually, although she didn't know it at the time) was a traveller. She hardly knew the man. She met him, briefly, when he was passing through. No pun intended. It was a brief *amour*, but productive.

The young woman's parents were not pleased. To escape their censorious ways and glances, she took to walking in the cemetery.

There, at least, she could cultivate the genial company of gentle folk who lived on the other side of caring. One day, as she was meandering among the marble and granite markers, she saw a familiar figure. He was passing between the stones, making notes and talking to himself. The young woman was about seven months pregnant at the time, and the sight of him nearly drove her into early labour.

"You! You! What are you doing here!"

"Have we met?" he asked, taking in the tub that was her middle.

Well! You could have knocked her over with a cruller! Met? Met? What a question! This was none other than the man who had planted the fruit that was ripening within her. She lost no time in reminding him of the greasy and intimate details of their only encounter. He took it all in, nodding.

"I wonder," he said, when she had finished upbraiding him for his forgetfulness, "if you might have mistaken me for my twin brother?"

It's a small world, my sons, and truer words than that were never spoken. I'll leave off being coy now, and cut to the chase. The fellow in the cemetery, the double of your father, was none other the man we have all come to know as Solomon Solomon, although that is not what he was called then. He is—or at least, he was—your uncle.

Surprised? I bet you are. It's for times like this that it's a good idea to carry a hip flask. Like your father, Solomon was a drifter. And like your father, he'd chosen a literary line of road work. He was an itinerant carver of epigraphs. He went from place to place and sculpted poetic summations on gravestones. He was versatile. He could chisel letters that were gothic or roman or that had a gentle italic lilt to them. And he would write verse to order, too. If his visit to any given place happened to coincide with a timely death, he would take the salient details of a biography and condense them into a couple of memorable lines. Otherwise, he would leave behind half a dozen stones marked with "one size fits all" snippets that were intended for families who, when the time came, might want something more stylish than RIP.

> Ashes to ashes and dust to dust,
> Not even once had he ever cussed.

Or:

> Dust to dust and ashes to ashes,
> Gosh she was pretty when batting her lashes.

Solomon had some old-fashioned ideas. It had been years since he'd last clapped eyes on his twin. Even so, he felt a certain responsibility toward his brother's bastard sons. He took to checking up on you, and on me, when his peregrinations brought him to our valley. You might recall how he would sit at the kitchen table of an afternoon, balancing you one on each knee, while he told you Mother Goose rhymes. Eventually, when rambling had worn him down, he decided to drop anchor here and build a cabin in the woods. That was when he hung up his chisel and set to work carving his own legend. That was when he started to call himself Solomon Solomon.

He loved me, as I think you know. I would rather it had been otherwise. As soon as he made his affections known, I told him not to hold out hope for reciprocation. I'm selfish. I like my life the way it is. I have no interest in hacking off a big piece and handing it over to someone else to play with. No, no, no. I told him all that, and yet he went on loving me. It was ridiculous. It was pathetic. But that's how it was.

Solomon had a hard life, and that's the truth of it. His love was unrequited. His work was undervalued. Day after day he cranked out his poems for *The Rumour*. It was his only source of income, save what I was able to slip him from time to time. He earned just about enough to keep himself in fudgsicles and tobacco. God, it was sad! And poverty takes its toll. I watched him grow stranger and stranger. Some days he would turn up unannounced at the door and talk for hours in his strange and circular way about angels and visions and read to me from his work in progress. It was a trial, and I don't mind saying so. But whom else could he turn to?

Once, he came with what I took to be good news. He'd been offered a commission to write a book for the schools.

"It's to be called *Hygiene for Boys: Good Clean Verse for Growing Minds*."

"Congratulations! Textbook writing pays well, doesn't it?"

"Feh! Prostitution! Lies! They'll want me to make ridiculous promises. Get lots of sleep and your life will be a feast. Wash your hands after you use the toilet and you'll never know sadness. It's all such nonsense! Why are they so afraid of the dark side? Why are they so afraid of the beast in us?"

He was very agitated. But I told him in no uncertain terms that he would be an idiot to turn this work down. Sometimes in a life, I told him, principle needs to give way to practicality. Sometimes, you have to plug your nose and swallow.

"I could never live with myself!"

"Nonsense. Listen here, Solomon. No one can escape compromise. All we do in our lives is make deals with ourselves. It's the only way to get by. So how about this? You sit down in the morning and write the text they want you to write. You talk about the evils of smoking, the importance of fresh fruit and the imperative of fresh air. And then, give yourself the afternoon to say what you truly feel. Write it down. Set it aside. One day, someone will find it. One day, the truth will out."

He snorted his contempt.

"The truth will out, you say? Ho ho! Not in my lifetime, missy! You can count on that!"

I hated it when he called me missy. It made me feel like someone out of *Gone with the Wind*.

"Maybe not," I told him. "Maybe not. You know what they say about a prophet in his own time and country. Perhaps you'll never be recognized while you're alive. That shouldn't really matter, though, should it? Not if you set down the truth. Truth transcends the temporal. Truth is bigger than space."

Sometimes, I amaze even myself with the things I can say without gagging. Anyhow, he took my words to heart. He set to work. He got into the spirit of the endeavour. He devised his silly little code, just to add to the mystique of the exercise. And that's the way *Tight Jeans for Boys: Probing Poems for Pubescent Punks* came to be. It was Solomon's way of washing the taste of unsavoury Puritanism from his mouth. It was a seed he thought to sow whimsically on the wind, with no idea which way it would blow or how it might grow. Nor will I ever know. But if you boys have had either the luck or the wit or the misfortune to find this notebook and to discover what I am writing now, then you will have also unearthed his manuscript and released the genie from the bottle. I hope it's been fun!

The world is powered, I am convinced, by accident and coincidence. Both have a role to play in our lives. Consider this strangeness, which came to light early on in my friendship with Solomon; a friendship that grew strained over time, but that at the beginning had a decidedly confessional air around it. In comparing notes, we determined that on the very day his brother and I were playing mechanic, if you catch my drift, Solomon was in Moosejaw, dallying in a hammock with a young woman. Their union was only half as fruitful as the one I endured with your father. She had one child, a boy. Her social situation, though different from my own, was every bit as awkward. She was married. Her husband was a schoolteacher. At the moment the son he was to raise as his own was being conceived, he was standing at a blackboard, trying to impart the significance of 1066 to a classroom full of bored and restive 10 o'clock scholars.

It was a great sadness to Solomon that he was never able to acknowledge paternity. Until he moved to the valley, he kept tabs, at a distance, on the growing lad, whose name he told me but I've forgotten. It was unusual. Cadbury, or Cardamom, I think. Evidently, he was the spit and image of his father. I must say I'm relieved that the two of you took after me, physically at least.

Two days ago, on Halloween morning, Solomon came to the door, looking even more distracted than usual. I could extract almost no sense from his ravings. He had the air of a mad seer who had just glimpsed something nasty in his crystal ball or mirror.

"The end is at hand, missy! I can feel it! I can feel its breath on my neck! Here! You take these! Make sure they don't fall into the wrong hands, or terrible things might happen!"

And he shoved at me his wadded ball of fudgsicle wrappers and scribbled up Kleenexes and annotated toilet paper rolls and loped off down the drive, his seeded dandelion thatch blowing this way and that with the wind. I never saw him again. I will put these traces of him in the safe and turn their future over to whatever mix of accident and coincidence might tumble along. Mrs. Rochester knows the combination, and I don't doubt that she will spill the beans when she's good and ready and the time is ripe.

How are you boys? Are you happy to hear from your old mother after all this time? Are you angry that I kept this from you? Do you believe me when I tell you I had your own best interests at heart? These are questions to which I'll never know the answers. I think I like it that way.

Love, Mother.

From *The International Bulletin of Weasel Spotting*

December 15, 199-

It has been six weeks since the mysterious disappearance of Polly Perch, the celebrated and sometimes controversial editor of *Interference*. Ms. Perch vanished on Halloween while visiting a little island valley where she had gone to judge a poetry contest. The valley, though isolated, is well known to weasel enthusiasts the world over as the breeding ground of a particularly amorous species of stoat.

Polly Perch was last seen wandering into the woods, only minutes before a freak electrical storm shook the whole vicinity. An intensive search turned up only her turban, a cigarette lighter and the heel of one shoe. Some have suggested that she was immolated by a bolt of lightning, but no forensic evidence has been advanced that might substantiate this. Nor is there any indication that she fell victim to foul play.

What happened to Polly Perch? We at the *International Bulletin of Weasel Spotting* would never dream of rubbing the salt of foolish speculation into the wound of bereavement. However, when the literal truth is unknown, some comfort can be derived from myth. And that is the spirit in which we remind friends and admirers of Polly Perch, who was herself a keen weasel spotter, of this snippet of ancient folklore.

It is said, in Cornwall and in Brittany, that once every hundred years, on Halloween, the King of the Weasels, who is as old as time and whose appetites are voracious, selects a human woman to be his bride. According to the legend, he and all his court descend from their vaunted kingdom to one of the holy sites of weaseldom and wait quietly in the forest for a suitable candidate to wander by. Then, he rears up and reveals himself in all his glory, and asks the wench whether or not she will come willingly with him to be the favoured wife in his harem. If she nods assent (for she would be too overwhelmed to speak), she is whisked away in a whirlwind and never seen on earth again.

It is naught but a pretty story. But what harm can be done by fancy, especially in a world where solace can be hard to find? And those who knew her know full well that there would be no more fitting Queen of the Weasels than Polly Perch.

Moffat Lindisfarne, Editor.

Altona gave me cologne

Altona gave me cologne last year for Christmas, a bracing scent called Fêted. It comes in a hexagonal blue bottle, with a label that shows a man of roughly half my age, standing alone on a white expanse of beach, leaning on a surfboard and shielding his eyes against a many-hued tropical sunset. A frothy wave crashes onto the sand, on which is inscribed the slogan: "Fêted: A Way to Smell, A Way to Feel."

Altona chooses her gifts with great care. She likes to think the presents she gives will expand the horizons of the recipient. Kits for making dulcimers, cactus garden starter sets, books on juggling: each of these, inscribed with my name, has made its way to a hallowed spot beneath our tree. I would never have thought to acquire any of these items for myself. Similarly, the cologne: I have never worn such stuff, never much liked the whiff of it on others. Altona watched me open the package with the happy vigilance of a vulture hovering over a truck-flattened rabbit.

"I picked it up from the duty-free at the airport when I was coming back from Vegas. It'll drive your girlfriends wild," she said, with a broad wink. "There was a bellhop at my hotel who wore it, and I could hardly hold myself back."

Of course I expressed surprise, which was genuine, and gratitude, which was a little more contrived. Every so often, Altona takes it into her head that I should make a foray into the world of dating. I'll find books or magazine articles with suggestive titles (*Romancing the Stone: Getting Involved After Fifty*) left at my breakfast place. Or someone will have mysteriously circled likely looking prospects in the "Companions Wanted" section of *The Rumour*. I interpreted this to be her subtextual purpose in giving me an aphrodisiacal unguent.

I could never be angry with her for so mild a tampering. She means well, always. She knows that my childhood bachelor vows remain firm, and that not even the most fervent prayers to St. Jude could lift from me the label of "hopeless cause" when it comes to romantic involvement. Even so, she likes to give me a shove in the direction of interpersonal union. Intellectually, she knows and accepts that I am happy as I am. But emotionally, she cannot see how this might be. She has too bountiful a heart. What's more, Altona is a born organizer. For her, life is one great filing system, and all the men and women merely folders. She can no more stanch the urge to reclassify her friends and associates, so that they fit in better with her masterplan, than a salmon can stop itself from swimming upriver to spawn.

I dutifully dabbed a drop or two of the amber liquid behind my ears. I could certainly understand how its aroma might arouse a nostalgia for the tropics, if not an overpowering urge to make love until the sun came up. I have never had the pleasure of smelling a grove littered with overripe, windfall papaya, but I shouldn't be surprised to learn it is close olfactory kin to Fêted. Mrs. Rochester, who had cosied up to the Christmas angel, looked down from her treetop roost and snickered, "The mandrakes give a smell and at our gates are all manner of pleasant fruits, new and old, which I have laid up for thee, O my beloved." Her meat is marbled with a thick streak of malice, that is for certain. Still, we all chuckled at her cleverness.

That was last year, when chuckling came easier. When the world was an altogether different place. Last year, Mrs. Rochester could quote as liberally as she liked from the Song of Solomon, and no one would blink or bat an eye. But ever since the pyrotechnic display at Halloween and the revelations that followed on, Solomon is a name we do not raise casually in conversation. You just never know what might happen.

Only a year ago! It hardly seems possible that so much has both come to light and been put to rest since just last Christmas. When I think back on the three of us sitting around the amply festooned tree under Mrs. Rochester's watchful gaze, exclaiming at our gifts, regaled by Waffle's occasional sneak attacks on the hanging baubles, I marvel that not one of us lifted a head to sniff the prevailing wind. Perhaps the smell of what was to come was obscured by the cloying presence of Fêted.

Only a year ago! Had I squinted through the telescope of time and seen myself on this Christmas Day, 365 days hence, would I have done things differently? Had I known that I would be sitting alone in my dressing gown at 11 in the morning, in front of a potted palm festooned only with a popcorn string and few strands of tinsel, drinking my sixth cup of coffee with the cat on my lap and a parrot on the wingback of the chair, all of us following the lyrics the record company thoughtfully enclosed with the Mitch Miller Sing-Along Christmas Album ("Pa-rum-pa-pum-pum," clucks Mrs. Rochester, along with "The Little Drummer Boy," which is her favourite carol); had I known all this, would I have been quite so dismissive of Altona's ham-fisted nudgings toward companionship?

You bet your sweet mistletoe. Nothing is so luscious as solitude when it has been freely chosen in lieu of chatty sociability. Ten days ago, we began our annual hiatus from the business of turning out breakfasts and turning down beds. Ten days ago, I waved goodbye to my regular housemates as they chugged off down the road in a southerly direction.

"You could come with us, you know," said Caedmon, as I helped load the luggage into Violetta. "There's lots of room."

"You *should* come with us," said Altona.

Hector nodded. "I think so, too. And when will you have another chance to visit Mexico?"

I smiled and shook my head. I hugged each of them warmly. I wished them godspeed.

"Drive carefully," I said to Caedmon as he slid behind the wheel and cranked the ignition.

"Happy holidays, cousin," he shouted above the rumble of Violetta's engine. Cousins! Whoever would have imagined it a year ago? I jogged after them down the drive, watched as they turned left, and waved until they rounded the bend in the road and the thatched roof of Violetta disappeared from view.

Their journey had evolved from one of Caedmon's inspirations. He was concerned that Francesca had been pining since the loss of Paolo. She showed no sign of coming out of it. Caedmon hoped a desert interlude would revive her flagging lizard spirits.

"I think Violetta might have a big trip left in her," he announced one morning. "I think I'll try for Arizona."

When Altona heard this, she pounced. For years, she has been trying to convince Hector that they should take a break from the grey and lacy rains of our winter and head off somewhere dependably sunny. Round about mid-November, she begins to bring over travel brochures and to pepper her conversation with names like Baja, Guadalupe, Acapulco. However, it is not for nothing that Hector is my brother. Like me, he can claim a stubborn aversion to straying from the home front. The dunes of the Oregon coast marked the limits of his tolerance for travel. But the extraordinary events of recent months have coaxed the adventurer in him to the fore. When Altona suggested they expand their horizons and hitch a ride to Phoenix, Hector astonished us all by saying, "Phoenix, heck! Let's all head for Mazatlan!"

"Wish you were here," reads the sweet cliché on the postcard I retrieved from the mailbox yesterday morning. The pictured scene was not unlike the one on the Fêted bottle. Altona had appended a P.S. "And a big, big kiss for little Martina!"

"Wake that little princess with a smooch," said an exhausted June, when I showed her the card, "and there'll be hell to pay. This is the longest she's slept all week." The baby dozed in her bassinet, which made an attractive centrepiece on one of the cafe tables. We stared down at this new traveller, marvelling at her impossibly clear skin, the faint blue traces of vein in her forehead, her tiny perfect hands that can grip so convincingly, and the pink, milk-encrusted mouth that June assures me is a miracle of suction. So new! So entirely new! I couldn't stop myself from leaning over and tracing a line with my finger around the button of her nose. So soft! So incredibly soft! There was a click, and the sound of film advancing.

"Couldn't resist," said Rae, setting down her camera.

Martina is only two weeks old. I would wager that in six months' time she'll have outstripped both Jacqueline Onassis and Elizabeth Taylor as the world's most-photographed human being. The community notice bulletin boards in the cafe have been given over entirely to the display of her pictures. Martina nursing, Martina crying, Martina sleeping, Martina burping, Martina being changed, Martina flat on her back and staring up at the photographer with a look that seems to me to say, "Enough! Enough! Enough already!"

I remembered I'd brought along a package for the baby archive. "Here," I said, pulling it from my coat pocket, "I just picked it up from Mac."

"Hooray!" cried Rae, rather too bumptiously. Martina stirred and grumbled, then thought better of it and drifted back to sleep. "Goody!" she whispered. "Let's watch it!"

"Oh, no!" June had a stricken look about her. "I don't think I'm ready to live through it again. I still hurt."

Rae was not to be dissuaded. "Come on! It's Christmas Eve morning! What better time to watch a miraculous birth?" She scampered to the video machine and stuck in the tape I'd just given her. Familiar faces filled the screen of the television behind the bar.

For almost twenty-five years, J. MacDonald Bellweather II has engineered a Christmas carol sing-along and potluck at his home on the second Sunday of the month. It's the real beginning of the party season. Everyone looks forward to it, and everyone comes. But in November, after the Solomon fiasco, Mac had gone into a self-imposed exile. We had all supposed that this year his lingering depression would rule out any gathering of the clans. Much to our collective surprise and delight, Mac proved himself resilient. The clouds around him lifted and the invitations appeared on schedule.

A sigh of relief was heard up and down the valley at this signal that normalcy was in the offing. We were all determined that this would be a potluck to remember. On the appointed day and at the assigned hour, we crowded into Mac's place, full of good will and laden with our finest offerings: shortbread, fruit cakes, all kinds of decorated cookies, stöllen, spreads, cheeses, squares and dainties of every stripe. Our host, who is a keen collector of gadgets, greeted everyone at the door with his new video camera: a get-well gift he'd bought for himself. For the next hour, he roamed the room, capturing the random images he later cobbled together into the record that unrolled before us.

As it transpired, Mac had not exorcised every bug from his camera, and though the picture was a model of high definition, there was no accompanying sound.

"Thank the Lord for small mercies," was June's response to that glitch. "Look! There's Abel, going straight for the punch bowl."

"And that would be my beloved brother, right behind him. Consistency, thy name is Hector."

"And there's Caedmon! Gosh! What a bow tie! No, no, wait! It's Francesca. And there's Altona! I loved her hot crab dip."

We kept up a running commentary as we watched our silent friends and mute neighbours swarm the groaning board. We filled in what bits of dialogue we remembered and invented lines, sometimes rather unkindly. We snickered at the charades and the *tableaux vivants* that preceded the musical portion of the evening, and then provided the soundtrack, as best we could, when the carolling began. "The Holly and the Ivy." "I Saw Three Ships." "The First Noël." "Silver Bells."

One of our long-standing carol sing staples has been Abel Wackaugh's performance of the famous French carol, "O, Holy Night." This year, as at Christmases past, he was accompanied by Mac's player piano, and by me fingering a bassoon obbligato against the old mechanical keyboard's strident noodling. How this tradition began, and why it gained such prominence, and why it continues, are among the abiding mysteries of the season. From a strictly musical standpoint, it has little to recommend it. The piano is tinny. My playing is generally undistinguished. And while Abel evinces tremendous enthusiasm for vocalizing, his voice is remarkable mostly for its shortcomings. It would be overstepping the bounds of the truth to say that his singing is pleasing to the ear. Not that it much matters, mind you. We look forward to his performance with the same joy and trepidation that we bring to the certainty of overeating. We know it will make us feel uncomfortable. We know it can't be good for us. But it belongs to the season and we crave it.

We watched the silent Abel move to his position adjacent to the player piano. He held his hands behind his back and paused for a moment or two of reflection. When he was adequately centred, he nodded to Hector, who threw the switch that set the roll in motion. The cylinder began to turn. The keys started in to play, seemingly of their own volition. I lifted the bassoon to my lips and began to blow. Abel's face was the very picture of divine rapture, and June, Rae and I hummed along as he mouthed the words.

"O, holy night! The stars are brightly shining!"

Mac, who must have been gaining confidence with his new toy, was trying some experimental shots. There were close-ups and slow dissolves. At one point, we had an alarming view into Caedmon's left nostril.

"Long lay the world in sin and error pining!"

There was Matthias Leodegar, sneaking a drink from the punch bowl. Altona was standing at the buffet, eating her own hot crab dip.

"The thrill of hope, the weary world rejoices!"

Caedmon hove into view, holding Francesca high above the heads of everyone in the room so that she might see Abel, who was picking up steam.

"Fall on your knees! Oh hear the angel voices!"

His adam's apple strained against his collar. His face was red with exertion and piety, and thick veins punctuated his forehead. I did not look much better as I worried away at my reed and navigated my way through a few of the more treacherous measures.

"O, night, divine! O, night, when Christ was born!"

Our soloist had long since freed his hands from their behind-the-back hiding place. He was holding them toward the heavens, as if anticipating the imminent delivery of stigmata. The camera panned across the audience, most of whom were biting their lips with anxiety. Everyone knew what was coming. Abel was working his way toward the high and ringing climax of the piece with the steadfast resolve of a mounted crusader hacking his way through ranks of Saracens. The tension was thickening. Never once, in all his years of trying, had he managed to squarely hit the high "C" that is the summit of "O, Holy Night." Year after year, Christmas after Christmas, he scoops his way into its proximity, and then bats away at the note from above and below for what seems an eternity, like a cat trying to swat a meddlesome butterfly. It is a grand and terrible moment, and can usually only be broken by the whole assembly bursting into applause, so that he can honourably extricate himself.

"Oh hea-a-a-a-r the angel voi-i-i-i-ces!"

Mac brought his camera to bear on June, whose face was a mask of concentration and horror. Her mouth was moving in little circles, and she seemed to be gasping for breath.

"Oh, God," she said, rocking Martina and turning away, "I look like I just swallowed a fish bone. Turn it off! Turn it off!"

"Oh, n-i-i-i-i-ght—"

Abel stopped and gulped for air.

"De-e-e-e-e-v-i-i-i-i-i—"

His eyes began to shift. He looked one way and another. Pandemonium was erupting around him. The camera pulled back and revealed June, her mouth as wide as Abel's. She had taken up his vowel and howl, both.

"A-i-i-i-i-i-i-e-e-e!"

The screen went blue. The tape was over. Martina opened her mouth and let forth a wail that was a perfect imitation, albeit in miniature, of her mother's scene-stealing ululation.

"I guess that was where Mac fainted," said Rae, pushing the rewind button on her remote control.

"I was surprised a baby could come out so quickly," I said. "I've always heard that first-borns dawdle and dally on their way into the world."

"Welcome to the world of precipitous labour," said June, positioning Martina to feed. "Yow! Talk about greased lightning. I think the ragtime on the player piano might have had something to do with it."

I stood to go, and ran my hand over the child's round head

feeling the little gullies where the skull plates had yet to fuse. Only two weeks ago I was part of the audience who watched agog as that same crown blossomed from between her mother's legs. Little Martina! I saw her turn her wrinkled, perfect gargoyle face toward us, saw her open her eyes even before she was fully extracted, heard the shocked mew that followed her first gulp of air. I have never seen anything so pretty or so holy, and feel sure I never will again.

"Do you have to leave so soon?" asked June.

"Miles to go before I sleep," I smiled, and blew them all a kiss on my way out the door. Then I got into my truck and headed up the road to my eagerly awaited rendezvous with a stranger. Every so often, I stopped to check the map and directions Altona had included with her Christmas present. This year, bless her heart, she hit the gift-giving nail bang on the head. *"Redeemable by bearer for one ride with Goatfoot the Balloonman"* was the promise on the certificate she slipped under my pillow on the morning of their leaving. I could not imagine a more perfect gift. Ever since I saw that rainbow-coloured aerial wonder drift across the valley this past spring, I have been wanting this. Dreaming about this. I have imagined myself, high and serene and silent, looking down on the world made new. It would have been sensible to wait for spring before cashing in my chit, but I didn't have the patience. I called Goatfoot and asked if I might spend my hour aloft early on Christmas Eve afternoon.

"I appreciate it's rather an odd time to make an appointment for such a thing . . ."

"Odd?"

"Well, with Christmas and all. Most people want to be with their families."

"Ha! All the same to me. Come around 1:30."

I found my exotic conveyance just where Altona's map promised it would be. I saw it at a distance, its red and blue vertical stripes rising up from a gondolalike contraption that was anchored smack dab in the middle of a stubbled field at the end of an unpaved road. I parked the truck and approached with a measure of trepidation. In my many rehearsals for the main event, I had always imagined myself plying the skies alone. But one look at the balloon, which loomed so much larger in life than it did on the small screen of my brain, and I understood the folly of that fantasy. It had a look of fierce independence about it.

Goatfoot leaned against the basket, looking into the middle distance, drawing now and again on his pipe. We nodded at each other as I approached.

"Ready?" he asked, and I wondered for a fitful moment if in fact he did plan to turn over the keys and tell me to drive it away.

"I guess."

He vaulted nimbly into the basket, extended an impressively callused hand to haul me in, and with no ceremony or blessing, we cast off and took to the air. Once we were clear of the ground and were passing above the trees, I was doubly glad he was there to crank up the heat and talk to the zephyrs and interpret the currents. It was all so much more complicated and involved than I had envisioned! And it turns out that ballooning is in no way silent, as I had thought it would be. Goatfoot was taciturn, but the upward blast of sustaining heat was plenty loud, and the wind sang lustily, and the dogs who congregated below saluted our passing with a raucous chorus. They tore around in circles in the fields as we passed over, barking and yapping and chasing our shadow and carrying on their canine cabals. Why dogs should find the passage of a balloon so unsettling is beyond me. Perhaps they feel honour bound to live up to the "Beware" signs that are nailed to fence posts here and there. Perhaps it all looks to them like the fulfilment of a dire prophecy, known only to mutts.

The afternoon was overcast and cool, and I was glad of my many woollies, especially as we gained altitude and the winds began to assert themselves, careering around and through the gondola. I peered over the side and down at the valley where I've spent all my days. It is so lovely! Lovelier than I ever knew, even at this time of year when the orchards are bare and the green in the meadows is verging on grey. We headed in a northerly direction, passing over the golf course, which was deserted, and over the cemetery, where the usual suspects waited for the Judgment Day roundup. As we passed above The Well of Loneliness, I activated my X-ray vision and squinted through the shingles at June, settling Martina for a nap.

"Be happy!" I whispered. "Be happy, wee dumpling!" There was a great snort of heat from the furnace and the balloon shuddered, lifting higher still. Below wound the gravel road that led up the hill to Abel Wackaugh's Hair Styling and Hardware. There was the shady grove where Solomon had chosen to build his house and planned his long-gestating revenge. Farther up the valley, the tree-tops gave way to the anomalous and protruding turrets that mark Mac's ancestral home: a Bavarian castle parachuted into the rain forest of the Pacific Northwest. We slipped easily in and out of the moist ribbons of low-hanging cloud, now and then losing sight of the landscape. I wondered if this was what a clairvoyant sees when she looks into her crystal ball: vague, amorphous images taking shape, then fading, till one rises up clear and strong.

"Look! Look!" I called out loud, and the balloonman obliged.

"Your house?"

"My house!"

I was so excited that I started in to wave. Goatfoot looked down with practised indifference.

"I figured. Everyone shows me his house."

He went back to fiddling with his dials and gauges. I couldn't understand his nonchalance. By golly! It's some pretty house; at least, when seen from such a vantage point. Summoning up my X-ray vision once more, I looked right through the roof and into the empty rooms. There was Waffle, snoozing on the blue chenille bed-spread in one of the guest rooms Caedmon had recently painted. There was Mrs. Rochester, head under wing, perched on the sewing dummy in the attic. There was Mother's room, her coins and miner-als, her test tubes and telescope. I scanned the empty library, with its orderly books, my bassoon and the portraits on the walls. There was the safe. I could have looked into it but chose not to. I peered into the kitchen, taking in the waffle iron and the coffee maker and the egg poacher and the toaster and the hundreds of useless bits and pieces that collect over the course of a life. It may not have had the high drama of seeing your life pass before your eyes while drowning. Still, as I gazed down from this unaccustomed height, with Goatfoot the Balloonman beside me, whistling far and wee, I felt I could read my whole story from the first grunts of "once upon a time" to the end of the middle chapters, on which I've latterly been working. I screwed up my eyes and squinted into the enveloping, translucent vapour, thinking that I might catch a glimpse, if only fleetingly, of what lay ahead: of what would unravel before the time came to say "happily ever after," or else, "amen."

"Yo ho!" called Goatfoot. "Have a gander below!"

I looked down, and much to my surprise saw that the land had slipped away, saw that we were scudding along above the water. The sea stretched out below us, rolling on forever, wave after booming wave testing the chipped and jagged rim of the earth. I don't think I'd ever been so surprised by anything as I was by its shining.

We live less than two miles from the shore, with its fine rocks for climbing and its tidepools full of periwinkles, jellyfish and sea anemones; with its long white beaches littered with contorted driftwood, skeletal traces of fish, kelp, clamshells and sand dollars. When our visitors ask after recreational possibilities other than reading and napping, I always recommend a trek to the beach. No one is ever disappointed. They come back with seagull feathers, pretty pink stones, odd bits of bone, floats that have escaped from nets.

"How lucky!" they say. "How lucky to live on an island! How lucky to live near the sea!" And I know that they have imputed to me the life they think they would lead themselves if they settled here: rising up early every morning and jogging on down to comb the sands for desirable, cast-up flotsam. It is a charming, romantic notion, and there are islanders who do just that. But I am not among them. While I can't say that the sea is wasted on me, precisely; while I am not impervious to its drama or its beauty or its thundering charms, I am nevertheless someone whose basic impulse is to turn inland. Forests, fields and gentle hills: this is the geography, the reassuring solidity, to which I resonate most ringingly. Hundreds and hundreds of years ago, in another land and in a time of more limited vocational possibilities than we now enjoy, I would have cast my lot with the men who chose to stay behind and mind the flocks and till the soil. I would have stood on the hillside and waved goodbye to the brave or foolish souls who adventured out to sea in ships.

"Beautiful, isn't it?" asked Goatfoot, who had left off his important rope-jimmying to scan the wide horizon. I jumped at the sound of his voice. "Nothing to speak of between us and Japan."

So much possibility! So much emptiness! A gull flew past, white and silent and swift: a restless shade, wandering the earth. As we hung there, suspended between heaven and the deep, with Japan just a wink away and with all the world and all its riches tumbling before me, I felt a tug somewhere deep within, as if my own flesh-bound ghost was eager to liberate itself there and then from the cage that was decaying around it, and strike out for exotic ports of call. Goatfoot spoke again, his voice muffled by the wind.

"Shall we just keep on going?"

I looked at him, wondering if I'd misunderstood.

"Pardon?"

"I said, shall we just keep on going?"

I forced a laugh. "Where? To Japan?"

He shrugged and looked again to whatever it was he saw beyond the join of sea and sky.

That I sit here now in my comfortable chair, savouring this solitary Christmas morning, with a fire in the hearth and Waffle massaging my ankles, all eager for me to set down this book at last and take her into my lap, will tell you how I answered the balloonman's seductive offer. Oh, I was tempted! Don't think I wasn't! Dangling up above the water, in a place that was really neither here nor there, a place governed by laws that seemed more spontaneous than scripted, don't think I didn't contemplate simply giving him the go-ahead to proceed. Why, I might have had the world! Everything I saw spread out before me could have been mine, simply by saying yes to the balloonman.

What would I have forsaken? This house that grows needier with age and might any day give way utterly to earthquake, flood or fire, but that contains within its four angled walls the evidence of everything I've done and learned and been. A brother and friends who know me so well they can read my moods in the set of my jaw and the tilt of my eyebrow. A small life that is more than half over. A past where nothing much has happened, and a future that promises more of the same. A cantankerous parrot, a supercilious cat, a baby so new she hasn't yet thought of learning to smile, an ongoing opportunity to practise, practise, practise the art of muffin making, and all the attendant possibilities of thereby attaining perfection. The sound of our visitors' footfalls up and down the stairs, the tangle of their stories. What? Abandon this? This island? My valley? My God! How much more of the world does any one man need? How much more could he stand?

"Home, home, home," called the reminding waves, as they tumbled one over the other in their pell-mell rush to get to shore. Goatfoot gave his habitual shrug and started tacking into the wind, bringing us around, taking us away from where the incomprehensible tides mutter their same old stories, gossiping endlessly among themselves. When we were two men on earth again, we shook hands, and I crossed the field, back to the truck. A few minutes later, rounding the top of the hill, I looked in the rearview mirror and saw what might have been his balloon, cutting a furrow through the low-hanging clouds, travelling west.

That was yesterday. I will never forget it. Today has its own exigencies. I'm expected at The Well for dinner and must exhume Mrs. Beeton from wherever she's buried on the cookbook shelf to look up her recipe for hard sauce. I've stretched my recreational solitude out as far and as long as I possibly can. Look at the time! It's 11:59! Christmas morning is on the very cusp of becoming Christmas afternoon. In just one minute we'll be entering the no man's land of noon.

When Hector and I were boys, we invented a noontime game. We watched the grandfather clock, waiting for its two hands to meet and for the first of the twelve chimes to ring out. Then taking turns, one after the other, we would make a wish, one for each stroke of the clock, six apiece. We told each other that if we managed to articulate our wishes before each respective pealing was done, they would be granted. It's harder than you might think, choosing half a dozen random wants from the vast catalogue of possibilities, especially when you factor in the pressures of competition and timing. If one of us failed to spit out his imagined needs in the allotted time, he was eliminated and the other brother was able to claim all the wishes as his own. It's a strange little game, I grant you, and one that is best played in pairs. But as I'm alone, and as the itch is on me, and as the clockwork whirl that ushers in the chimes has just kicked in, and even though I haven't tried this in years, I'll give it a solitary go.

One, I wish you a comfortable bed.
Two, a roof to withstand every storm.
Three, a pillow to cushion your head.
Four, an angel to keep you from harm.
Five, I wish you remembrance of dreams.
Six, I wish you the love you require.
Seven, in summer, the sheltering shade.
Eight, in winter, a welcoming fire.
Nine, I wish you the comfort of friends.
Ten, I wish you an absence of fear.
Eleven's a wish for the right wish to end.
Twelve and it's over. I wish you were here.